D0309634

A FLASH OF RED

Tyler Vance thought he'd left the violence behind when he quit the military twenty years ago and moved to North Carolina. Now a freelance gun writer and the father of four-year-old Cullen, he wants nothing more than to forget those days, but that was before the bank robber pointed a gun at him, before Vance's instincts took over and he dropped the gunman first, before he found out just whom he'd killed and what it meant. For the gunman had family too, and they definitely believe in an eye for an eye . . . or maybe two.

CLAY HARVEY

A FLASH
OF RED

Complete and Unabridged

NIAGARA

Ulverscroft Group Limited
England - USA - Canada
Australia - New Zealand

First published in the
United States of America

First Niagara Edition
published 1997
by arrangement with
Putnam Berkley Group, Inc.
New York

ISBN 0–7089–5890–7

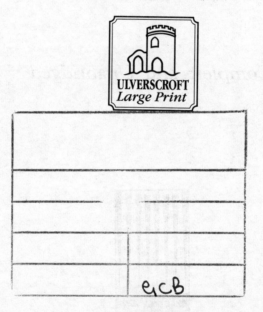

ULVERSCROFT
Large Print

Published by
F. A. Thorpe (Publishing) Ltd.
Anstey, Leicestershire
Set by Words & Graphics Ltd.
Anstey, Leicestershire
Printed and bound in Great Britain by
T. J. International Ltd., Padstow, Cornwall

My thanks to God for two incomparable gifts:

His Son, and mine.

Acknowledgments

Through help from the following, this book exists.

My father, Odie, who provided me, both genetically and through example, with a sense of humor.

My mother, Leola, who from early on never failed to bolster my self-confidence when there were signs of it flagging.

My wife, Barbara, who gave me love, the blessing of being a father, encouragement, no-punches-pulled editing, and who shouldered more than her share of the bills for far too long. Maybe now she'll get that new sofa . . .

My son, Christopher, who provided the inspiration. I wrote this book for him.

My sister, Anne, who, through incessant hazing when I was but a tender shoot, made me scrappy.

Although God gave me whatever writing talents I possess, He left it to Emma Lee Laine, my tenth-grade English teacher, to point them out. She did, and in such a way as to make me thirst to write, just to please her.

My pal Mike Holloway, archetype for Dave Michaels. A finer man there isn't.

Alphabetically: Debra Baker, the small lady with the huge heart, head ego booster and political-correctness adviser; Nancy Holloway, quiet, calm, dropping whatever she was doing at any time to critique a work in progress; Debbie Ortiz, faithful whip cracker, chief monitor for improprieties, plot inconsistencies, grammatical gaffes, and who always laughed in the right places; Becka Powers, poet, savant, dramatist, who steered me clear of more than one rocky shoal. If on occasion I ignored the advice of this erudite quartet, it's not their fault.

Officer Ed Humburg, close friend, squinty-eyed scrutinizer of my wanderings through police procedure.

While I choreographed a whuppin', martial arts expert Malik Pearsall looked over my shoulder.

David Best, M.D., supervised my medical esoterica, fielding questions at odd hours that would make a mortician blanch.

Elizabeth Grant, my Texas buddy, who spurred me on, shooed me under the wing of . . .

. . . stellar agent David Smith. All nascent novelists should be so fortunate as to land David.

Last, maybe most, my heartfelt appreciation to editor Neil Nyren. Here's hoping my work justifies his faith.

"Once in an age the biter should be bit."

— Thomas d'Urfey

Prologue

I DIDN'T want to shoot him, I really didn't. He gave me no choice, poking the barrel of his revolver straight at me and yelling, "Get out of the truck!"

God knows I've killed enough men. They often come to me in the night, disembodied. But not faceless. Never faceless.

At home there was a four-year-old who called me Daddy.

Six months ago a drunk driver took his mom.

Crossed the median. *Wham*, just like that.

For three days he didn't speak. When he did he just asked, "Why?"

It nearly killed me.

Now here was a guy who might take his daddy. *Bam*, just like that.

No . . .

1

WHEN I pulled into the bank's parking lot en route to the drive-in window, I found myself behind a bronze Olds four-door of late vintage which sat, engine idling, a few yards this side of the window, blocking both "open" lanes. Odd. Maybe the driver was making out a deposit slip and had failed to notice that the car in front of him had finished conducting its banking business. Assuming of course that there had been a car in front of him.

I reached over and punched off the radio with my thumb, stilling the silken cello of Yo-Yo Ma. A thin veil of exhaust fumes rose from the Olds's tailpipe, muting the dying rays of the sun. I waited a few seconds, almost honked my horn, noticed that the driver was not looking down but was rubbernecking like a first-time bather at a nude beach, his head never still. Very, very nervous.

A marked police car sped by the bank, blue lights ablaze but bereft of siren accompaniment. On the way to an accident? The strain of its presence was too much for the driver of the Oldsmobile. He stood on the gas, his car fishtailing and fighting for traction as its tires painted twin black marks on the asphalt. Five seconds, tops, and he was squirting out of the parking lot, barely avoiding a rusted

Nissan whose occupants saluted him in concert, poking their middle fingers skyward. Undaunted by their derision, he roared off westward, the compass heading opposite that of the departed police car.

Strange, these goings-on.

Having a keen sense of self-preservation augmented years ago by Uncle Sam under conditions that were less than serene, I stayed right where I was. Did *not* pull up to the drive-in teller's window to make a withdrawal, withdrawing instead from my glove compartment a Colt .45 automatic. I racked its slide to chamber a round, then rested the gun — still in hand — on my right leg. And awaited developments.

Which were not long in coming. Out the side door of the bank, perhaps thirty feet from my truck, popped a medium-sized man sporting lavender sweatpants, an olive turtleneck sweater, an orange ski mask, and a stainless-steel Smith & Wesson .357 Magnum. I transferred the .45 to my left hand, holding the gun against the door panel out of sight. With my right hand, I shifted into reverse. For many reasons, I wanted no part of a robbery in progress. My best way out would be to make a run for it, with backward being the safest route.

Lavender Pants stared in the direction of the now out-of-sight Oldsmobile, stomped his foot, and mouthed the common street euphemism for excrement. Clearly upset, this colorfully clad miscreant.

He reached up, grasped the ski mask at its crown, jerked it off angrily, exposing a coarse black beard mottled with gray. His right ear boasted four jeweled adornments that were completely ineffectual at belying his obvious aggressiveness.

Trying my best to blend with the scenery, I assessed the probability of ducking low in the seat, punching the throttle, and driving my way out of this situation without acquiring painful perforations to my anatomy. I judged my chances to be slim.

What if I backed up, swung around, put some sheet metal, sponge rubber, and upholstery between his gun and my skin? *Might work*, I thought, just as he yelled, "Get out of the truck!"

Ah, well.

I now had two viable options, in my view. One, I could drop the .45 onto the floorboard and relinquish my truck, hoping he wouldn't shoot me, pistol-whip me, or secure me as a hostage. Such an alternative went against my gut feeling, my knowledge of human nature, my philosophy of social decorum, and my extensive — albeit long-past — training in handling violent confrontations.

I went with option two.

I shot him in the beard.

The impact of the heavy hollow-point bullet snapped his head back. He gave a spasmodic kick with his right foot, then fell over backward, his revolver clattering on the concrete. I didn't see him hit the sidewalk, being too busy getting

5

the hell out of my truck.

The side door of the bank had slammed open just as old Lavender Pants and I were getting acquainted. Not figuring the tall, ski-masked individual standing in the doorway to be the governor with my lottery check, I just fired the one shot and exited stage right, through the passenger door. Real fast.

It couldn't have taken me more than three seconds to clear the truck, but by the time my shoes hit the tarmac I had two pounds of shattered glass in my hair. My ancient Toyota pickup was being demolished by a hail of jacketed 9 mm bullets as I crouched beside its protective right front wheel. *Sounds like an UZI*, I thought, as I knelt there trying to make myself tiny. The barrage ended as abruptly as it had begun, the sudden silence punctuated by the clack of changing magazines. I duckwalked to the front bumper. The report of a single shot rang out; the nasty little bullet whacked into the offside of my truck, stopping the motor forthwith. *Probably hit the fuel pump. Better it than me.*

Why just one shot? Gun jammed? Did he have a handgun as well as the UZI? A partner? I risked a peek around the front of the truck, poking my head out and tucking it back in like a rattlesnake on speed.

I saw just the lanky guy, snapping back the bolt on his automatic weapon. As I took a longer second look, he pulled the trigger, receiving for his effort a heavy *click* as the firing pin snapped forward on an empty chamber.

6

No jam, I reflected. *He didn't shove the magazine home.*

Steadying my left elbow into a headlight recess, I silhouetted the black sights of my pistol against the milky white of his jacket while his attention was directed at his recalcitrant firearm, and yelled, "Drop it!"

Hard to intimidate a man with an UZI. He lifted his head, looked me fixedly in the eye, smacked the magazine's floor plate with the heel of his left hand. The magazine snapped into place.

As he reached upward to retract the bolt, I shot him where his heart should've been. He grabbed his chest with his left hand, staggered, nearly dropping the gun, then sagged to both knees, his right hand closed tightly on the trigger, spraying 9 mm slugs into the cement walkway, wickedly whining ricochets merging with staccato muzzle blasts as the gun purged itself. I shot him again, hoping to stanch the burst, my second bullet producing no visible effect. The shooting did not stop until he fell forward onto his face and lay still.

I watched him over my gun's sights for what seemed like several minutes. No one moved within my range of vision. Especially me.

The squeal of tires brought my head around as a shiny red Volvo wagon spun out of the parking lot on the other side of the bank, then disappeared from view. It was hard to tell from where I crouched, but there appeared to be three people in the car, including the ski-masked driver.

I stood up, keeping a wary eye on my downed assailants. A marked police car bounced over the grassy verge separating the bank parking lot from the street, blue lights flashing. They'd likely been called to quell a robbery. Had they been informed it had escalated into a shoot-out? I laid my gun carefully atop the hood of my defunct Toyota and stepped out of reach, so as not to make anyone more nervous than they already were. There I waited with my hands well out from my body, palms forward, for the long-familiar but nearly forgotten adrenaline surge to abate.

2

"YOU'RE a what?"

"A writer."

"What kind of writer?"

"Books, magazine articles, monographs . . . "

"The hell's a monograph?"

"Short treatise on a specific, limited subject. Like fly-fishing."

"You write about fishing?"

"No."

"Then why'd you bring it up?"

"Never mind."

No mental giant, Detective Carl McDuffy. He leaned against the only table in the room — a metal industrial-strength job bolted to the tile floor — arms folded across his flat chest. Longish red hair spilled down his brow into his eyes. He brushed it away with an index finger. Whatever happened to department regulations? Good grooming? Unobstructed vision?

I had been escorted to this room, deep within the confines of the Greensboro police annex, by a uniformed patrolman who had subsequently turned me over to the scarlet-plumed McDuffy. Immediately following the shoot-out at the bank, approximately four million police officers had arrived amid much screeching of tires, flashing of lights, and drawing of guns. I had stood politely — and safely — beside the remains of my faithful Toyota while steely-eyed guys and gals in blue surrounded, searched, identified, and grilled me, making me feel as popular as a Twinkie salesman at a Weight Watchers convention.

After determining that I had been duly disarmed, subjugated, and scrutinized, the bulk of the policefolk turned their attention to more important matters. What little information I could catch, as I waited there under guard, indicated that a multitude of witnesses had related to the gendarmerie the following: Four men had staged a holdup at the bank; two of them had attempted an exit through the west entrance of the bank building, encountering a good deal of difficulty; I was personally and solely responsible for said difficulty and either "incredibly brave" or "a fucking idiot," depending upon whose opinion you subscribed to; the remaining pair of robbers had grabbed an unfortunate teller and her car keys, and escaped through the east-side entrance.

A final, almost tearful comment was proffered by the branch manager, a professorial, tuberous stub of a man dressed in a pale green suit of neither plant nor animal origin. The gist was that despite the best efforts of the "gentleman in the diminutive truck" (me) to "thwart" the robbery, two "dregs of society" had, alas, "absconded" with funds the "precise aggregate of which has yet to be determined."

Pedants, everywhere you look.

Shortly following the manager's somber fiscal revelation, I was whisked off to the station house and ensconced in the lackluster interrogation

10

room in which I now sat. It was large enough, barely, to contain the metal table, three chairs with yellow plastic seats shaped like ice cream scoops, and maybe four or five adult-sized humans if they all used Dial. White walls and ceiling, maroon-tiled floor, no windows, one door. On the long institutional table were two small aluminum ashtrays, a pack of Juicy Fruit, and McDuffy's rear end.

Would they offer me gum? Probably not.

Through the one door strode a big man wearing a medium grey suit of fashionable cut, a pink shirt, and a tie featuring many colorful geometric shapes. His angular face had been recently shaved, his hair newly shorn to the length of a drill sergeant's. Prominent ears, blue eyes, blunt fingers, and, I would soon learn, an equally blunt manner. He was maybe a half-foot taller than I — making him six two — and carried at least 235 pounds lightly on big feet, like a puma. Much gold jewelry in evidence, none of it in his earlobes. Or nose. He padded across the room, rounded the table, sat.

The big man said, in a guttural rasp that could have come from a jaguar if jaguars could talk, "Carl, get off the table."

Instant compliance. McDuffy shifted his carcass upright and milled around like a shy, pimply teenager at the senior prom. Obvious who was in charge here.

Again the throaty voice: "I am Lieutenant John T. Fanner, Homicide. Your name, I have been told, is Tyler Vance. Is that correct?"

Tough. No-nonsense. Intent on setting the

11

pace. We'd see about that.

I said, "Pass the gum?"

"I beg your pardon?"

"Gum. There's some on the table. Hand it over. My throat's dry."

They glared at me, flint-eyed.

"The two of you keep looking mean at me, I might faint from terror, fall over, maybe sustain a bump on my noggin, be compelled to sue." I planned to win them over with my keen wit.

"Here, smartass," McDuffy said, tossing me the pack of Juicy Fruit. Had I won him over? No matter; I had the gum. Popped a piece into my mouth and chewed contentedly.

"Are you comfortable? Is your throat relieved?" asked Lieutenant John T. Fanner.

I smiled pleasantly.

"I assume that we may now continue. I would like to talk with you about your shooting two citizens."

I snorted. "Those *citizens*" — I stressed the word theatrically — "tried their damnedest to shoot *me*. At least, one of them did. The other might have been satisfied with taking my truck."

"They were less than completely successful, since you are here and they are not." He talked like Mattie Ross in *True Grit*, using no contractions.

"Well, my truck is certainly the worse for wear," I countered.

"Just how did you determine that the intentions of the first man you shot were not only unlawful but threatening?"

12

"The guy came out of the bank wearing a ski mask, brandishing a magnum six-gun, obviously looking for a getaway car which had just got away, peeling rubber all over the parking lot in its haste. That seemed a little suspicious to me, how about you?"

"How did you know that the vehicle was in fact a . . . as you put it, getaway car?"

"I'd been watching the driver since I pulled up behind him. He was sitting well back from the drive-in window, motor running, looking this way and that. Nervous as a rabbit up a flagpole. When a cop car whizzed by on Cornwallis, he took off in a big hurry.

"The bearded guy showing up, face covered and waving his .357 around and all, confirmed my suspicions. When he told me to get out of my truck, I demurred."

"You certainly did," said Fanner.

McDuffy waded in. "If he was wearing a mask, tough guy, why didn't it have a hole in it where you shot him?"

"Because he jerked it off in disgust when he saw the Oldsmobile was gone," I answered. "By the way, it was a late model, maybe two, three years old, copper or bronze in color. Didn't catch the plate."

"You sure it was an Olds, not a Chevy?" McDuffy pressed.

"Well, I can't be certain," I said, "but it had 'O-L-D-S-M-O-B-I-L-E' on the back in great big letters. Maybe it was a Studebaker."

"Why would he go to such trouble to conceal his identity just to expose himself at the first sign of trouble?" Fanner asked.

"I didn't say he was smart, just mad. Maybe his mask itched. How the hell do I know? You think I shot the guy for nothing?"

"No, I do not think that," said Fanner. "I simply wanted to hear your side of it. Several witnesses corroborate your story."

"Then why am I still here?" I said, and stood up.

McDuffy stepped in front of me. Close. Too close. A conditioned response, long dormant, welled up in me, tightening my chest. For an instant I surveyed his anatomy, mental faculties on auto scan, seeking the proper spot for instant incapacitation without an attendant risk of death.

Well, only a slight risk.

"What I want to know," he said, poised like a bantam rooster protecting the henhouse, "is why you shot the dude in the face instead of his shoulder or something. Seems like you wanted to kill him, not just stop him."

"Ever drawn your gun other than to clean it, McDuffy?" I looked him over ruefully, then shook my head. "My guess is no."

His face was suddenly inches from mine, ruddy, irate, quivering with anger. "What's it to you!"

"McDuffy!" Fanner snapped.

But McDuffy didn't budge. I put my hands in my back pockets, slowly, afraid to have them out in the open. He had no idea how vulnerable he was, the rube. He thought he was a tough nut to crack.

14

Fanner's chair squeaked on the tile floor as he shoved it backward. McDuffy swiveled his head in the direction of the sound, then back to me, torn between anger and subordination. And saving face. For a moment, I thought he was going to take a swing. The moment passed. He turned on his heel and went to a corner of the little room, breathing deeply, only partially subdued.

Probably liked to think of himself as explosive, what with the red hair and all. And he was, but only in the way a Fourth of July firecracker is explosive. If his temper went off, I doubted much carnage would ensue.

Fanner was quite another matter. He'd be capable of more mayhem in his sleep than McDuffy could manage in the throes of uncontrollable fury.

"I am curious. Would you answer Sergeant McDuffy's question, please?"

"You mean why I didn't try to cowboy my way out, shoot the gun out of his hand, wing him in the uvula?"

He almost smiled, but caught himself. "More or less, yes."

"The quickest way I know of to lose a gunfight — aside from throwing up your hands, wetting your pants, and yelling 'HELP!' — is to try to shoot your opponent around the edges, hoping not to kill the poor soul, who is, after all, only trying to shoot you. The man was virtually at arm's length, Fanner, revolver in hand, and he had all the room in the world to maneuver. My own gun was below the windowsill, in my weak

15

hand, and me with no room to move and no effective cover. The only thing I could do to survive was put him out of commission really, really fast. So I did."

"I'll say" — from McDuffy's corner.

"You worked all of that out while you were sitting there under his gun?" asked Fanner.

"Yes."

He pondered that, studying me closely. Then he said, "I would like to hear about the gun. How did you happen to have it so close at hand?"

"I was planning to cash a royalty check I'd just received in the mail. Since it was for nearly forty-five hundred bucks, I carried my own, shall we say, insurance, right there on the seat beside me." Well, not exactly on the seat, but carrying one in an unlocked glove compartment is illegal in my state. A small fib, but who was to know?

"What did you want with forty-five hundred dollars in cash?" McDuffy asked.

"I was thinking about buying a Studebaker," I answered.

He gave me a withering look. I tried not to wither, at least not right there in front of him.

From Fanner: "Are you perchance a Vietnam veteran? You are too old for Desert Storm, unless perhaps you serve in the guard or reserves."

I didn't like this shift of direction, but I concealed my discomfiture artfully, resorting to acerbic levity. "Thanks. Pardon me while I take a sip of Geritol. I went regular Army right out of high school, stationed in Korea for eighteen months — '73, '74."

His blue eyes probed.

"Korea, in the 1970s. There was not much action then. At least not publicized. Were you infantry?"

I nodded uneasily.

"Stationed at any time north of the Imjin River? Did you ever patrol the demilitarized zone?"

Fanner was no dummy. Nor was he uninformed.

"No," I lied.

"Never in a firefight?"

"No." Another lie. Seemed to be becoming a habit.

"Hmm," he responded thoughtfully, tugging at his ear. I didn't think he'd bought it, not all of it. He suspected I was holding back. He was right. I had no choice; information about my Korea escapades was classified. Highly classified. Divulging information — however tenuous in specifics — to a civilian could land me in Leavenworth or some other federal funhouse. No thanks.

Besides, after thirteen months of cleaning house for Uncle Sam, I'd developed a deep-rooted aversion to talking about it, even during my final military debriefing. Not only that, I'd refused to continue covert ops in the Korea DMZ, even under the threat of court-martial and serious jail time, not because of a failure of nerve but an extreme repugnance toward my duties as military-trained attack dog. The gory details of my tenure as a solitary operative in the "Z" still haunted me. They always would.

Fanner said, "I suppose that is all. This appears to be a case of self-defense, justifiable homicide witnessed by a number of solid citizens. Physical evidence supports that premise. There will likely be a grand jury hearing, going through the motions. Such an event will work in your favor should a family member sue you for wrongful death."

"Now there's a happy thought," I said.

"Unfortunately, things like that happen all the time." He held out a pawlike hand. I shook it. His grip was akin to getting your hand wedged in a car door, but he didn't abuse it. I was glad. Might want to use that hand later.

He turned to McDuffy. "Arrange a ride for Mr. Vance — his vehicle seems to be in disrepair. And keep your temper on a leash." With that, he turned and left the room.

McDuffy turned up the wick on his Clint Eastwood stare. It wasn't difficult to keep my knees from buckling, though it was tough sledding indeed not to laugh out loud.

"Where to, bucko?" said McDuffy.

"My address is in your report. When do I get my gun back?"

"Never, I got anything to do with it. Evidence disappears all the time, security not being all that tight around here."

He stepped closer. "I don't give a muskrat turd what Fanner says, you're a cocky bastard that needs deflating. Whack two guys, then walk. Shit. That's not your job. It's mine.

18

"Go out to the front desk and wait. I'll find someone to take you home, some rookie doesn't care who he rides with."

He put his face close to mine and added, "But I'm betting I'll be seeing you here again, soon."

"Then I hope you'll brush your teeth," I said, and walked out.

3

I WAS hustled out a side entrance, to avoid any lingering journalists. We were successful; nothing moved on the street. Which wasn't really surprising. It was after midnight.

A plainclothes cop dropped me at my father's home, waited long enough for me to make the curb so he wouldn't run over my foot, and departed. Didn't even tell me good night.

I got even. I didn't wave when he pulled off.

My dad's Chrysler was parked in the carport, as usual. What was unusual was the squat brown sedan with military plates pulled in behind it. I looked it over for a moment before going up the back steps. It was from a Fort Bragg motor pool.

Wonderful.

I unlocked the back door with my key, negotiated the breakfast room, kitchen, dining room, and entered the living room. There sat my dad in his high-mileage rocker, a glass of milk at hand. Across the room, sitting on the edge of the sofa, elbows resting on his knees as if he were about to leap to his feet and yell 'GERONIMO!' was Rufus Earl McElroy, Colonel, United States Army, whom I'd last seen twenty years before when he'd been a mere captain.

I'd missed him not a whit.

The implications of this surprise visit washed over me, leaving me not only mildly apprehensive but a tad miffed. After an initial glance of recognition, I ignored him, crossed the floor to enter the front bedroom.

My son, Cullen, was asleep in the middle of the oversized, marshmallow-soft mattress on the ancient double bed in which my maternal grandparents had slept during much of my boyhood. I leaned over and kissed him gently on the forehead, noticing that he'd had his bath; his thick brown hair was redolent of shampoo. His breathing was soft and regular, unlike mine, and his mouth was slightly upturned at the corners. He was enjoying immensely the dreamland in which his subliminal self cavorted.

I sat beside the bed and watched him sleep. The focal point of my life.

In the other room I heard Colonel McElroy rise, speak to my dad. And I heard Dad say, "Sit down. He'll be out in a minute. He's rechargin' his batt'ries."

The officer muttered something. Dad said, "This is my house, Colonel. You can either sit down or leave, but you ain't goin' into that room."

Dad was seventy-two, overweight; the colonel was more than twenty years younger and in great shape, unless he'd changed his habits over the years. Nonetheless, I bet myself a nickel that McElroy sat down.

I kissed Cullen once more and joined the duo in the living room. There was no conversation to interrupt as I entered. The two were just sitting

21

there, my dad sipping his milk, the good colonel simply glaring. McElroy turned off the glare, stood, and approached when I entered, hand out. I looked at the hand but didn't take it.

"I'd like to hear what you want before I shake your hand, Colonel, if you don't mind."

He dropped his hand, nodded amicably, and reset. I joined him on the couch. Crossed my legs.

McElroy said, "How'd things go at the police station?"

"What are you doing here?" I returned.

"Looking out for you," he said, then turned pointedly to my father. "Mr. Vance, would you mind . . . ?"

Dad preempted by rising and stating, "Think I'll go to the back bedroom and watch Jay Leno. Carson McCullers might be guestin'." He ambled out, leaving the milk glass on the end table, where it rested in a ring of condensation.

"Leno into séances, now?"

"Ah. Familiar with Ms. McCullers, are you?"

"I endured college English. Barely."

"Pay Dad no heed. He was yanking your chain."

"Must run in the family."

"You can't mean me. Heavens, I was your obedient annihilator all those months in Korea."

"Obedient. Right. That always was your strong suit."

"Colonel, exactly why are you here?"

"As I said, running interference for you. With the authorities."

22

"How did you know I was in consultation with the authorities?"

He chuckled. "Consultation. That's rich. We got a call from your liaison," he continued. "He'd been informed about your little skirmish at the bank — "

"What do you mean, my liaison? Who the hell is my liaison?"

"When you left Korea in '74, I gave you a name in case you ever ran into, ah, difficulties related to your military background."

I vaguely remembered something about that, but not the person's name. Never expecting to encounter any difficulties relative to my record, I'd promptly placed Mr. Whoever's name in my mental file 13.

"This situation today at the bank," he continued, "is a perfect example of the type of problems that have sometimes cropped up with your, um, comrades. It's why we keep very close tabs on all of you."

"Just who are my comrades?"

"Sergeant Vance . . . "

"I'm not a sergeant anymore."

"Mr. Vance . . . since the Korean War, and up through Vietnam of course, there have been only fourteen soldiers given similar training and, ah, opportunities as yours. Five are still alive, counting you. The first one ran into trouble just three months after he completed his tour. Got into a knife fight with three bikers in a Tulsa topless bar. He gutted two of them, broke the other's arms and ripped out his windpipe. And they had the knives, not him. Word was our boy started the fight. The three were local rednecks. 'Just out for a little fun's all,' said the chief of po-leece, related by blood, incestual like as not, to two of the cycle freaks. So they locked our man up and fed the key to the chief's Weimaraner.

"Our toughie wrote to his papa, a retired master sergeant who knew, we don't know how, the scoop on his son. Daddy made a call to the Pentagon. They scrambled to fly a military representative down to speak with the Okie chief.

"This effort at diplomacy did not fare well. The lad stayed in stir. The representative flew back to Washington to huddle with the brass. It was decided that the risk of a security breach was serious, and intolerable. So they brought in a Marine, mean bastard, and got him tossed on a drunk and disorderly. Wound up in the showers with our friend. An argument ensued. Only the Marine came out breathing.

"The other jailbirds claimed our ex-soldier boy started the fray but wasn't up to concluding it. And there it stopped. The Marine served thirty days on the D and D and walked out. Of jail. The Marines. The country. As we speak, he's living in Sri Lanka, courtesy of a generous pension provided by a grateful government. He was a member of our elite little club, one of the best hand-to-hands we ever had. As you can imagine from your own training and experience, that's pretty damn good," concluded McElroy.

"You mean to tell me that I'm part of a closely monitored group, and that a member

24

of that group killed one of its own?"

"At the time, there were only four alumni. The Pentagon considered it essential that none of the four ever mentioned their combat history to anyone who might leak it to the public. The soldier who picked the fight with the three motorcyclists was going round the bend, and for all practical purposes had been put out of the Army's reach. So they sent a man in. It was necessary."

"You don't know for sure the guy would have talked."

"But he might have. They couldn't take the chance."

"What's this 'they' shit, Tonto?"

"It all happened in the late fifties, before my time."

I mulled over the implications of the foregoing tale, and the possible reasons behind McElroy's relating it to me. "So, are you here to sound me out? Or take me out?"

"Sergeant — Mr. Vance, we have no doubts about your loyalty. You've never done anything to cast suspicion on yourself. Not in twenty years. I'm simply here to offer any assistance that might prove useful. In fact, I've already been of assistance."

"How?"

"Didn't spend much time being interrogated by the cops, did you?"

"No. And I wondered why not."

"Now you know. I brought the word from on high, routed through Bragg, of course, since it's close by. Didn't have to be me. I just happened to be TDY with the Eighty-second, Special Ops. Since I'd been your control in Korea, it was expedient that I handle the situation."

"So you buttonholed the cops while I was being held incommunicado at the station for four hours."

"Correct."

"Told them to lay off, or go easy, or kiss my ass."

"In a nutshell."

"Fanner must have loved that," I murmured.

"Who?"

"Homicide Lieutenant John T. Fanner. Savvy hombre. Very conscientious. I'll bet he's in a back room right now, grinding his teeth."

"Bear in mind," said the colonel, "that this miniature firefight was cut-and-dried. You simply defended yourself. The cops may have raked you over the coals to make themselves look good in the papers, but you were in absolutely no danger of being arrested. There were sixteen witnesses."

"Then why'd you bother slipping a word into someone's ear?"

He shifted on the couch, scratched his head, cleared his throat.

But he didn't answer.

Light dawned. I said, "You were afraid I'd made it look too easy. There I was, two baaad dudes coming at me, one armed with a submachine gun, and I drop them both. Three shots, one of those not even necessary. Could an average civilian, even one who is known to

26

be an accomplished gun handler, manage such a feat? Not likely.

"Your boys 'on high' figured the local constabulary might be suspicious, dig into my past a little, uncover some interesting tidbits involving my military career. You were sent along to check things out, nip an investigation in the bud if possible, assess for damage control if not."

He looked very uncomfortable.

"And what if I had unburdened my soul, McElroy? Fessed up to my horrible past? Given dates, details, named names, pointed my bloody finger?"

"Then you'd be in a federal slammer right now, for violation of the Official Secrets Act."

He had me there. And he knew it.

"This pleasant visit," I said, "doesn't have anything to do with your offering me help. Your superiors simply wanted to remind me that I'd better keep my yap shut about specific sordid, suspect, and highly illegal military operations run two decades ago, just in case I'd forgotten.

"Well, Colonel, pass the word along that not only will I keep my counsel, but the public doesn't give a toot anyway. Besides," I added, "I wouldn't want anyone to know what I was involved in."

"Good," he responded, rising. "Make sure you keep it that way."

I showed him the door. He showed me his back.

★ ★ ★

27

Dad must have heard the front door close, because when I turned away from the knob he was standing by the fireplace looking worried.

"Want to talk a spell?" he said.

"Sure, Pop. Sit."

We did — I in the wing chair by the hearth, he in his ubiquitous rocker, God bless him.

"Son, you gonna be okay?"

"You bet. I just got a little glass in my hair, a cut here and there. That's all. I'm fine."

"That ain't what I meant and you know it," he snapped. "When you called from the bank," he went on, "I turned off the TV. Didn't want Cullen seein' his daddy on the six o'clock news, surrounded by police. He'd have wondered what you'd done, or had done to you. Woulda scared the little dude."

"You did exactly right. You always do where Cullen's concerned."

"Always tried to where you were concerned too, when you was growin' up."

"I know you did. Most of our arguments were my fault. When adolescence takes you by the glands, you suddenly know everything there is to know. Takes ten years to realize that you didn't know anything at all."

"What's been worryin' me," he said, "is how this brouhaha will affect you. I remembered when you came home from Korea, the weight of the world on those broad shoulders. Me and your momma couldn't sleep at night frettin' over how overseas had taken such a toll on you.

"Over the years, you improved a sight. But not all the way back to how you used to be.

28

When you married Tess, now that helped, but it was Cullen that turned you around.

"Your losin' Tess had me wonderin' whether you could handle all the grief or if you'd just backslide. You needed to be strong for Cullen, especially since it was his momma that died. And you did good, supportin' your baby son in every way a man can, though a man ain't no momma.

"Still, none of those things was your fault. Shootin' them fellows today, well, maybe it wasn't your fault, but you did do the shootin'. I'd hate to see you slip into another brown study like after Korea.

"You never told me much about what went on over there, but there wasn't supposed to be any serious problems since '68, when those Commies come south intendin' to shoot up the Blue House and our boys on the *Pueblo* were being held prisoner.

"Just the same, I minded how my brother James acted when he came back from the Pacific in nineteen an' forty-five. Quit huntin', cold turkey, and he'd done it like it made him money all his natural life. Wouldn't talk about the war neither. Never.

"Nigh to thirty years later, my son goes off overseas, then comes home a wreck, never talkin' about why. Gives up huntin', even for squirrels. So I figured, though I never mentioned it to your momma, that you'd got into a scrape over there, a shootin' scrape, and that was that.

"Now that you're nearly back to the way you were when you was growin' up, laughin' and jokin', maybe even huntin' again so Cullen can give it a stab, I don't want to see that go down the drain on account of two miserable bank robbers who was tryin' their best to fill you plumb full of holes. No sir. I surely wouldn't."

It was the longest speech I'd ever heard my father give.

I went over and patted his arm. His eyes were misted; I pretended not to notice.

"I'm okay, Dad. I promise."

But I wasn't.

* * *

Later, Dad gone to bed and night sounds surrounding me, a third cup of Colombian in my hand — handle warm to the touch, rich coffee aroma deep in my nostrils — I sat in the swing on the screened-in back porch. Absorbing events, disturbed. My response at the bank, two more men's blood on my hands, McElroy's unexpected appearance — too much from my past, too abruptly, my head thick with Korea . . .

* * *

There came a rap on the door. Not loud, just a light *tap-tap*, shave-and-a-haircut-two-bits. I knew the knock.

"Come on in, Dave," I enjoined.

The door swung open, creaking on its rusted hinges, and in strolled the aforementioned David

30

Michaels himself. More than six feet, more than two hundred, more than a friend. His handsome face was set in a dour expression, uncharacteristic for him; he smiled more often than anyone I knew, except Cullen.

He sat beside me on the swing, easing his bulk into position not unlike berthing a barge. One of steel, not wood. Solidity.

"Why so glum? I'm the one who had to ace two guys today," I greeted him, with more acerbity than intended.

"So you get to take it out on me, right?"

"Sorry."

"Forget it. Odie called me right after you phoned him from the bank. I was at the store working on a batch of TVs. Said he didn't want me hearing it on the radio. Considerate man, your dad. So here I am, offering you succor.

"Succor?"

"Read it in *Reader's Digest*. When I got here," he continued, "there was an army vehicle in the drive. I parked down the street, hoofed it back, and sat in that old lounge chair in the basement, read that article of yours in the current *Petersen's Handguns*. On the .454 Casull. Bet the guy who runs the company will call your editor and raise hell.

"Anyway, when I saw a set of headlights swing past the window, I figured the conference was over and the guest, or guests, were gone."

We waxed silent, beset, I suspect, by similar distant and unpleasant memories, his of one Asian country, mine another. Dave and I could reside in each other's shadow for

31

hours without feeling the need for verbal communication. So it had been since Mrs. Flanderwort's third-grade class. We'd backed each other in many a playground confrontation; coursed the woods like young wolves, hunting deer; gone off separately to do battle in far-off lands, returning physically healthy but scarred emotionally; ridden side by side during our thirty-something years on powerful, socially irresponsible Yamahas, his an XS1100, mine a V-Max. We rode them very fast.

Then along came Cullen. I figured he might someday want his ol' dad to see him graduate from high school, so I gave up motorcycling. Not without remorse, but what the hey, the child hadn't asked to be born. A next-door neighbor congratulated me on my forthright conversion to responsibility and respectability. What she really appreciated was the peace and quiet.

Dave curtailed our reverie. "What's eating you about this turn of events?"

I didn't answer.

"Speak."

I coalesced my thoughts, said, "When I came back from Korea, I told you what went on. Not all, enough for you to fill in the voids for yourself. After Vietnam, I figured you'd have little trouble."

He nodded. "So what? Why're you sitting here beating yourself up over this thing at the bank? That's what I want to know."

"Overseas, people were generally shooting at me, lobbing grenades, planting mines for me to step on. I was always outnumbered, confronted

32

by men who wanted dearly to nail my hide to the barn door. But not today."

I looked at my watch: 1:15. "Well, yesterday. The first guy I shot didn't have a chance in the world, not one. He didn't even threaten me, at least verbally. Just told me to get out of the truck — "

"That's a load of horse poop and you know it!" Dave interjected. "The guy had a gun out. You had to figure he'd use it. Any other attitude would have been nuts. Cullen needs a father, not a photo on the bureau. You did what was necessary to stay alive. Now you're saying you took advantage of the poor schmuck?"

"When I made the choice, it was like flipping a mental switch," I said, "deciding my only way out was to take *him* out. So I snuffed him, just like . . . " I snapped my fingers. "No second thoughts, no regrets. Like it used to be in Korea, just glad to be alive. I thought I'd gotten past it."

"Past what?"

"The ability to take lives, then shut it out, like it's no big deal."

"I see. You think you're such a deadly hombre this guy didn't have a chance. He was just a simple feller, down on his luck, caught in a pissing contest with the head hippo."

He turned to face me, and put a big hand on my shoulder. "Tyler, my boy, you may be good, but not that good. Nobody is. Your mind-set was what kept you alive. You were willing. He wasn't. Or at least not as willing as you. Don't forget that. Every time you look at Cullen, thank

33

God for whatever it is that sets you apart from the norm. Without it, your son would be an orphan.

"Besides, you didn't ask that jerk to single you out. He made that move on his own."

"He didn't know what he was up against," I said.

"Yes he did. He just didn't know *who* he was up against. His mistake. Anyhow, it's done. Live with it. He's obviously got plenty of company in your skeleton closet."

True.

4

"**D**ADDY. You're on TV."

"Mphmphht."

"Daddy! Paw-paw said to wake you up. You're on TV."

I rolled over, took the pillow out of my mouth.

"Daddeee!"

"I'm awake."

"You're on TV. Paw-paw's taping it."

"Do I look handsome?"

"No. Bored."

"Oh."

Well, that was something. At least I didn't look dead.

Cullen graciously allowed me to sleep another hour and a half. Since he seldom allows the sun to rise before he does, his noisy play had intermittently disturbed me all morning. I was used to it, so managed to doze while eighteen-wheelers prowled amongst the furniture in the music room, helicopters buzzed loftily in the dining room, and Conan the Barbarian engaged the entire free world in swordplay.

Directly, I managed to coax my logy body into a vertical orientation and shrug into one of my father's bathrobes. He had two. I wore the one stained from the effects of Cullen's incontinent babyhood. My ecology-conscious wife had insisted on cloth diapers, which, though

35

kind to the landfills, were leaky.

Padding into the kitchen, I dug out the required paraphernalia and set to work scrambling eggs. Cullen burst in, slid to a stop by the counter, watched me poking at the pan with a wooden fork, said, "Can I have some?" Then, remembering, added, "Please."

"Where's my good-morning kiss and hug?"

I bent over, felt his little arms slide around me neck, squeezing tight, and received a buss on the lips. Away he sped, tossing a parting shot over his shoulder as he disappeared into the big bedroom: "Not too done. And with salt, please. But no pepper" — this last floating back as if on the wind, the words fading as he distanced himself.

I cracked another egg, one-handed, as Tess had taught me. She'd been a whiz in the kitchen. Her mother had seen to that.

The doctorate in history Tess had seen to herself.

I heard the back-porch screen door slam, then the inner door. The clipped *tock-tock-tock* of a woman in high heels. Through the kitchen door strode Ethyl Cullowee, Cullen's maternal grandmother. My mother-in-law. My dad's nemesis.

The look on her face would have peeled paint off aluminum siding. She spoke through her teeth, snapping off each word as if it had a rancid flavor. "Have you seen the morning paper?" In her eyes danced motes of anger.

"No. Dad doesn't subscribe. What's Jesse Helms said now?"

36

She slapped the offending organ down on the countertop, gritted, "The blimp," and whirled out of the room in search of Cullen. Dad had likely heard her coming and slipped out the front door. Coward.

I rotated the paper so I could read it without getting a headache. On the front page of the *Herald-Tribune* — above the fold, three-column head — was a story about me, complete with a photo that made me look like an ax murderer with a hangover. It gave accurate details about the robbery, the shooting, the kidnapping of teller Felita Hutchins, the tire-smoking getaway, all the while hinting that if I hadn't resisted with such vehemence, only the money might be gone and not the hapless Ms. Hutchins.

I wondered for a moment if that could be true. Probably not. Since the holdup men had vacated the bank on the side opposite mine, I doubted they'd been concerned much with me.

The story went on to lament mildly that I hadn't been held by the police, merely questioned and released. The fact that a dozen witnesses exonerated me of blame obviously set ill with the writer — surprise, surprise.

It was about what I expected from the *Trib*, but it still made me feel liverish.

I turned the eggs out of the pan and onto some plates, yelled, "Cullen, your eggs are ready!" then listened for answering footfalls.

Didn't hear any.

"Cullen! Your food will get cold!"

"Why're you yelling?" he said, stepping out of the breakfast room practically at my elbow.

37

"Sorry, I thought you were in the front of the house with Grandma."

The home I grew up in was rambling, having been added onto several times and moved once. All the rooms had at least two entrances; most were connecting. Picture a maze in the shape of a big, loose U with a fence connecting the open ends and you won't be far off.

"We came through the bathroom," Cullen was saying. "You didn't need to holler."

"Sit." I gestured at the plates. "Eat."

He did. To Grandma, I said, "Would you like some eggs? Toast? Coffee? Oreos?"

Seating herself, she responded, "I believe I'll have a cup of tea."

Of course she would; I'd need to prepare that, and my eggs would get cold.

"Where's Dad?" I queried gingerly.

"He probably saw me drive up and slunk out the front door. Don't blame him. Got a bone to pick with that man. But never you mind. Did you read that blubberball's story?"

"What's a blubberball?" asked my son, around a mouthful of egg.

"A large person," quipped his grandmother. "Now eat your food and let the grownups talk."

"I read it all right. About par for old Rita."

The gentlewoman of whom I spoke, Rita Snipes, had been one of Tess's undergraduate classmates at the University of North Carolina. She was an abbreviated but corpulent correspondent, roughly thirty-five years old, whose venomous prose had castigated me more than once in the public press. Anyone who had anything at all to do with hunting or shooting often found themselves on the receiving end of her poison pen. (Metaphorically speaking: her handwriting, according to Tess, had been so indecipherable even Rita couldn't read her own notes in college, and so had acquired a tape recorder after her first semester.)

Ms. Snipes was suspected of venality, and it was a known fact that she could be induced to imbibe alcohol on occasion.

Any occasion.

Ethyl tilted her regal head at me, arching an eyebrow. Although such scathing body language had reduced many a male to but a stuttering resemblance of his normal self, I was used to her. "The gall," Ethyl said. "'Endangering many innocent bystanders.' What did she expect you to do? Fall to your knees and beg for mercy? Blimp! Forget the tea." With that, she reached over to kiss Cullen on the cheek, ignoring snippets of egg clinging to the vicinity, and popped up. Out the back door she went, in search of a target for her ire.

I hoped Dad had walked down to the lake.

Aside from a trillion calls from well-wishers, ill-wishers, and one insurance salesman, the rest of the day passed uneventfully. No word from the police on who my assailants had been, or who their partners were thought to have been.

For two hours of sweaty seclusion, I performed my daily physical regimen. Did my t'ai chi kata, not as fluidly as I might have. Then three sets of one-arm push-ups, fifty reps per, and four sets of chins in groups of twenty-five. On the last two sets I tied a twenty-pound dumbbell to my feet. Five hundred crunches in a stretch, legs crossed at the ankles, hands behind my head, flat on my back. No mat.

Tough, wasn't I? The Big Four-oh looming in my immediate future daunted me not. Birthday candles are for blowing out, not fretting over.

I finished with 250 incline sit-ups a 25-pound plate under my chin for added fun. After enough rope skipping to make my legs rubbery, I dragged my 165 pounds into the shower, almost too tired to lather properly.

★ ★ ★

Cullen and I climbed into my dad's car in midafternoon. When I switched the ignition on, Rush Limbaugh came over the radio, in full battle with a liberal schoolteacher from Des Moines over what level of income constituted "rich." By her reckoning, I was rich.

She was right.

I reached over and put a hand on my fortune. He smiled back at me. "Can I turn on some music?"

"Sure."

He poked the AM/FM button with a little forefinger and Randy Travis filled the car.

" . . . we all thought his heart was made of solid rock. But that was long before we found the box."

At the conclusion of the song, Rod Davis came on and tried to sell me a Chevrolet. To

40

avoid being tempted, I turned off the radio.

"Why are we riding in Paw-paw's car?" Cullen asked.

"My truck was pretty shot up at the bank."

"Aw, shoot! I love that truck. Can they fix it?"

"I doubt it."

"Why did all those police look mad at you on TV?"

"That's one of the things the police do well. Look mad at people."

"When I first saw you on TV, I got scared. A little. So I went into your room on tippy, tippy-toe, and watched you asleep. Your mouth was open. Are you 'posed to sleep with your mouth open?"

"However suits you."

"What if a bug crawls in?"

"Don't chew."

"Yuk. Anyway, I watched you a whole long time and you seemed okay. So I snuck back out and watched some more TV."

He was quiet for a spell. "What if those men had shot you?"

"They didn't. Try not to dwell on it."

"But they coulda. Right?"

"It's possible."

He unbuckled his seat belt and slid over close to me. Put his head on my bicep, little hand on my forearm.

"I know Mommy's in heaven, with Jesus, and can look down and see me anytime, and she still loves me." His voice was husky. "But I can't see her, except in here." He pointed at his temple.

41

"I couldn't stand it if you went away like Mommy did. I just couldn't." He rubbed my arm with the side of his head.

"I won't then."

"Promise?"

"Promise."

He fell asleep, there in my dad's car, clinging to my arm. Once home, I turned off the phones and imitated Cullen. To perfection.

We got up around six that evening. Fixed sandwiches and watched the news. Some stations treated me like a hero, others like a pariah. As expected.

Cullen seemed bored by all the media attention. He didn't care what they were saying; he'd already formed his opinion about me.

Munching snacks of rice-and-popcorn cakes, we watched *ET*, a semiannual event for us, both of us blubbering at the end as always.

After brushing my teeth, I turned on the phones and turned down the beds. Tucked Cullen in, listened to his prayers, read *Tell Me a Mitzi* till he fell asleep. As I was double-checking the doors, the phone rang.

"Hello."

"Mr. Vance, please."

"You got him."

"Not yet. I will, however."

"I beg your pardon?"

Click. Broken connection.

The voice was baritone, heavily accented though geographically indistinct, calm, assured, menacing, resonant with the dulcet tones that hint of a higher education.

I didn't like it much.

After reporting the call to the police, I lifted Cullen's sleeping form out of his bed and moved it to mine. From the gun safe came a Ruger P-94 9 mm pistol. I snapped in a loaded magazine and put two extras beside the gun, on the nightstand, within easy reach. Locked the bedroom door, then pushed the heavy chest of drawers against it.

I sat up all night. Beside my son. And slept not a wink.

5

"**A**M I getting a new mom?"

"Now what brought on that question?" We were eating lunch, more or less; I was having a postprandial cup of Gevalia hazelnut, and Cullen was avoiding his lima beans by engaging me in conversation.

"Barry says that his mom and you have been, uh, dating for a real long time now, and that y'all are gonna get married. Then she'll be my new mom and Barry will be my brother."

Cullen's mother had been gone for less than a year, and he wasn't keen on acquiring a replacement. Nor was I intent on providing him with one, despite my recent (two weeks — a "long time" to Cullen) and casual interest in the mother of one of his neighborhood cronies. Cullen and I were a team, quite comfortable with each other and our lot, and what with my dad and mother-in-law around to assist in his upbringing, not without plenty of loving support. I certainly enjoyed the company of women, but sustained no overwhelming need to move in with another one.

Besides, I wasn't acquainted with any who might answer in the affirmative should I ask.

"Son, you'll never have a new mother. You might gain a stepmother someday if I were to be married again, but you had only one real mom. No one can take her place."

44

"What's dating mean?"

"Dating is when two grownups go out to dinner, or maybe to a movie together."

"And smooch?"

"Not always, but if they like each other, sometimes they do."

He mulled that over. "When you date a lady for a long time, do you have to marry her?"

"No, although some of them do view it differently."

His little brow knit thoughtfully. "So you're not gonna marry Mrs. Cranford?"

"No. In fact, we're not planning to go out together anymore."

His face relaxed, the tension easing palpably. "Good."

"Why is it good?"

"I don't really like her that much, though I'd never tell Barry. Might hurt his feelings."

"You wouldn't want to do that."

"I know. I like him a lot."

"So what's the problem with Mrs. Cranford?"

"Her eyes are too long."

I chewed on my upper lip to maintain a serious expression. It wasn't easy. I asked, with all the gravity I could muster, "What do you mean?"

He poked at the limes with his spoon, grimaced, took a tiny bite, grimaced again, and said, "She sees everything me and Barry do, no matter how far away we are. The day after yesterday we were in his tree house playing Power Rangers, and I took out my pitcher of Buzz Aldrich — "

"Aldrin."

"Aldrin, to show Barry, and he wanted to swap me a clump of printzels — "

"Clump of what?"

"Printzels. The straight skinny kind, not the loopy ones, but they didn't have much salt on 'em 'cause he had licked most of it off before he put 'em in his pocket. Please don't keep interrupting."

"Sorry."

"It's okay. Anyhow, Mrs. Cranford yelled out, 'Don't you give Cullen any of those printzels! You had 'em in your mouth!'" He imitated the lady under discussion, holding his hands up to his mouth like a megaphone.

"Like that, you know, real loud. You know how far away it is from their back porch to the tree house? She can see really good. It's spooky."

I sipped my coffee as he regarded his beans balefully. He looked up, eyes awash with pleading, then back down at the bowl. "Do I have to eat all of 'em?"

I could see me through Cullen's eyes. I'd hated lima beans as a kid too.

"Each and every one," I said, cringing internally.

He winced as if struck by a water balloon. "Aw, Daaad! I hate 'em!" he declared.

Over the rim of my cup, I answered, "I know."

"*You* eat 'em." Defiant. One of his endearing qualities. Obviously from his mother's side of the family.

"I already ate mine."

"Why do I have to eat lima beans? Why can't I have some yogrit?"

"Yo-*gurt*."

"Yeah. Why not?"

"Because limas are good for you. You need fiber. The pizza you just inhaled doesn't have much. Neither does yogurt. Limas do."

"'Cause they're a veg'table?"

"That's correct."

"You told me mushrooms were veg'tables. The pizza had lots of mushrooms. Do mushrooms have fiber?"

"Some. Not enough."

"Oh." Resigned, he changed the subject. But he didn't eat another bean.

I let it go. Choose your battles.

"You promised me a Happy Meal tonight, with a toy."

"Sorry. Something came up. I have to go see Mrs. Patterson."

"Web's mom? What you seeing her for?"

"I'm not sure. She left a message on the machine asking me to call her. I did, and she asked me out to dinner tonight. Said she had a favor to ask. Maybe tomorrow we'll go to McDonald's, if you're good at Paw-paw's this afternoon." Paw-paw is southern for grandpater, and I don't apologize for my son's use of the locution. Neither does he.

A beatific smile. "Oh, I'll be good. Real good. So you promise? About McDonald's?"

"I promise."

But I was wrong. We wouldn't be having

a Happy Meal the next day, or the next. McDonald's would not serve hot provender to the Tylers, father and son, for quite some time in the future. We'd both be different then. If I had known what was in store, I wouldn't have taken him to my dad's, or anywhere else. I'd have stayed home, barricaded in the bedroom, with Cullen clutched protectively to my chest.

★ ★ ★

While Cullen played in the backyard with our pair of West Highland white terriers, Nubbin and Miss Priss, I loaded my shooting gear into car number two, a nearly new bright red Supra. In went the shooting box, loaded with such gear as stapler, cleaning rods, screwdrivers, and whatnot. Two rifles. Large cardboard box filled brimful with ammunition of two calibers in several brands and bullet weights. Targets. Sandbags and benchrest pedestal. A sissy bag in case the big-bore number was unusually irritating to my shoulder. (I may be sturdy and resolute as hell, but recoil takes its toil. Some days more than others.)

Then Cullen climbed in, and off to Paw-paw's we went.

★ ★ ★

I was anticipating the rifle's prodigious kick, but anticipating and prepared for aren't exactly the same, if you catch my drift. No one can absorb for long the punishment dished out at the aft

48

end of a rifle capable of decking a triceratops with one shot, at least not without some deleterious effect on accuracy. Such backthrust can't be controlled totally; the best I could do was hang on and ride it out. As the roar of internal powder combustion assaulted my eardrums — despite the dual protection provided by earplugs and muff-type sound reducers — the big .416 Weatherby slammed rearward, compressing my scapulae, mashing my right shoulder, whapping my cheekbone painfully. Groan.

Some people claim to enjoy such punishment. Old-time gun scribe Elmer Keith was one of them. I never set much store by what he wrote, anyway.

A major part of my job as a firearms writer involved testing new guns and cartridges — "wringing them out," in shooters' parlance. But doing much firing from a benchrest with the likes of the .416 Weatherby left me wondering just who got wrung out! It's much more enjoyable testing a lightweight synthetic-stocked .243 deer rifle, or a .308 heavy-barreled target number like the second gun I'd been shooting that day, a paramilitary prototype from a European maker who wanted his chunk of American SWAT money. From such ordnance there was less wear and tear on ears, joints, and nerves. (I'll be the first to admit that the more years I accumulate, the more reluctant I am to accept the discomfort.)

Checking to make certain no one was looking, I rubbed my shoulder, then peered through the spotting scope to note with satisfaction the close proximity of the last bullet on target to the four preceding it. Five shots in about an inch and a half. Not bad accuracy from such a stout-kicking piece, especially with factory ammunition. I stood up and rotated my head, to considerable creaking accompaniment from my neck. Returned the long, heavy gun to its even longer, heavier metal carrying case, with some relief, I must confess.

It was getting late; I still had to shower and shave before my soiree with Heather Patterson, she of the liquid eyes, legs clear up to her clavicles, bouncing golden tresses that tossed sunlight and a hint of invitation toward unsuspecting and unprotected admirers in her wake. Why in the world she'd asked me out was a mystery. In her thirties, slim and athletic, with family money and a high-paying job as editor of a local children's magazine, she was capable of bewitching any swain within eyeshot with but one long-lashed, emerald wink, although I wasn't sure she was totally aware of it. I'd heard that all attractive women know they're attractive. In Heather's case, I questioned the validity of that aphorism.

I'd met her and her son Web at Lake Daniel Park when Cullen was still endiapered. Over time, the boys became friends; both currently played T-ball on the team I coached. When my wife Tess died, Heather had been one of my and Cullen's staunchest supporters, bringing food and doing the laundry and cleaning up after two grief-stricken males too numb to look

50

after themselves. She didn't try to close in, perhaps afraid she might create an intrusion, come between us at a very difficult time.

After the mourning period passed, she more or less faded from view. She'd bring Web to ball practice, leave, pick him up afterward. I was too busy during the actual games to look for her, so never knew if she came. Web always left with the family of another player.

But here she was back in my life, at least tentatively. Tonight, for the small investment of a modicum of Mexican food, I'd bask in her radiance, maybe get another shot at her. I'd have to turn on the charm, dazzle her, get a second date on my terms. Perhaps I should yodel a few bars from *The Music Man*, like when I'm in the shower.

Then again, maybe not.

Even loyal, devoted Cullen — to whom I'd been singing since he was a fetus, my mouth to his momma's expanding belly — blanched when I did "Seventy-six Trombones."

I glanced at my watch: 4:31.

I glanced at my wallet: numerous photos of Tess and Cullen and a couple of lonely one-dollar bills, plus the royalty check I'd never gotten around to cashing yesterday, what with the excitement and all. I doubted that two bucks would buy many enchiladas. Would Heather spring for the evening?

Fat chance.

I hustled my gear into the car, considered going to the bank to cash my check, decided I may never go to a bank again. I'd run by

51

Dave's store and write a personal check.

Trailing a cloud of dust, I wheeled the red Toyota down the gravel track toward the paved road. At the gate — which consisted of a twelve-foot length of heavy chain welded to an upright metal pipe and affixed to another one by a robust padlock — I stopped, got out and dropped the chain, drove the Supra through the opening, then reversed the procedure with the chain. My sunglasses slipped down the bridge of my nose from the exertion. I pushed them back into place with a forefinger.

As I pulled onto the hardtop, I waved to Herb Archer, owner of the shooting range, and pondered whether a passerby might mistake me for Arnold Schwarzenegger. Probably not; he's too tall, too European. Stallone? Naw. Too swarthy, too intense.

By the time of my arrival at Dave's electronics emporium, The Lion's Din, I had settled on Mel Gibson.

A glance in the mirror caused me to rethink that assessment. I'm better looking.

★ ★ ★

When I walked through his door, Dave looked up from the VCR whose innards he'd been prodding with a long pointed instrument.

"You the proctologist?" I greeted him.

"Feeling better today, are we?"

"Shut up and cash this." I handed him the royalty check.

"Could I refuse such a polite request?" he said,

glancing at the amount. "Thanks, but you're confusing me with one of the Rockefellers. You got one with fewer digits?"

I handed him the check I'd written while waiting impatiently at a red light, Tracy Chapman singing "Fast Car" to me, all chalky and sullen.

"This any good?" he said.

"How should I know? I found it in the parking lot."

"Guess I better not ask for ID then."

"No problem. I have several."

He handed me forty bucks. "I'll take a chance on the check if you'll just leave. Don't like riffraff hanging around the store. Bad for our image."

"You think this joint's got an image?"

"Don't call my dump a joint."

I took my twenties and left. That'd teach him.

6

SHE opened the door, gave me a temperate smile, and extended a slender hand. Clear nail polish, manicure, graceful, firm grip. Her hair had been recently catered to by a professional with a deft touch, perhaps Bobby Atkinson at Leon's. Those in the know with the dough went to Bobby.

She wore a pastel flower-print dress, cream background, belted at the waist. Simple strand of pearls, pearl-colored. Pumps, so she wouldn't be taller than me. How thoughtful.

Her makeup was understated; you couldn't tell it was there unless you looked hard. I did, trying not to squint. A little eyeliner, hint of blush. She didn't need any, not with her skin.

"You look very nice." I said.

She enhanced the smile ten or twelve watts, shut the door and locked it, dropping the keys into her purse. Pirouetting lightly, she said, "Thanks. You too," then walked to my car, her hip movements rhythmical, languid, sensual. And natural, no put-on.

Zing!

I helped her into the car, and when I thought my voice wouldn't crack, said, "Casa Gallardo okay with you?"

"Just fine."

I pulled away from the curb, priapism be damned. She didn't sit in my lap on the way to the restaurant, but she didn't hug her door either.

Our first problem came about when she punched the car's cigarette lighter and began to rummage in her bag.

"Please don't smoke," I petitioned.

She turned both emerald orbs on me, hesitated for the count of five, grimaced, said, "Sorry, new habit. Does smoke bother you?"

"Only when I breathe."

A tiny glint of humor flashed. "Okay, I can wait. Do you avoid people who smoke?"

"I can't think of any specific group of people I avoid. I simply avoid smoke when I can."

"Do you have any friends who smoke?"

"Several. One of my best friends, from early childhood, was a smoker."

"Was?"

"He died, at thirty-nine. Lung cancer. His older sister, who also smokes, has emphysema, angina, and bunions. I'm not sure if smoking caused the bunions."

She chuckled deep in her throat. The Supra tracked along, most of its 320 horses in reserve. She looked around the car, took in the dash, leather upholstery, the CD player.

"Nice car," she offered. "Didn't you used to drive a little pickup truck?"

"It's . . . indisposed. But I still have it. Thought you'd prefer to ride in this."

"Especially if it rains."

"Beg your pardon?"

"Your truck might leak pretty badly, with all those holes."

"Ah. You follow the news."

"Mind telling me about it?"

"Not particularly." So I did.

She listened attentively, not interrupting once, eyes on my face as I talked and drove and relived. When I had finished, she said, "It bothered you, didn't it?"

"Nearly being shot?"

"No, having to shoot those men. I watched you as you related the story. You spoke with no bravado. If anything, a twinge of remorse."

"I'm not proud of it."

"A lot of men would be."

Yeah, well, a lot of men never saw a group of close friends shot to doll-rags by a North Korean patrol, then, while the Koreans were preoccupied with dismemberment, came up from behind and killed them all. I'm not proud of that, either.

What I said was, "Is there anything else you want to know about it?"

She continued to watch me carefully, turned sideways in her seat. "I think not."

We made small talk the rest of the way to the restaurant. Occasionally, she put her hand on my arm when stressing a point, giving it a firm but poignant squeeze.

Be still, my heart.

We arrived, went in, her arm intertwined in mine, and joined a queue of fellow patrons. Every male in the place eyed Heather, either overtly or covertly, regardless of whether they had a female of their own in evidence.

Heather seemed oblivious to anyone but me.

Quite a lady, this. She knew how to focus

56

her attention on her escort, instead of looking around as if comparison shopping.

I appreciated how rare that was and told her so. She smiled enigmatically. "Why should I look around? I'll stick with you."

I was about to faint from pleasure when our greeter singled us out of the throng and asked, "Smoking or non?"

Before I could answer, Heather said, "Non, please."

I was in love.

We followed our short, stout, balding host to a small for-two table stuck in a corner near the kitchen. As she pulled out Heather's chair, I asked, "Can you cash a check for more than the amount of purchase?"

Porcine eyes blinking rapidly, as if caught in an April shower, he queried as to the amount of the check.

"Forty-five hundred dollars, more or less."

She blinked even more rapidly, if that was possible. A mole on her chin quivered, causing several thick black hairs to quake noticeably.

"I'm sorry, sir."

"I was afraid not." We sat, ordered drinks — beer all around — then bellied up to the menus.

★ ★ ★

An hour later, our meal having been disposed of and the residue removed, we got to the *raison d'étre*. Or at least Ms. Patterson did.

"Have you been wondering why I asked you

57

out tonight?" she opened.

"It crossed my mind. And whether you plan to pay the bill."

"Oh, of course . . . "

I held up a hand. "My pleasure, my treat."

"No, really . . . "

"I was needling you, Heather. Bad habit, I know. Not everyone appreciates my humor."

She looked uncomfortable. Something was eating at her.

Girding her loins, she plunged in. "A problem has arisen. With Web."

I smiled encouragingly.

She fiddled with her fork, her napkin. Eyes on the table, not me.

"At preschool, he's becoming somewhat of a discipline problem."

"Getting into fights?"

"Yes."

"Talking back? Rebelling at authority?" Animated, looking up now, she said, "Yes! Exactly. Cullen too?"

I shook my head. "No. Me."

She frowned. "When you were a child?"

"Then too."

"I'm serious."

"So am I." I went on. "How can I help with this?"

She inhaled, exhaled, looked away, looked back, then forged ahead. "Web needs a father figure." She sat straight in her chair, exuding relief, defiance, discomfiture, as if thinking, *There, I said it.*

"This a proposal?"

58

Fluttery laugh. "No, no, nothing like . . . You're kidding again."

I nodded. "Coaches, even at the T-ball level, are a type of mentor, role model. Don't you agree?"

"Certainly. But I think Web needs one more like full-time."

I was taken aback. "You mean have him move in with us?"

"Oh, no. Not move in. Just spend more time with you and Cullen. You know, going fishing, throwing a ball back and forth, roughhousing . . . "

"Guy stuff."

She gave me embarrassed again. "You know what I mean. I'm not being sexist."

"Sure you are, but it's okay. We are, after all, of different sexes."

I had no idea where Web's dad fit into his life, or even if he did. He and Heather had divorced some time before Tess died. So I said, "What about your ex-husband?"

She muttered, "He's not a role model for anyone."

"Why not?"

"My husband has nothing whatever to do with Web. He has no visitation. In fact, there is a restraining order that prevents his even seeing him."

I was very uncomfortable with the way this was going.

"Why?" I queried.

She shook her head.

"There any uncles, maybe a grandfather?"

59

"No uncles, on either side. My parents live in Charlotte. Dad owns an electrical contracting firm. He's into money and sports, and browbeats Web every time we go to visit.

"To be frank with you," she went on, "Web's main problem is that there are no men in his life right now. The consequences of that are beginning to get out of hand."

"You haven't any, uh, romantic interests at the moment?"

"No need to be delicate," she said, proving it by looking me right in the eye. "I have absolutely no luck with men. Never have. The ones I like either don't like me, are unhappy that I have a child, or simply want to spend all our time together in the sack."

Her eyes, rather abruptly, seemed to be sizzling. Must have inadvertently prodded a nerve. *Tread carefully around any mention of significant others*, I told myself.

But hey, was I not happy that there were no significant others in her life? Yes indeedy.

At the next table, a corpulent fellow with a large nose and wing-tip shoes dug into his jacket, withdrew a cigar the size and shape of a hoagie, and lit it, despite a No Smoking sign at arm's length. I considered jerking it out of his hand to set his toupee afire, but thought better of it. I'm too well-mannered. Would have made me feel better, though.

Trying not to inhale, I steered Heather back into safer waters. "So what does Web think of this idea?"

"He nearly worships you. During ball season,

60

he talked about you all the time. It's 'Coach Vance said this, Coach Vance did that.' Watching you during games, I noticed how you treated all of your players with respect, and genuine affection. That's why I'm asking you specifically to do this for Web. He needs a man to pay attention to him, be firm but not simply negative, like his grandfather."

"I'm flattered. Though I'm not certain how much it'll help, I'll be happy to spend time with Web, and I'm sure Cullen will enjoy having a playmate his age. He spends a lot of his day at my dad's, who's keeping him this evening. The homeplace covers more than seventy acres, with a big lake for swimming, fishing, boating, getting bit by mosquitoes. Dad's retired, and my mother passed on years ago. His main pursuit in life is having Cullen around to keep him young. That, and dodging my mother-in-law."

She laughed politely, then said, "You can't know how much I appreciate this. Since I work such long hours, Web spends too much time in the care of those who don't love him, if you know what I mean. With the divorce and everything, he hasn't had the easiest of childhoods. You're the first man outside the family who's really paid attention to him. With his dad and mine out of the picture, at least as much as I can manage, he needs a man around who likes him."

"I love children in general, but Web stands out on his own merit."

She beamed at the praise, then waxed wistful. "I wish his father . . . " The thought trailed off;

her face tightened. "No matter." She closed that door. On to other things.

"Do you think you could get him tomorrow? He's at preschool from seven-thirty until six or so. I drop him on the way to work, then get him on the way home. I'll arrange it so you can pick him up whenever you want."

"Before we settle on anything, let me check with my dad. I'll call you tomorrow."

"Okay."

"Not wishing to flog a dead steed, but how do you really feel about that little fiasco at the bank yesterday?"

"How should I feel? Did you go there on business?"

"I did."

"Did someone try to impound your truck at gunpoint?"

"They did."

"Did another someone try to mow you down with a machine gun?"

"Machine pistol," I corrected.

"Whatever."

"He did indeed."

"Did you defend yourself in accordance with state and local laws?"

"Not to mention Blackstone."

"Well then."

"You have no problem with it?"

"Why should I?"

"I don't think you should."

"Neither do I," she agreed.

"Okay. One final item on the agenda."

"And that is?"

"What do I get in return for becoming Web's mentor?"

Arched brow, my altruism under instant scrutiny. "What do you want?"

"A date."

"A date? I thought this was a date."

"Doesn't count."

"Why not?"

"You had an ulterior motive."

"Oh. A real date, huh?"

"Uh-huh."

She considered me for a long moment.

"Do you like me?" she said.

"Yep."

"I have a child, you know."

"Heard that. Doesn't scare me away."

"I don't like to spend all my time being groped."

"Can we hold hands in the moonlight?"

Another considering gaze, then: "Maybe. On the second date."

"Goody."

"But no groping," she clarified.

"You've got a deal."

That settled, we paid up and went for a ride in the gloaming.

★ ★ ★

We tooled out I–40 to Highway 68, turning north toward Oak Ridge Military Academy. We drove past the old mill with its red-painted waterwheel, which always made me want to run in and buy a big bag of meal, then rush home and bake a pan of corn bread. I resisted the urge. In retrospect, things would have turned out better if I hadn't. After thirty minutes of driving, the darkness now complete, Heather requested something sweet. I asked what she had a taste for. She said a sundae, so we headed for The Sweetery on Battleground Avenue. The entire front of the restaurant was constructed of glass, so that the patrons were on display as they gobbled succulent goodies. We entered the swinging doors at the left front of the single serving room. The counter for eat-in customers ran off to the right and circled to form a U as it neared the right-hand wall. Short stools lined the counter, a few filled to spillover by ample backsides, male and female.

Since it was a Wednesday night, the place wasn't very crowded; we pretty much had our choice of seats. We walked around the curved portion of the counter and seated ourselves opposite the entryway, backs to the far wall, facing out toward the parking lot.

For Heather a chocolate nut sundae; *pour moi* a coffee milk shake. A perky college coed dubbed Naomi took our orders. Directly, they were presented with a little flourish I found delightful from a lass working late at night, and probably for minimum wage.

Heather lit into her ice cream with genteel gusto. She didn't even get hot fudge on her lips. When I ate a sundae, I generally had to run myself through a car wash after.

With her thus engaged, I glanced out at the parking lot. A black BMW 633 pulled into the parking space next to my Supra and cut its lights. Its occupants did not join our little group of dessert consumers, simply sat in the car.

A part of my mind went on alert status, tasting the night, hackles raised. Disjointed perceptions coursed through my brain in jumbled succession, but nothing specific. Something ominous, incorporeal; not concrete, recognizable.

I'd had this feeling many times before. It was never pleasant.

I glanced at our server, standing by the cash register chatting with another employee. Nothing out of sync. The few other guests were eating, drinking, conversing affably. No one else seemed disturbingly prescient.

A pair of indistinct forms were visible in the front seats of the Beemer. No movement, though. Nobody got out. The car sat heavy and sleek, a squat German toad staring with lightless eyes. Tension plucked at my nerves, walked with tiny electric feet up my spine.

"What's the matter?"

I'd forgotten Heather was there. I looked at her, then back at the BMW.

"Nothing," I answered.

"Then why do you look like my father's Doberman when she hears a noise outside the house?"

Good question.

Good analogy.

The door on the passenger side had opened, its window down. Odd. It wasn't cold outside, but too cold for riding with the window all the way down.

65

A very, very large man stepped out of the passenger seat and stood looking in the glass front of the restaurant. At me. Wide-brimmed hat, pulled low to conceal his face. Overcoat. Unusual stance. His left arm was bent at the elbow, the forearm angling across the front of his body. His right elbow was tucked into his right side. I squinted to see better. Five years ago, I wouldn't have had to squint.

On the windowsill of the car door, I could vaguely discern a small circular outline perhaps an inch in diameter. Looked like the end of a length of pipe.

Or a shotgun barrel.

Heather was saying something when I grabbed her by the arms, jerked her tightly to my body, and spun backward off the stool, pulling her down to the floor as I fell. When I hit the floor, cushioning her fall with my body, I spun again, pinning her to the tile. I couldn't hear what she was yelling. The subdued hum of the restaurant had plunged precipitously into a dazing cacophony of gun blasts, shattering glass, and hysterical screams.

7

"**D**ON'T move," I told Heather, then vaulted the counter twice and ran out into the parking lot through a window where only seconds before a pane had stood. The BMW screeched north on Battleground Avenue, cars diving for the curb in its wake. I didn't make the plate.

Back inside, bedlam. At least four people were bleeding, one elderly woman from multiple wounds. Heather knelt beside her, using a wad of paper napkins as a pressure bandage. She spoke to the lady soothingly, in low tones, to keep her as calm as possible. It seemed to be working.

Our friendly hostess was sitting on the floor behind the register atop a crushed mound of ice cream cones, crying heartily into her apron. No one was paying her any attention, so I jumped the counter and squatted on my heels beside her. She glanced at me, snuffled, then lapsed into chest-heaving sobs.

I put a hand behind her head and held it to me, surreptitiously examining her for damage. No blood. She cried and cried, her breathing shallow and erratic. Made me want to cry too, but that would have been counterproductive. So I just held on. Directly, her sobs depreciated into steady but controlled drippiness. She looked up at me, mumbled a quiet "Thank you," then stood and leaned against the counter. Made of stout stuff, our ice cream lady.

I checked on Heather, who had moved to a teenaged boy lying on his back on the floor, a six-inch shard of glass protruding from his right arm near the elbow. He was pale but coherent, and appeared to be reasonably comfortable. She'd fashioned a tourniquet from her belt and applied it to his upper arm; the wound was barely seeping.

I put my hand on her shoulder. She looked up, said, "I'm okay. How about you?"

"Fine. I'm going to check on the guy in the corner."

She nodded and I went to check on the guy in the corner.

* * *

The guy in the corner was dead. Four buckshot pellets had taken him high in the back, and that was that. I covered his face with my shirt and went to meet the first police officer to arrive, saying to him as he came through the door, "We've got one dead, maybe a half-dozen sufficiently damaged for external bleeding. The girl over by the bathroom door appears to be in shock. She's conscious but totally unresponsive."

"You are?" — from the officer.

"Tyler Vance. But that's not important. There are several people bleeding here, one of them badly enough to require a tourniquet. We need an ambulance right now."

68

I don't know if he said anything in response, because I had left him by then.

A lady cop named Rodriguez, whom I remembered from the bank, had just stepped into the room. She spotted me and walked over. "Why is it whenever I see blood all over the place, there you are?"

I explained the situation to her; she took a quick scan of the place, then made a call. Soon the parking lot was full of ambulances, police cars, cops and medical personnel.

I sat shirtless at the counter with Heather, shivering in the chill air, until McDuffy came in to heat me up with his connate mental flatulence.

★ ★ ★

"Describe the car."

"Black BMW 633."

"License?"

"Vanity plate. Had 'ARMAGEDDON' on it."

"Sure it did, asshole."

"There was no plate on the front, McDuffy. This is North Carolina, you know."

"Any other distinguishing characteristics?"

"Darkly tinted windshield. Cellular antenna. White sidewalls, which I've never seen on a 633. Kind of like wearing spats."

"Didn't you look for a plate when the car peeled off?"

"I was on the floor at that moment. I didn't see anything."

"Some tough guy. Here I thought you was a real stand-up hombre when the lead flies, but where were you? On the floor. Counting tiles, huh?"

"Looking for a slime trail, to see if you were in the vicinity."

He rotated his head at the shoulders, as if trying to loosen a kink, never taking his eyes off my face. Intimidating.

"Let's start over, Sergeant. You ask, and if the questions aren't impertinent, irrelevant, or irrational, I'll answer them to the best of my knowledge."

"You'll answer them anyway, either here or downtown. Wanta go downtown, tough guy? Me and you, in a back room? Alone?"

"Only if you shower first."

"Listen, numbnuts — "

"Sergeant." Heather speaking.

"What?"

"Are you normally such a cretin, or did we simply catch you at a bad time?"

"Listen, lady — "

"No, you listen. This gentleman and I have just been shot at, along with many others in this room. One person was killed. If you don't exhibit a significant attitude adjustment immediately, I promise to spend the remainder of this evening in the company of a newspaper reporter whose name you would recognize instantly but without affection. Do we understand one another?"

Although clearly upset, McDuffy realized that he had been clearly out-threatened. Whatever professionalism he possessed reasserted itself.

He breathed in deeply, held for a count of eight, exhaled, and said, "You're right, ma'am. I let my dislike for your boyfriend color my judgment. I apologize. The fellow that did the shooting, did either of you see him?"

"Yeah," I said. "Big guy, six eight, two-ninety or better. Had an outback-style hat pulled low over his forehead, I suppose so no one could see his face. Wore a heavy, dark frock coat, like Kevin Costner in *Wyatt Earp*. Huge as he is, he shouldn't be hard to spot. He'd stand out in a group of Dallas linemen.

"Anyway, when he climbed out of the car — and I literally mean climbed — he stood with the door open. Didn't shut it and come on in like a customer. I noticed that his window was down, which I thought was odd. It's not especially warm outside tonight."

"Then why don't you have on a shirt?"

"I laid it over that fellow in the corner," I said, indicating the direction with a tilt of my head.

McDuffy looked over and said, "Oh. Right."

"Anyway, I spotted his gun barrel resting on the windowsill, although for a moment I didn't realize it was a gun barrel. Once it dawned on me that it was, and that I was looking right down its muzzle, I grabbed Heather and took her to the floor. The front of the building disintegrated; pellets whacked into everything. I covered her with my body and prayed. Obviously, God heard me. Things could have been much worse. In fact, considering the number of rounds the guy fired, it's a miracle half these folks aren't dead."

"Any thoughts on just what this jazbo was after?"

Before taking my dive, I'd locked eyes with the giant, his prodigious threatening bulk limned by a streetlight down the block. Vividly he'd projected from soulless, sharklike eyes an evil, unalterable intent.

"Yeah. He was after me."

* * *

Heather and I were sitting at the bullet-chewed counter, drinking coffee, bone tired. I'd called my dad; she'd called her sitter.

"Are you all right?" I gestured with a hand at the disarray. "About all this?"

"Do you mean being shot at by a guy the size of a Dempsey Dumpster, or having to minister to the wounded?"

"Either. Both," I said.

"I was first on the scene of a really terrible wreck my second year at Wake Forest. Three people died, one so badly mangled he was barely recognizable. I was holding his head in my lap when he went, trying to comfort him since I obviously could do nothing to fix him. I cried for days, not just because he died, but because I had been so . . . ineffectual. After that I took paramedic training in my spare time. Learned CPR. I never had to use any of it, until now. Tonight, my knowledge paid off, at least in a small way."

"More than a small way. That youngster might have bled to death if you hadn't stanched the blood flow."

Shake of her head. "You'd have done it."

"He might not have lain there for me like he did for you."

"Then you'd have knocked him out. I still can't get over your lack of hesitation . . . If you hadn't pulled me down as quickly as you did, I probably would have been killed myself. Have you noticed the wall behind where we were sitting?"

I nodded grimly.

"There's not much left of it," she went on. "Then like a flash you went over that counter and on outside without the slightest hint of indecision. What if he'd just been reloading?"

"I was watching as I jumped the counter. If he had come back out of the car, I'd have tried to draw his fire away from you and the others."

"Nice. Then you'd be dead now."

"No sense the rest of you going with me. Besides, I've been shot at before. There are ways to evade," I continued with my line of bullshit, "although against a scattergun at close quarters, not many." That was certainly true enough.

"Tyler Vance."

"Yes ma'am?"

"My daddy's been hunting ducks for thirty years."

Puzzled, I said, "So?"

"At the end of my junior year in high school, I pretended an interest in the sport, a transparent attempt to please Dad, and convince him I

73

should never go off to college without a red Corvette."

I encouraged her to continue, although I had no idea where this was going.

"I spent hours and dollars — lots of each — at a trap and skeet range. Became as familiar with a Remington 1100 twelve-bore auto as I was with my much used tennis racket. That fall, Dad and I hunted out of the same blind every weekend of the season, side by side, both of us getting our limits on ducks, geese, even swans down at Pamlico."

"And?"

"So cut the crap. If that mountain-sized bozo had popped out of the Beemer again with you that close and no cover, he'd have cut you to ribbons. And I don't care how evasive you tried to be."

"Maybe I did understate the situation a little."

"A little. Do me a favor. Treat me like a big girl. No sugarcoating, no coddling. And never, ever lie to me."

"Okay."

"Now drink your coffee and let me think. I'm trying to remember more details about that BMW."

Glancing at the parking lot, I saw Fanner get out of an unmarked car and saunter toward the front door — what was left of it. "All right. I'll go speak with the gent coming through the door."

"He a friend of yours?"

"Not so's you'd notice."

On the way to Fanner, I was ambushed by a newly arrived rookie, solicitous, officious, and pushy.

"Here, sir. Sit down. Have you been hurt?"

"No, I'm fine. Thanks anyway."

"Are you sure?"

"I'm absolutely certain." I tried to sidestep. No good. The officer blocked my path.

"Where's your shirt?"

Enough was enough. "What shirt?"

"Yours. You don't have one on."

"I don't?"

"No. Did you get blood on it? Use it for a bandage?"

"I don't think so. Maybe I didn't have one on when I came in."

"You don't remember?"

"I'm not sure. You'd think I'd know, wouldn't you? Maybe I lost it. Or someone stole it off my back. Is Newt Gingrich in here?"

"That's not funny, sir. I happen to be a supporter of Speaker — " she started.

"I'll bet you are. Look, there's Larry King," I said, pointing. When she turned to look, I slipped past.

As I walked away, I said, "Why don't you talk to that lady at the counter? She got a good look at the car."

With the gleam of Mission in her eye, she scurried off to be officious and solicitous and pushy to Heather, while I sought Lieutenant John T. Fanner's ear.

75

"I was informed you were not hurt," said Fanner, looking me over carefully.

"I'm not. But thanks for your concern."

"Where is your shirt?"

I told him what I'd used it for.

"A pity," he said.

"We need to talk," I told him. "Privately."

"Indeed we do. I was going to suggest my office. There have been developments, and lack of same. Is right now convenient for you? It is most imperative."

"Damn right. About the urgency, that is. As for the timing, I have a date I need to get home. Then I'll meet you at the station."

Fanner said, "I wish to stress the importance of what I have to tell you, especially in view of what happened here tonight. One of my officers will be happy to convey your guest to her home. We really must talk as soon as possible."

"Thanks, but no thanks. I brung her, I'll tote her home. I'll meet you within an hour. She doesn't live far."

He looked uncomfortable, under pressure. Leaning forward, he asked sotto voce, "Have you a gun in your car?"

Startled, I replied in the affirmative.

"Be sure to keep it on the seat beside you, in plain sight, of course, where it is legal. And within reach."

Suspending our discussion, he said, "An hour then. My office. Ask at the desk."

★ ★ ★

"Did you really tell her that you couldn't remember whether you had on a shirt?" Heather asked.

"Not my fault. She asked for it."

"She wasn't pleased with you."

"Can I help it if she's humor-impaired?"

Slight smile. Not much of one, though.

In contrast to our most recent ride in my Supra, from Casa Gallardo to The Sweetery, the conversation was subdued. She did make a game attempt at banter, and so did I.

We spoke of my appointment with Fanner and speculated on what he might have uncovered about my friends at the bank that necessitated such a pressing meeting. Our consensus was that I'd have to wait and see.

We arrived at her condo. I cut the engine, went around to her side of the car, opened the door, and helped her out. I escorted her to the stoop, in no great hurry for the evening to end.

"You'll call me as soon as you're through with Fanner, right?"

"It'll be late," I protested.

"You'll call me as soon as you're through with Fanner, right?"

"Right."

She stepped close . . .

"Thanks for tonight," she said, and I responded with, "My pleasure."

Even closer . . .

"For the meal, the company, the candor," she

77

said, and I responded with, "Sure," about an octave too high.

Really close . . .

"And maybe my life," she said, and I responded with, "Anytime," then cleared my throat.

Had I never dated before?

Sure I had. About the time Teddy Roosevelt stormed San Juan Hill.

"Don't be so nervous, I'm just a woman."

"I know, and I haven't been this close to one in a long time."

She withdrew a step. But just a short one. "Think you could get used to it?"

"I think so."

"Do you want to get used to it?"

"If it's you."

Slow smile, the first since the shooting. "On our first real date?"

"As long as it's soon."

"Deal," she said, and opened her door, and walked in.

8

I WAS shown into Lieutenant Fanner's office by a pleasant enough patrolman named Jennings. Fanner sat stolidly behind a formidable walnut desk, dinged and besplintered here and there, both he and it. The pockmarks of experience.

Into a chair placed directly front and center, I settled. Draped one leg over the other, grasped the top leg at the knee, fingers entwined, and relaxed. More or less.

"I trust you escorted your friend home without incident."

"Sure, and made it here all by myself."

"How fortunate," he responded. Then, getting down to business, he said, "I ran a check on you, through sources I have cultivated over time, civilian and military. I was CID during the early Vietnam years."

Uh-oh.

"I cashed in a bundle of chits, twisted more than a few arms, cajoled and threatened and made deals. Information about you is more difficult to obtain than financial dirt on the President, but I achieved some degree of success. I was informed, with uncharacteristic lack of specific details, that your military background is not quite so innocuous as you indicated in our previous interview. It would seem that you have, shall we say, been over the hill to see the elephant."

79

"Okay, let's say that," I replied.

"Based on the assumption of your having considerable professional experience along these lines, what is your assessment of the situation at the ice cream store?"

"I don't want the papers getting hold of this."

He lifted a hammy mitt, palm out, toward me. "Not to worry. Whatever you say here is for my ears only, not even interdepartmental use. No one else is ken to what I have managed to unearth through my own modest information network. The data is stored here" — he tapped his temple — "and nowhere else. You have my word."

I nodded.

"All right, here goes. In my opinion, the guy in the BMW was after me. Just me. He looked neither right nor left, but straight at me. And he waited until I looked him in the eye, as if he wanted me to know who the hitter was and what it was for. But I don't.

"I think it was probably related to the bank job, and the threatening follow-up call. Nothing else I've done in twenty years would bring on something like this. Not even close.

"I've thought about it a lot. Only thing I can come up with is that the two gents who got away from the bank were uncommonly loyal to the pair left behind."

Fanner said, "You may have put your finger on it, at least partially."

He gazed thoughtfully at the desktop, drummed his thick fingers, and tugged at a meaty ear.

Picking up a notepad, he said, "Let me read to you about one of your victims."

I cringed inwardly at his use of the term "victims."

"Irving Jacob Hooker," he read, "aka Irving Talbott, aka Talbott Jacobs. Born June 11, 1958, Atlanta, Georgia. Five feet nine inches tall, hundred and fifty-two pounds, dark complexion, medium build. Usually wears a beard, sometimes just a mustache. Distinguishing marks: scar from knife wound under left eye; appendectomy scar. Criminal record: conviction, armed robbery; conviction, assault to murder; conviction, petty larceny. Served total of eight years in various penal institutions, both here and in New York State.

"Prison scuttlebutt is that he garroted a man while imprisoned, but was never brought up on charges. No witnesses. He had a reputation for being a 'bad' man, if none too bright.

"This is the gentleman whose face you ventilated."

"I suspected as much. How about Old Slim, the machine gun aficionado?"

"We have been unable to identify him."

I leaned forward in my chair. "The hell you say. You've had two *days*."

"That is true, we have. Nonetheless, we have no idea who he is. Was."

"I'll assume you ran his prints."

"Thanks," he said dryly, "for the assumption."

"Since the FBI's involved," I said, "it being a bank robbery, it's a good bet that they've also run a check."

"A good bet, yes."

"And still you've come up with zip?"

"As have the INS, the armed services, the SBI, and my palmist," he said.

Good grief, the man had a rudimentary sense of humor. Who'd've thought? I felt better about him. A little.

I asked, "Coroner check dental records?"

"Now why did we not think of that? *Of course he did*," he growled. "However lame and bumbling this department can be at times, we are not jackasses, Mr. Vance. We investigate homicides regularly, often successfully."

"Sure. No offence."

"Uh-hmm" was all he said.

Figuring I'd denigrated him and his staff more than sufficiently, I decided to conciliate. "About his teeth, any clues?"

"Yes. He obviously brushed and flossed regularly. 'Immaculate' is the word the coroner used, I believe."

"I'm presuming the deceased carried no ID, no traceable jewelry, bore no gigantic tattoo on his back saying, 'My mom lives in Burbank,'" I said.

"Unfortunately not. We have made an official request to both Interpol and the CIA," he continued, "though whether the latter would cooperate even if they could is moot."

"What about the car?"

"No one made the plate number."

"How many black 633s are there in this town, for Pete's sake!"

"We are looking for the car, but what do you

82

think the chances are that it was stolen, and has been ditched by now?"

"Right," I answered, chastised.

"Right," he agreed.

"Any news on the bank teller?"

He shook his leonine head sadly.

"So what do you have in mind?"

"Relative to what?"

"Protecting me."

"I will have a marked car cruise by your home periodically to check things out."

"Oh well then. My worries are over."

"What would you have me do?"

"I'd have you keep this monstrous anchovy and his pal off my back any way you can."

"How?"

"Put someone in my house, or outside. Around the clock. Have a car follow me all day. My son and I spend a lot of time together, so he's in danger too."

Fanner said, "Even if I agreed with you about all that, we do not have the mandate or the manpower to serve as a buffer between a specific citizen and a criminal, especially when we have not the slightest clue who the criminal, more correctly, criminals, are. The police serve primarily to apprehend perpetrators after a crime has been committed, not to act as a deterrent factor, except where the fear of being caught serves that function. I am sorry I cannot do more."

"In other words, you'll pursue these characters after they shoot me."

"With zeal."

"Somehow, I am not comforted," I said.

He looked at me pointedly. "If I had your resources," he said, "I might dig for a little information myself. Get to know my enemy, so to speak. Before he becomes a cancer that cannot be removed."

"You think I've got special connections, do you?"

"Are you saying you do not?"

I thought about it.

"Maybe I do at that."

★ ★ ★

After just one ring, "What?"

"Dave?"

"Yeah. You still at the police annex?"

"Leaving now. I wanted to check on things."

"Quiet as a frog eating crackers."

"Cullen asleep?"

"No, he's playing the tuba. It's after midnight, Ty. What do you think?"

"Sorry. I'm wound up, is all. Things don't feel right."

"Forget it. Listen, your daddy and his M1 carbine are outside somewhere with Nubbin, who'll bark if a gnat farts. Priss is in the house with Cullen and me. She barks if a gnat *thinks* about farting. Your mother-in-law is sitting on the back-porch swing, in the dark, with a Benelli 12 gauge in her lap. A SEAL team might get into this house, but two half-ass bank robbers sure as hell won't."

"Okay," I said, taking a deep, deep breath.

84

"I'll honk when I pull into the driveway."

"You better, or Granmaw just might shoot you."

9

MY imagination ran amuck on the way
to my dad's, conjuring boogeymen
behind every pin oak, and I didn't
pay much attention to my surroundings. Or what
was behind me. All I can offer in retrospect is
that I probably figured two tries in one night
was unlikely.

Wrong.

As I followed Bryan Boulevard where it
splits from Benjamin Parkway, I glanced in
the mirror. Caught a dark-hued Camaro Z-28
in the amber splash of a streetlight. Lucky for
me the streetlamp was there when I happened
to look back. The Zee was running with its
lights off.

*Now there's a coincidence, I thought. Both
headlights burned out. No parking lights either.
Guy too drunk to know he's driving blind? Let's
find out.*

At the first exit, I made an abrupt move onto
the off-ramp, ran the light, then headed left
across the overpass.

The Z-28 switched on its lights and came
after me.

*Unmarked car tapping me for running a red
light? No. Not even a highway patrolman would
run blackout at night just to hand out a ticket.
Would he?*

I decided to make sure. Back on Benjamin

Parkway, with its forty-five-mile-an-hour zone, I eased off the gas, downshifted to second, held the tech right in the meat of the power band. The Camaro charged up to me, changed lanes, and drew up nearly even, to my left. As I swiveled my head to see who was on board, the passenger window descended and a shotgun barrel poked into view.

I punched the throttle, felt the torque surge at the small of my back, an invisible force shove me deep into my seat. The tachometer needle swung almost instantly to its 6800-rpm redline. I rammed an upshift to avoid awakening the rev limiter with its attendant governing effect. The rear tires chirped as all 320 horses pawed and whinnied, fighting their traces. This, after all, was what they were made for.

The Zee had lost ground and was trying hard to make it up, when I braked, downshifted, and spun the wheel for a right onto Green Valley Road. Downshift to second, tires clawing for grip, finding it. Controlled drift, oversteering slightly as I let the Japanese thoroughbred have its head. With Toyota's twin-turbo system, boost was instantaneous; virtually no turbo lag, no waiting for internal mechanical gizmos to spool up. The car simply thrust itself down the blacktop, like a Phantom jet heaving itself across a few hundred feet of carrier deck.

I turned right again at the bank, hoping to lose myself among the maze of buildings in Friendly Shopping Center. I slowed, nearly sideswiped an elderly man in a green Buick, who looked as if he'd swallowed his pacemaker. Don't know why;

I missed him by a good six inches.

Swung around Swenson's, putting a building between the Z-28 and myself, and slipped cleverly into a . . . cul-de-sac.

Oops.

I U-turned to get out and the Camaro spotted me, the rumble of its big V-8 ominous as the howl of wind shear in the belly of a thunderstorm. I zoomed past the ABC store, another bank, a shoe emporium, the Zee in hot pursuit. Down Pembroke, right at the Terrace Theater, past Scott Seed, shooting the light to the entrance ramp for Wendover Avenue.

Down the ramp, out onto the six-lane, tech needle hugging six grand in third gear. Really moving. Palms sweating.

Here came the Zee, careening down the ramp, nearly losing it at the bottom, hustling after me.

I popped the clutch and grabbed fourth, for the first time since the chase began. The engine was pulling strongly, coolant temperature at midrange on the gauge. Beginning to hit her stride, my Supra.

And along came Jones.

We hit the West Market overpass at 120 or better and began the descent. Two pickup trucks were chugging up the on-ramp to my right, an old red Ford and a new yellow Ford. I checked the mirror; the Zee was right behind me. The red truck pulled out into the center lane; the yellow one kept straight, in the far right, merge lane. That left me one lane, the outside.

I aimed for it.

So did the old red Ford.

Cutting back like a well-trained quarterhorse, the Supra ducked for the center lane, which was about to be vacated — I hoped — by the red Ford. I zipped between the trucks like a squirt of toothpaste.

My sudden passage must have startled their drivers. The old Ford swerved partially into the center lane, straddling the white line. The yellow truck shifted a mite to port, over toward the old Ford, and straddled the other white line.

The Zee found itself caught between a truck and a hard place.

But the driver pulled it off. Not smoothly, but the car didn't pile up either. The Camaro's tail came around and sideswiped the yellow truck at just the right angle, then caromed off and spun out in front of the red Ford. Both trucks, neither going especially fast, simply stopped and watched the Zee spin doughnuts down Wendover.

Alas, when the car stopped it was headed in the right direction, after a fashion, and, smoke roiling from its rear wheels, it roared defiantly in my wake.

This guy could drive.

I took the Holden exit so fast I wasn't sure I could stop at the bottom.

I couldn't.

With the Supra marshaling all its suspension wiles, and its brakes inhibiting our progress to the limit of tire adhesion, I bulldozed through the intersection sideways, corrected, straightened, and punched the gas once more.

The fuel injectors did their job and I squealed off, the car's rear end oscillating like a crazed fire hose.

The Camaro came down the ramp and entered the Holden Road intersection with about the same degree of control I'd so deftly maintained. Just enough to remain right side up. I ran the signal at Walker Avenue, to the severe discomfiture of a young woman in an MGB, who had green on her side. The Zee dodged her, ending up on the grassy median digging up the city's azaleas. Didn't seem to slow it down all that much. I sped through the Market Street traffic light — for once green in my direction — with the Z-28 nosing my bumper.

Trying to shove my foot through the firewall, I once again put space between the Supra and our pursuers. Not much, you understand. But space nevertheless.

Madison Avenue, which ran ribbonlike through a quiet, upscale residential section and was known to teenage hotrodders as the Chute, was coming up on my left. For most of its mile-long expanse, it featured stately homes on its northern flank, a wooded city park on its south side, here and there punctuated with open play areas, biking paths, and in one place, a sizable lake. Speed limit was twenty-five; some of its turns were tricky at that speed. Just the escape route for a fleet-footed Japanese semi-racecar; anathema for a slug-footed slab of Detroit sheet metal, even with a master wheelman at its helm.

I hoped.

If I were wrong, things could get pretty exciting in a hurry.

I spurred left onto Madison, removing paint from a parked Nissan. I'd come back and leave my number later.

The first dip and a hard left-hander were no problem, although I did run onto the shoulder a time or two. Past Kemp Road came a tough bend to starboard. I made that one, barely (at sixty), eliciting an involuntary glottal resonation that was not only unseemly from a strapping he-man like myself, but indicative of an untimely lag in self-confidence.

The park, mostly wooded at this point, was to my left, houses on the right. The fourth dip, leading as it did into a sharp right curve, caused trouble. As I passed Battle Road, control was a sometime thing. It quickly became an elusive thing. It finally disappeared altogether in a tight righthand turn marked on the left side of the road by a bright row of reflectors. I zigzagged all over what narrow street there was, tagged one of the reflectors, swerved back to the right, jumped the curb, and plowed a furrow in a freshly mown lawn, stopping just short of a fire hydrant.

Fire hydrant, I thought, *in the middle of a yard?*

I found reverse, backed into the street. Once again in first gear, I eased out the clutch pedal. Stopped. Listened. Thought.

In the immediate distance, I could hear the squealing protestations of tortured rubber as the Z-28 approached the hairy right turn I'd just negotiated. Switching off my lights, I sat in the center of the narrow street, eyes glued to the rearview mirror.

I shifted into reverse. Foot off the brake, so no brake lights. Hiding in the middle of the street. Good thing there were no streetlights immediately adjacent.

I sat back, pressing my body deeply into the cushiony safety of the seat. Deluding myself, probably. Comforting nonetheless. Head tight against the headrest.

Slick palms, dry mouth, ostrich egg in my throat.

Watching the mirror.

Watching . . .

There!

Headlights loomed, coming fast, the stench of burning radials mingling with the foggy dampness. Pungent. Frighteningly near.

Now!

I switched on my lights, simultaneously dumping the clutch. Tires spinning uncontrollably, the Supra lurched rearward just as the Camaro hove into view. As I'd hoped, the driver's reaction to the sudden obstacle — me — was to steer left, avoiding impact. Unfortunately for him, that course took him straight toward the apex of the curve. And beyond. Into the park.

A slight embankment — perhaps three feet high — bordered the road on the left. The Z-28 slid down it at high speed, rose up on the two left wheels, fell heavily on its side, and continued over onto its top, all the while retaining a substantial forward speed. It crashed into a maple tree, rebounded, twisted

180 degrees, and came to a halt, once again upright.

I watched briefly, debated inspecting the aftermath, and decided it was a matter for the police. Besides, the pair might have survived. And they had at least one shotgun; I had a handgun, with no extra magazines. The park was relatively open here; not much cover. If they flanked me. I'd be in deep shit.

This might be the time, but it was not the place. One or both might be dead or severely injured. Better to hope for luck than walk into a quagmire.

Lights were coming on in the houses around me. Soon folks would be out on their lawns, peering inquisitively at the wreck. Then, cops.

Supra and I limped off to my dad's.

★ ★ ★

We were holding a council of war at the Vance ancestral homestead, the four of us humans. Nub and Miss Priss stood watch in Cullen's bedroom.

Ethyl asked, "You going to call what's his name?"

"You mean Lieutenant Fanner."

"Himself."

"He'd probably have me arrested for speeding, careless and reckless driving, leaving the scene of an accident, assault on a parked Nissan, and trespass."

"Wouldn't call him, then," she said, and went to check for the eleventh time on Cullen.

"Besides, he already told me that there's not much he can do about the situation," I said to her departing back. "Maybe now he'd have a patrol car come by every thirty minutes instead of on the hour."

It was after four in the morning. My eyes felt as though the sandman had been dumping his surplus beneath their lids.

Dad said, "You look a little green around the gills," and took a sip of milk.

"Thanks. I needed that. I've been going over in my mind all the nasty things that could have happened if I hadn't noticed the Camaro in the streetlight, hadn't been able to outrun it, hadn't — "

Dave said, "You reflect too much. You do that much thinking in Korea?"

"Different there. Only me to think about."

"Now there's Cullen."

"You bet."

"That's not gonna make it easy on you, should they keep at this. Assuming the wreck didn't squash them, of course."

"I realize that, and it looks like Fanner and the rest of GPD are going to be more hindrance than assistance."

Dave nodded. "You may have to do this yourself."

"Thought about that. If I go hunting trouble, find it and take care of it, it's a given that some assistant DA out to make a name will stick me in a cell. Then I'd have to cough up big bucks to a lawyer out to make a name by trying to get me out."

"Where'd Cullen be all that time?" Dad asked.

"Exactly," I concurred.

"Maybe Fanner had a good idea. Why don't you ring up McElroy, see can he find out a thing or two? Couldn't hurt," Dad suggested.

Oh yes it could. I'd already thought of that, but the unpleasant aftertaste of Korea was still on my mind.

Shit. Any way I turned led into a dark and endless tunnel, with Cullen's quality of life — and maybe physical safety — in the balance.

Ethyl rejoined us. I looked a question at her. She nodded. "He's fine. One dog's asleep on one side, the other's on the other."

I smiled a thank-you, my lips feeling oddly disconnected. Tired.

The phone rang. Dave snatched it up and barked, "What?" at it. Then: "He's right here."

Handing the phone to me, he mouthed, "Fanner."

The conversation took maybe two minutes. I replaced the receiver on its base.

Dave said, "Yes?"

"Fanner said they examined the remains of a burned Z–28 tonight. Found a Mossberg riot gun, eight-shot, and they matched it to shells recovered from the ice cream parlor. Primer indentations, he said. A flat-brimmed, western-style hat was in the wreckage, and some blood. B-negative. Small amount.

"No bodies. Said witnesses saw two men run into the park and disappear. One of them was 'quite large,' is how he put it."

"That's our friends all right," Dave said.

"He wanted to know if I knew anything about the wreck. I denied any knowledge. Think it's best if I just lay low."

"What if someone could ID your car?" — from Dave.

"Then I'll come clean. No other choice. Unless that problem presents itself, I want to stay out of the limelight until I get things figured out. Then we'll see."

I went on. "Fanner says the Camaro was stolen, tonight. From a local nightclub. Owner was found in a trash pile, concussed but alive. Out like a light. BMW was reported stolen an hour ago. Owner lives in Kernersville. Just got home from Myrtle Beach and discovered it missing."

"Resourceful pair," said Dave.

Dad asked, "Any word on that teller they grabbed?"

"Didn't say. If there were, he'd likely have mentioned it."

"Now what?" asked Ethyl.

"I'm going to sleep for a few hours. The heat's on these guys. Should be safe for a while. First thing in the morning, I'll call McElroy. Then we'll see."

I dragged myself into the bedroom, took off my shoes, moved Nubbin over and lay down beside my boy. With a Browning 9 mm in one hand and Cullen's small fingers clasped in the other, I fell asleep.

10

ACQUIRING McElroy's ear proved more difficult than I'd assumed. I finally reached a party who admitted knowledge of his whereabouts and promised to relay a message for him to call ASAP. I hung up and went to work on breakfast.

Thick slices of ham; chopped raw apples, dates, and bananas; buttermilk biscuits. Cullen walked in bleary-eyed and sat down at the breakfast room table. Loquacity was not one of his early-morning traits.

"What would you like for breakfast, my boy?" I queried, W. C. Fields-like.

"Grips."

"Takes a while to make grits. Will your tummy wait?"

"I guess."

"Want a hot biscuit and honey while I'm fixing the grits?"

Sleepy nod.

"You mean, 'Yes, thank you'?"

"Yes, thank you."

I plucked a steaming biscuit from the stack, replaced the covering cloth, split it horizontally with a serrated blade, slathered on heated honey from a small crock on the stove, and handed it to my scion, who consumed it greedily.

A healthy appetite *is* one of his early-morning traits.

Dad came in, nigh as weary as Cullen, worn out from an all-night vigil, I suspected. I wasn't aware of how they'd worked out the watch for the remainder of the night and early morning, but wouldn't have been surprised if none of them had slept. Ethyl and Dave had left shortly after my awakening, spurning my offer for breakfast.

Hard to imagine, turning down food.

They'd each had a last cup of coffee (the pot had remained filled and steaming all night long), and departed with the admonishment to stick close to the house and watch out for the "baby."

Pop nursed his coffee, with Cullen coming awake gradually. The conversation was desultory until my dad mentioned that he'd taught Cullen how to play poker the night before. Cullen chimed in with how many hands he'd won, what a pile of kitchen matches he'd accumulated.

Stirring the grits, I asked Dad, "How many ranks of hands can he keep track of, pairs and three of a kind?"

"Shoot, no," answered Cullen. "I know straights and toilets, too."

Dad and I looked at each other, back at our heir, and asked simultaneously: "Toilets?"

Cullen's little brow knit thoughtfully. Behind hazel eyes whirred adept mental machinery. Finding what he sought, he brightened, and the tiny vertical crease between his brows erased itself.

"Flush!" he corrected. "A straight and a *flush*."

Three generations of male Vances laughed together, savoring, enhancing the moment. Tightly bound, united in spirit as well as genealogy. Only two of the multitude of Vance uncles, aunts, and cousins I'd met over the years had exhibited any hint of humor deficiency. Errant synapses, no doubt. No such evidenced in this trio.

Miss Priss and Nubbin overheard the gaiety, bounded in on padded feet and watched us enjoying each other, tails wagging in approval. I tossed Nub a discarded piece of ham, abnormally pinguid for such expensive pork, and he gobbled it with gusto, then licked his chops and lay down on his belly, legs at all four corners ready to spring should another delicacy materialize.

Not so Miss Priss. Too dignified. She lay in the doorway and feigned indifference, her uncontrollably watering mouth belying the sham. I slipped Nubbin another morsel, which he relished with no pretence at humility. Priss heard him smack his lips and cocked an ear, but she refused to turn her head.

I pointed at Nub with my right index finger, held for a count of three, the hand signal for *Stay*. Then I dropped an especially juicy piece of meat in front of Priss, who pretended not to see it.

Nubbin stayed where he was, quivering all over, having a gastric attack. Dad looked at them, then at me, and shook his head.

As I returned to the stove and my simmering pot of grits, I heard the muted click of canine teeth, *snap!* like that. I waited an appropriate span of time, then glanced over at Priss. The ham was gone.

She tried hard not to look smug.

Nubbin stopped quivering and rested his head on one forepaw. Sighed.

"You're a hard man, Tyler," bespoke the elder Vance.

"He got two to her one," I said. "Besides, who taught me how to train dogs?"

My father, who had trained more coon dogs in his life — and won more field trials — than anyone in the state, flipped a hand. "I confess," he said.

"Well then."

Cullen, not following the drift, said, "Are my grips ready?"

To which I replied, "Indeed they are," and spooned him up a bowlful.

★ ★ ★

The phone rang. Dad got it, greeted the caller, listened, then offered it to me. I asked, "McElroy?"

He shook his head.

It was Heather, harried and out of breath. I immediately apologized for forgetting to call her the night before, after my meeting with Fanner. Before I could tell her why, she interrupted with, "That's not important. I don't know how else to phrase this, so I'll simply plunge ahead. Do you expect a repeat of last night's shoot-out?"

"Good grief, I hope not. What makes you think there might be?"

100

"Nothing . . . it's just, I don't know what else to do."

"About what, Heather?"

"My father had a mild stroke this morning. He blacked out and they haven't been able to revive him. There's serious blockage of his carotid artery, and they're going in to clean it out. If the operation doesn't go well . . . "

"Think positive."

"He could die."

"He could also snap right out of it."

There was a long pause, then a barely audible, "I know."

I said, "Is there anything I can do?"

"No . . . Yes, well, I'm not sure. It's just . . . " She trailed off.

"Are you at the hospital?"

"No, I'm at work. The hospital just called. Mom is sedated. It's Web."

"What about him?"

"He's at preschool. They want me to come to Charlotte right away." Long pause again. Holding her emotions in check. Hard at times like this.

"You don't want to take Web?"

"God, no. If he saw his granddaddy like that . . . But what if I have to stay?"

"Are you afraid you won't get back in time to pick him up this evening?"

A halting "Yes."

"Would you like for me to get him?"

No answer.

Aha. How obtuse could I be?

"You're afraid to leave Web with me, in case

101

they make another try."

She began to cry softly over the wire. "I'm so ashamed. After all you did last — "

"No, no. You've nothing to be ashamed of. What kind of parent would you be if something like this didn't scare the hell out of you? It sure scares the hell out of me. All I can say is that Cullen is going to be with me, all the time. I can't guarantee Web's safety, of course, but if I had any serious concerns, I wouldn't keep my own son by my side.

"By the way, there's been a further development." I told her about the car chase.

"Those guys aren't going to quit."

"Oh yeah, they will. One way or the other." More silence. "I don't know what to do."

"There any other options? How about Web's father?"

"No!"

"This appears to be an emergency — "

"*No!* That's out of the question."

"Okay." I let it slide. "Any friends you could call?"

"Only one family, and they're at Disney World." Lengthy pause again; then she apparently made a decision.

"Can you meet me at Four Seasons Mall in an hour?"

"Sure," I said.

"I'll have Web. I can't think of anything else to do."

"Heather, we can't let a pair of thugs control our lives."

She sucked in a breath I could hear over the

phone. "Right. See you there." She gave me a specific meeting place and rang off. I told Cullen who was coming. He was delighted.

I cleaned up the breakfast mess while Cullen and the dogs romped on the big screened-in back porch, just as I had done at an identical age with a little mixed breed named Nippy. Much good-natured growling and gurgly laughter suggested that they were playing tug-of-war with the old towel Dad kept for that express purpose. All participants, human and canine, delighted in the revelry.

To lessen the risk of jerking loose a dog's tooth, I reminded Cullen to be careful how hard he tugged. He said he'd remember, and went back to his work. I let them play a half hour or so, until they all began to show a lack of enthusiasm from fatigue. (Tough on dogs, getting slung around on one end of a towel by a nearly-five-year-old.) Then I fed everyone a light snack; dogs too. Dad was sound asleep in the back bedroom; I left him a note, and we hied off to the mall. I drove my dad's car, a Smith & Wesson 9 mm in the glove compartment, chamber empty, full magazine.

I wouldn't let two thugs control my life, but I couldn't let them catch me with my guard down either.

★ ★ ★

When we arrived at the mall, I retrieved the compact Smith double-action automatic from the dash, unobtrusively chambered a cartridge,

103

and secured the gun in a waistband holster at the small of my back, under a lightweight blue windbreaker. The little Smith was flat, unobtrusive, and stuffed with Federal 115-grain Plus-P-Plus jacketed hollow points, in case I ran into a crack-crazed yeti.

Or a very large felon with a twelve-gauge.

Carrying a concealed weapon was not legal in my home state. I took the risk. Better my fighting a misdemeanor charge in court than my son's visiting me in the cemetery. Since the police had disclaimed themselves as my protectors, I reckoned I'd have to look after myself and my young charges. The bitty Smith 9 mm might help me do that.

We met Heather and Web at the White Mountain Creamery, our favorite mall snack shop. The owner, Gary Barney, was mixing up a batch of chocolate chip muffin batter when we arrived. He offered each of the boys a freshly baked sample. I gave Cullen the Look; he gave me the Shrug, to wit: *It's only a muffin, Daddy*.

Heather lingered awhile, obviously reluctant to leave, which was all right with me. Finally, she decided it was time. She hugged Web tightly, kissed him a half-dozen times, him straining at the leash, ready to go to Homer's Corner. I said to Heather, "Hope your father'll be all right. Don't worry about Web. Think about one problem at a time."

"I'll call as soon as I know." She smiled, squeezed my arm, and left.

The boys and I escalated to the lower floor.

(Cullen eschewed the elevators as too crowded and the staircase as too boring — no moving parts.) Homer's Corner was an active child's playground paradise, with elevated tunnels, rubber matting, slides of all descriptions, ropes to climb, bars to swing from, diminutive trampolines to pounce on. The whole shebang was indoors and the play area was trammeled for safety, although many of the kids seemed to enjoy climbing the rope netting as much as anything else they did. Fortunately, it was made from sturdy stuff.

Web, although claiming never to have been there before, followed Cullen's lead, plunging headfirst into the first opening they spotted after the cashier had placed plastic ID bands around their wrists. I got one too. Children could leave the premises only with an adult whose bracelet matched theirs.

Good plan.

Carrying the cup of hot coffee Gary had thrown in with the muffins, I found a booth from which to view the barely controlled pandemonium reigning around me. I tipped the plastic lid off carefully, burning a finger anyway, then raised the container to my lips, the aroma strong in my nostrils as steam eddied about my face.

Took a sip.

Ah . . .

Coffee.

Even decaf.

Late morning spun slowly into early afternoon, accompanied by gleeful cries, laughter, an occasional shriek, usually from a little girl, if you'll pardon the sexist observation. The boys took a break for pizza and juice. Their pizza came out of a machine, was in fact baked therein, its crust shellacked with a thin coating of what I assume was tomato paste, with some scraps of white cheese tossed on top. And while it had the patina and texture of recycled cardboard, at least it tasted bad and cost a lot.

During the morning I had become peripherally aware of a man; not an especially alarming gentleman, average height and build, pleasant of expression, casual but dapper in dress. When I first noticed him, he stood near the cashier, leaning on the countertop. Later I observed him sitting on a bench near the bathrooms, another time standing by the computer games being played by the older children. Watching. Always watching.

Cullen. Always watching *Cullen.*

My nape hair stood on end, seemingly waving like seaweed in a strong current. Tingling.

I looked for Cullen. He and Web were in the submarine, facing one another and hooting, mimicking the metallic clamor a sub makes when it needs to DIVE! DIVE! DIVE!

Back to the man. I didn't want to jump to conclusions here. The guy had made no threatening moves, no overt gestures of hostility. In fact, the only odd thing about his behavior was that he seemed to be avoiding whatever spot Cullen was enjoying at any moment, as if he didn't want to be seen by him.

106

But he was definitely observing Cullen, no doubt of that.

I examined him more intently. He was beginning to act nervous. Running fingers through his hair, shuffling his feet, he kept watching my boy as if trying to make up his mind about something.

What if he was part of a team sent to grab my son? Maybe he had a partner I had either not seen or failed to notice, one set to get me out of the way so this gent could snag Cullen and be off. Then they could arrange any kind of scenario they wanted to, using my son as the lever.

Maybe.

I looked around; no one seemed remotely sinister.

But this guy didn't have the look.

Then again, if he was really good, he wouldn't have the look.

Still . . . it didn't feel right.

I moved closer to him, as casually as possible. I didn't put my hand near my gun, feeling I wouldn't need it unless he was armed. I doubted that. Jacketless, colorful Alexander Julian knit shirt, tight Calvin Kleins: no room for even an ankle holster. Blade maybe, but if all he had was a knife, I wouldn't worry. I'd stuck an enemy soldier once, with his own bayonet.

Blades I could handle.

He made up my mind for me by putting his right hand in his pocket and stepping forward just as the boys came looping by, headed for the bathroom. They were oblivious to him, chattering, walking stiffly as boys do when they've ignored their bladders for too long, twenty feet from him.

I was *five* feet from him, in his path. My abrupt presence drew his attention and he stopped, turned uncertainly, glanced toward the boys as they entered the rest room doorway.

He looked at me, hand coming out of his pocket, frown forming, surprised.

I wasn't. I stepped closer, where only he could hear, and said, "When your hand comes out of that pocket, it had better be empty. If it isn't, your hospital stay will be long and painful."

11

HIS hand didn't come out empty. It didn't come out at all. He shoved it deeper into his pocket while he stood there gawking at me.

Still very close, I said, "Why have you been watching my son?"

"*Your* son?" he said, genuinely surprised. "I've been watching my son." Uncomfortable with my closeness, as I'd intended, he backed up a pace.

I asked, "Who is your son?"

"Web Patterson," he replied. Then: "Are you a cop?"

I smiled, from relief largely, but also to reassure him and to defuse the potentially volatile situation my paranoia, understandable as it might have been, had created.

"No," I said, "I'm Cullen Vance's father."

He looked vague.

"The boy your son is with?"

"Oh," he said, visibly relaxing. I held out a hand. He took it, though reluctantly, I confess. Couldn't blame him.

"You scared the hell out of me," he said. "There's a . . . "

"I know, a restraining order."

He nodded.

"Here." I gestured to my booth. "Let's sit, talk, be civilized. Then maybe you can see your son."

"Maybe?" he said, bristling a bit. "Who are you to — "

"The guy who, like it or not, is acting as your boy's guardian, with his mother's permission. Let us not argue, but discuss. I'm not the enemy here."

He settled into the booth, arms on the tabletop, Rolex in plain view just as if he wasn't ashamed of it. Ran nervous fingers through thick, curly, expensively coiffed hair. Smiled. A bit self-deprecating, I thought, but engaging nonetheless. I couldn't help but feel for the guy, being deprived of his child as he was.

I wondered why he had been.

He said, "I suppose you're wondering."

"About the restraining order?" I asked.

"Yeah."

"I must admit it."

"Is this just between us?"

I shrugged. "Depends. No guarantees."

He thought about it. The boys, obviously happy and well drained, scampered out of the bathroom, crossing the floor. Cullen looked my way, reassured himself that I was around, took in my confrere with a glance, followed Web into the play area.

"If we're going to get anywhere, I'll have to trust you. And your better judgment."

"That'll be unique," I said, grinning. "No one I know thinks I *have* better judgment, about anything."

Again the self-conscious smile. "You're trying to make it easier for me. I appreciate it."

I waited. He fidgeted. Fooled with his hands,

110

looked away toward the last place we'd seen the boys, checked the time.

"Nice watch," I said. Encouraging, priming the pump.

"I'm afraid if Web sees me, he'll come over."

"You two are pretty close?"

He nodded. "Very. Always have been. I put the first bottle in his mouth, changed his first diaper . . . " He trailed off.

"Then what's the problem? Why are you and Heather at odds?"

He took a deep breath, held it, let it out slowly through his nose, then looked straight at me, challenging. There was a hint of shame, balanced by pride.

"I'm gay," he said quietly, matter-of-factly. No defiance, no apology.

"So?"

He blinked at me. Twice. "So?"

"That's what I said."

"Heather's dad is the epitome of a gay basher. Won't hire one, won't — "

"What's her dad got to do with it?"

"He maintains a great deal of control in her life. Or at least influence."

"I don't know her well, yet. But from what I've observed, that doesn't sound like Heather. She strikes me as being her own gal. Excuse me." I looked around. "I meant woman. Feminists may be lurking."

Once again I turned upon him my most disarming smile. Shoot, in another minute I'd have him so charmed he might blast forth three complete sentences in a row. Must learn to control this power.

He hesitated. "I cheated on her. When we were still together. She found out. She is not a forgiving person, at least not about that."

See? Four sentences. Well, three and a fragment.

I hesitated. "With a woman?"

We hesitated, then said "No" at the same time.

We smiled at our simultaneous eruptions, mine manly and forthright, his a tad winsome and subdued. Or maybe the other way around.

"That's different," I said.

"Why?"

"Dunno, but it is. I had a buddy once, in Army AIT, before going overseas. Name was Bill. Really loved his wife. Wallet full of pictures. High school sweethearts, that sort of thing. He was from the Midwest somewhere, not exactly a bastion of tolerance.

"He got a letter from Louise . . . strange I should remember her name. Anyhow, old Louise dropped him a little note. Said she had taken a lover while Bill was in basic training. Couldn't help it, she said. Just happened.

"Bill was despondent. Crushed. Couldn't do his job. Chaplain got him time off duty to try to recoup, beat the thing. He just couldn't.

"So he wrote her a letter, wanting to know who the guy was. What he had that Bill didn't.

"Week later, he got this postcard. A fucking *postcard* she sent. Told him there was no guy.

There was a gal. That's all. No 'I'm sorry,' no 'Kiss my ass,' no nothing else. Just 'He's a she, Bill. Yours truly, Louise.'

"Bill laid the postcard on his bunk, visited the chaplain, who heard his confession. Then he got into his '62 Chevy convertible, headed out State Road one-eighteen, and drove into a bridge abutment at a hundred and ten miles an hour.

"Had to have a closed-casket funeral. He was so rearranged the coroner almost gagged.

"My point is that it seems to get to some people more than others, this crossing of sexual boundaries. If she'd dallied with a man, Bill might have snapped out of it. Who's to say?

"Perhaps Heather has a problem with losing you to a man, not a woman.

"By the way," I continued, "let me introduce myself. My name is Tyler Vance. I have no problem with you talking to Web since you're here. I'll speak to Heather about what to do in the future. You okay with that?"

"Guess I have no choice, do I?"

I shook my head.

He nodded, said, "My name's Jason," then went over to see his son.

He had to call Web's name to get his attention, but when the boy spotted him, he ran over. There was no doubt he was delighted to see his father. They hugged and kissed; Jason swung him around in a circle, eliciting giggles and entreaties to do it again.

My heart felt decidedly chilled toward Heather at that moment. No one has the right to keep

113

parent and child apart, barring abuse, of course, and there was no discernible evidence of that here. As I'd learned the hard way in Korea, holding a grudge spiritually destroys the grudger, not the grudgee.

If Heather wanted me to act as Web's father figure, we were going to have to come to an agreement about what, if any, problems arose from the boy's biological male parent fulfilling that role.

★ ★ ★

The next day Heather was home from Charlotte. She'd had business at her office that demanded her personal attention. Her dad was still critical, although he had briefly regained consciousness. Currently, they were trying drug therapy, but on the morrow the surgeons would scrub up. At the moment, I was at her condo and she was in my face. "You did what!"

She was hot, fit to be tied, foaming at the mouth, pissed off, burned up, livid. Choose your cliché.

"You heard me," I replied, in that soothing way I have, not unlike Robert Redford's down-home suave in *The Chase*. I smiled and tilted my head charmingly.

"What the hell made you think you had the right to make such a decision?"

She didn't appear charmed. Well, Redford *had* been killed at the movie's end. Maybe charm has its limits.

Might directness be better? I plunged in. "You

114

gave me the right when you left Web in my charge."

"I told you there was a restraining order out against my ex-husband. Why would — "

"Jason."

"Yes! Jason! You think I don't remember his name?"

"I've never heard you use it. It's always 'my ex-husband,' or 'Web's father.' That way you dehumanize him. Just wanted to remind you he has a name, that's all."

"Are you defending him?"

"From what?"

"From being a schmuck!"

"I've no opinion in that regard, or at least only a partial one, and that based primarily on Web's reaction to seeing him. The kid was enraptured."

"So what? Web's always doted on his father. I told you the court ruled that he couldn't see him, and — "

"You didn't tell me why."

"That's none of your business!"

"It is if I'm going to be in any way responsible for Web, and his wellbeing. Does all this have to do with Jason's sexual bias?"

"Sexual *bias*? He's a queer, for God's sake."

Playing devil's advocate, as with Jason, I said, "So?"

"So? What the hell do you mean, *so*?"

"Do you liken this proclivity to communicable disease?" I answered. "Believe Web will catch it from him, maybe it'll rub off? Do you think Jason *wants* his son to grow up gay,

115

will try to influence him in that direction? Are you afraid of child abuse, unaware that statistically there's a greater risk of a straight parent's sexually abusing a child, regardless of gender? Is it the risk of AIDS that has you in a dither?

"Or," I asked pointedly, "is it none of the above?"

"It's none of your concern, is what it is."

I got up from the couch on which I'd been resting, in the living room of Heather's condo. Blue fabric of a tight expensive weave, small floral print, matching chair across the room next to the fireplace.

At one end of the couch sat an oak end table, covered with expensive bric-a-brac and a picture of Web in a little sailor costume. Cute. It was even money Grandpapa was ex-Navy. I bet he also had more than a little to do with the restraining order, and Heather's athwart attitude.

There was a thirty-inch TV, VCR, sound system more expensive than Jason's watch, all housed in a custom-built teak cabinet, which clashed nicely with the oak end table and its elongated sibling, in front of the sofa, littered with oversized books: *The Random House Children's Encyclopedia* and *My First Science Book* and *Stone Soup*.

I stood, rocking on my heels, whistling "You Are My Sunshine."

"Sit back down. Please."

"In that chair over there?" referring to a big maple rocker in the corner, which gave me three

116

types of wood to admire. "Puts me out of your reach."

She looked up at me from her end of the couch. "I'm sorry. This whole subject just gets me all up in the air."

"Why?"

She shifted uneasily, shot an emerald glare in my direction. "How much did he . . . Jason . . . tell you?"

"Not a lot," I answered, standing over her. "Said he cheated on you, while you were still together."

"He say who with?"

"Not specifically. Told me the gender."

"And?"

"And what?"

"Didn't it make you sick?" she asked.

"Marital infidelity makes me sick. If you don't intend to be true to someone, don't marry them."

"Well, it never happened to you. You couldn't know how it feels."

"To be cheated on? Happened to me a time or two, not with a spouse. Trusted girlfriends in school. It hurt, but I didn't die."

"Any of them run off with another woman?"

"Not as far as I know. What difference would it make? Cheating's cheating."

"What difference would it make? I'll tell you what difference it makes — all the difference in the world. You feel like you're not enough . . . woman . . . for a man. Like maybe he switched genders, not just people, because somehow you . . . "

In the back of what feeble brain I possess, a

hundred watt bulb appeared. "Didn't have what it took? To satisfy a man? And we men, lustful creatures all, are notoriously easy to please," I said.

She looked away, genuinely miserable.

I looked at her. "Had you been around much when you met Jason?"

Shook her head, eyes on the carpet.

"He the first?"

Again a headshake.

"Not many, though, right?"

Nod. No eye contact.

"Post-Jason?"

"A few." Tears welling. "I can't seem to satisfy anyone, in any way. Or even keep them around long enough to . . . " Pause.

"Get to know you?" I finished for her.

Nod. Tracks of her tears. Puddling soon, in her lap, where her hands lay, clasping each other as if in prayer. For support. She needed it.

For nothing.

She had no more to do with Jason's homosexuality than did my Aunt Flo. And the fleeting affairs, or whatever they had been, were because she hadn't met the right men, not because of any deficiency of hers, that I had observed, anyway.

So I told her so.

She cried some more, and held on to me as if fresh off the *Titanic*. I looked through her sliding patio doors at the boys playing outside, oblivious to her plight and heartache, as they should be. In years to come, despite our best efforts, they'd have more than enough of their own.

118

12

WHEN Cullen and I got to my dad's that evening, he told me McElroy had phoned twice, leaving an unlisted number. Before returning the colonel's calls, I tried Fanner. He was in.

I asked whether anything further had turned up on my unidentified corpse. Fanner informed me that nothing concrete had materialized, but that after interviewing all the bank employees and customers, plus witnesses outside the bank who had seen the two robbers flee, teller in tow, he had deduced one thing. The smaller of the duo was quite likely related to the mystery male I had shot.

You mean family? Kinfolk? I asked him.

Indeed, he agreed, then went on to say that the two were of about the same size, both being tall and thin, and had similar mannerisms. Further, the two never spoke aloud. Any conferring between them was done mouth to ear.

Suggesting either highly individualistic voices or a foreign tongue, or at least a distinctive, perhaps recognizable accent, I surmised.

He agreed. Further, Fanner told me, both men had very prominent noses, obvious even through ski masks, dark — nearly black — eyes, pale skin tones with hairy hands and wrists.

Perhaps Eastern European, I injected.

Perhaps, he assented.

So, I went on, what we have is this: ectomorph, pale complexion, aristocratic proboscis, hirsute. I explained that hirsute meant hairy, to which he rejoined that he was aware of that, thank you very much.

Fun, playing with Fanner.

I'm not sure he thought so; he broke our connection with the curtest of closings.

Next, McElroy, long-distance to Spring Lake, North Carolina.

"McElroy," he said sleepily, after the first ring.

"Tyler Vance."

He rubbed the cobwebs out of his ears for a second, then: "More troubles?"

I told him all about them.

After a moment's assimilation, he asked, "You need protection? I can send troops, on the QT of course, to keep an eye on you. They'll blend with the scenery."

"I remember how *I* used to," I said, "but right now I need information. These guys aren't pro hitters — at least I don't think so. They've not had much luck so far."

"But look who they're trying to hit."

I thought about it. He was right. Underestimation of my enemy could get me killed.

On the other hand, considering my experiences with McElroy in the past, I wanted to keep him and his organization at a comfortable distance. If I set foot in his privy, how hard would it be to scrape him off my shoe when this was over? At the end in Korea, he'd tried his damnedest

120

to have me court-martialed.

"I'll think about your offer. For now, this is what I need." I gave him the description of my UZI-carrying attacker.

"Got it. I agree with you on likely region of origin. I'll send a photographer to Greensboro, get a pic of the guy in the morgue. Show it around a bit, here and there. Someone'll know someone who'll know someone."

"I assume you're still tied into CID."

"Sure, but they'd take a year and you might be pushing up gardenias. Or in an urn on the mantelpiece. I'm linked to Delta here at Bragg. If any outfit can pinpoint this dead guy, or his cousin or whoever the hell he is, they can. And quick. I'll call 'em now, get a move on. You certain you don't want a couple of shadows?"

"I think not, but I appreciate it. Might change my mind later."

"You say the word and they're yours."

He gave me two more numbers where he could be reached, a mobile and his beeper. Call night or day.

I asked, "By the way, why're you in bed so early?" My watch read 8:44. "If memory serves, you were quite a night owl in the old days."

He chuckled. "Still am, hoss. Didn't get any sleep at *all* last night. Busy getting my ashes hauled."

"All night?"

He chuckled some more and hung up.

He was ten years older than me.

Wonder what he ate.

Dad said, "McElroy any help?"

I ran through both phone calls as close to verbatim as I could recall.

"You gonna lay low till McElroy finds out somethin' Fanner can chew on?"

"I don't expect much from Fanner, Pop. This whole things smells out of his league. But I am planning to keep a low profile. Dave's coming tonight, isn't he?"

"Yes. Said look for him around tennish. He has lots of repair work to catch up on at the store."

Looking dyspeptic, he said, "Ethyl's comin' too. Dang that woman."

"What're you two feuding about now?"

"Just never you mind. Ain't nobody's business but ours. I reckon we can use all the eyes and ears we can get," he went on. "Hers work pretty good, mouth too." He got up to fetch a glass of milk, his chair continuing to rock in rhythmical, ever diminishing arcs as he left the room.

I walked over to check on Cullen, sound asleep on the floor in front of Dad's ancient Zenith, covered with a beach towel, head propped on a stuffed Snoopy. A small purple Barney lay just out of reach of one outstretched hand. Calm little face; light dusting of freckles beneath the eyes. He breathed regularly, openmouthed, like his mom used to when she was really tired and sleeping on her back.

I wished she was seeing him right now.

122

She probably was.

I picked him up and held him to my chest. He barely stirred, his head lolling back against my forearm. Into the front bedroom we went. I tucked him in and turned on the night-light and covered him up and kissed his cheek, twice.

Back in the living room, dad was once again comfortable in his chair, tall glass of cold milk in one hand, a chocolate cookie the size of a Frisbee in the other.

"I'm going to take the dogs home when Dave gets here," I said. "One of you gonna sleep in the room with Cullen?"

"You so het up from worry you don't know what you're sayin'?" said my father around a mouthful of cookie.

"Sorry. Stupid question. I withdraw it. Don't those things play hell with your dentures?"

He threw the remaining portion at me. I dodged, then withdrew to the breakfast room and had three cups of Stockholm roast, waiting for my relief.

★ ★ ★

Nubbin and Miss Priss were ecstatic, running up the stairs, sniffing here and there. Although my house was smaller than my father's, and my property much — *much* — less extensive, it was still home to my pooches. They'd lived most of their lives there. It was filled with their scent, favored snoozing spots, their toys, their memories.

123

Each of them liked Dad's place, but this was Home.

They explored, making sure everything was in order, then settled down. It had been a long day. Nub lay on the floor beneath my feet as I began research for an article on Colt single actions. Priss curled up on the sofa, her favorite piece of furniture in all the world. She'd slept so often in one corner of that old couch, the cushion had developed a depression roughly approximating her slumbering form.

As I sat at the dining room table reading, taking notes, the late-night traffic hummed outside. Around midnight, I stopped to listen. The traffic had abated. Seemed to be quieter than usual. Few cars, little evidence of the coming and going of my immediate neighbors.

I collected the H&K P9S .45 that had taken up residence recently in an upper kitchen cabinet — empty, of course — out of Cullen's reach. Retrieved its magazine, *not* empty, from inside a coffee can on another tall shelf, and shoved it into the butt of the big black autoloader. Racked a round up its chamber. The pistol boasted tritium night sights, good for dancing in the dark with large, malevolent, shotgun-toting gentlemen.

Nub climbed to his feet and sniffed the air, catching my suspicious mood. Outside we went, where we stood on the front porch, taking in the night.

Nothing much to take in. During the five minutes we stood like cigar store totems, not a car moved on my street. No closing doors,

124

nary a TV, just a taste of Pearl Jam from down the street with too much bass and too many decibels.

We went back in. My stomach reminded whatever portion of my brain that monitors such matters that it hadn't eaten in a while. I called for a take-out pizza. (Mushrooms and sausage.) They said twenty minutes. I waited ten and got up to go.

Nubbin, no longer sleepy, was bouncing around the dining room, full of piss and vinegar. I gave him the option of a ride to the pizza parlor, and invited Miss Priss to chaperon the excursion; she declined by politely raising her chin, gazing at me through limpid, intelligent eyes, then curling in more tightly on herself.

She sighed comfortably.

So we left her there, alone, all fluffy and white and content with her lot in life.

★ ★ ★

Six minutes to the pizza joint, three to acquire and pay for the pie, six minutes home, even in my dad's anemic old Chrysler. (Dave and I had transferred the Supra from Dad's place to my driveway earlier that night. I'd decided to stick with Dad's car on the chance that my adversaries hadn't spotted it yet.) All the while, Nubbin sat beside me, eyes glued to the redolent flat pizza box, mouth at flood stage.

When I pulled up in front of my house, there were several police cruisers in evidence, including two in my driveway, their flashing lights illuminating like strobes the grim faces of a score of onlookers. I stood on the brakes, squawked to a stop, switched off the engine, and got out, locking Nubbin in the car. The front door of my house was standing open, a pair of curious neighbors peering in. They saw me approaching and stepped aside. I looked more closely at the door.

I'd been wrong; it was not standing open. It had been shot off its hinges and was leaning tiredly against the doorjamb, cratered, splintered, full of holes.

Inside was worse. The staircase, railing, dining table, chairs, and front window casings were fraught with bullet holes. Shattered glass, everywhere. A uniformed officer was writing on a notepad. He spotted me and asked, "You live here?"

I nodded vacantly.

"Your name Vance?"

Again I nodded. Something was dreadfully wrong here, but my mind was too numbed to isolate it.

The policeman was speaking. " . . . hell of a mess."

I nodded a third time, and as I did I spied the matted blood and hair on the carpet. My eyes focused on the spot as through a zoom lens. A thin trail of gore led away from my feet, crossing the foyer to the living room.

I felt like I had to throw up, my stomach knotted so tightly I could scarcely breathe. My insides convulsed, but what came up was a sound so primordial it seemed to emanate from another species.

Witnesses swore it came from me.

Shoving cops aside; loudly, harshly, gut-wrenchingly:

"PRIIISSSSSSSS!!!!!!"

13

SHE was stretched out on the floor, a pathetic little mass of pain, blood soaking the carpet beneath her. Her back legs trailed uselessly behind her, the result of a broken spine. Using her front legs, she had tried to drag herself under her beloved sofa, haven from the thunder and hurt.

She hadn't made it.

Her face was remarkably placid, the only part of her small body not dripping crimson. When she heard me, she tried to lift her head to reassure herself that I was finally home. I knelt beside her, rubbed her muzzle lightly with a finger.

I tried to speak comfortingly to her, but the constriction in my throat made speech impossible. She licked my hand weakly. *It's all right*, she was saying. *You're here now. I waited for you.*

I felt a hand on my shoulder. "It's no use, pal. She's not going to make it."

Priss looked up at me, black almond eyes beseeching. *We'll do this together*, she was saying. *Like always.*

Her image was a watery blur.

I managed to say, "Get out of here."

The cop leaned closer. "Didn't hear you."

"I said get the hell out of here! Now! Right fucking now!"

He hesitated a second, then left the two of us alone together.

The silence of dying. A ticking clock, the wheeze from Priss's laboring lungs, occasional liquid lap of her tongue, timpanic thud of my heart. The business phone ringing.

Ringing.

Ringing.

I cradled her stalwart body — caressing her, caressing — for a very long time.

And then she left me.

14

ICALLED Dad and told him about the situation at my home.

"I'm sorry about Miss Priss," he said. "House a mess?"

"The front of it, and the furniture near the door. The carpet . . . " Couldn't continue.

After a moment, my father said, "Dave and I'll get right on it in the mornin'. Don't you worry none about Cullen. We'll cover him like Saran Wrap, bring him with us tomorrow.

"Oh yeah, Heather called. Asked would I have you phone her soon as possible. I said I would if I heard from you."

"Okay. Put Dave on, please."

It took a minute, so I figured Dad had filled Dave in by the time he picked up.

"Times are hard," he said as an opener.

"Not as hard as they're gonna be."

"Anything I can do?"

"Put down a pallet for Cullen in the center of the house. Likely the best spot is between the dining room table and the sideboard. Pull the curtains so no one can see in even if they climb up the outside wall, or down from the roof. You cover the entrance off the living room, let Dad have the one from the kitchen.

"I've got to dig a hole out in the backyard; then I'm going to take a long nap.

"Dad said you two could do some cleanup

and repairs in the morning. Can you spare that much time away from the store?"

"Thurman will cover it, so far as walk-in traffic is concerned. I'll do the repair work when I can. Don't worry about it."

"I owe you."

"Don't want to hear about owe."

"Okay."

"We'll try to let you sleep tomorrow," he went on, "be quiet as we can. How you plan to lock the front door?"

"They're posting a deputy here for a while. He'll cover the front door. I'll have the bedroom door locked and barricaded in case anyone gets past him. Doubt they will. They may believe they got me, won't know one way or the other till the news comes on in the morning."

"What's on your agenda for tomorrow?"

"Talk to Fanner, see if he's uncovered any more info on my mystery corpse. Try to reach McElroy, same reason. I need to get a handle on this. Being on the defensive all the time is not only getting old, it's getting ever more dangerous."

"And wearisome."

"That too."

A pause. Then he asked, "You need help digging that hole?"

I swallowed hard, said no, and hung up. Not being rude, just unable. Dave knew the difference.

★ ★ ★

131

It was very late, but Heather had asked for me to call, so I did.

There was no sleep in her voice when she picked up.

"You're awake." Not a question, an observation. "Tyler?"

"It's me. Dad said you'd called."

"What's happened?"

"How do you know anything has happened?"

"I may be beautiful, even blond, but not stupid. That's a myth perpetuated by men and dark-haired women."

I didn't say anything.

"I can hear the strain in your voice, Ty."

Still nothing from me.

"*And* your silence."

More nothing. What a conversationalist.

"You're scaring me."

Trying to keep my voice as even as possible, I told her what had transpired.

"Oh, God. I'm so sorry. Is there anything I can do? Anything at all?"

"Bring me the guys who did it."

"If I could, they'd be on your doorstep right now. Tied hand and foot. I'd be boiling the oil, heating up the pokers, getting out the dentist's drill."

I tried hard not to feel better, and was mostly successful. But the ache *had* lessened. This woman was infectious.

"Thanks," I said.

"I mean it."

"I know you do. And I'm grateful."

"I called about Web. My dad is being operated

132

on in the morning, so I'm leaving for Charlotte around six-thirty. Jason phoned. He wants to take Web on a picnic lunch tomorrow, since he's driving to Asheville the following day, for a week. With the restraining order still in effect, he can't pick Web up at the preschool, even with my permission. He wanted me to ask you to get Web so he could come by your place and pick him up at one o'clock. All that's out of the question now."

"I don't see why."

"Well, your place isn't exactly a safe house, is it? What are you going to do with Cullen?"

"Either Dad or Dave Michaels — a good friend of mine — or I will be with Cullen at all times. Sometimes all three of us. He won't be allowed to play outside where he might be seen. There's a sheriff's car out front, so I can't imagine another attempt here at the house. I won't ever have Cullen in the car with me unless it's absolutely necessary, so another stab at me won't endanger him.

"Last night, it must have appeared that I was home working, or watching late-night TV, with all my lights on. My Supra was there in the driveway — I took my dad's car to get the pizza. It was a pretty safe move for them, as long as they hit quick, then took off, like at The Sweetery.

"I feel Cullen will be fine here, with us three crusty combat vets to look after him. It's possible he'd be more secure in a basement room down at police headquarters with Rambo and Judge Dredd by his side, but I doubt it."

She thought about it a while longer. I waited. It was up to her, made no difference to me.

"Several burly, armed men will be in the house with the boys at all times? They'll be limited to indoor play? There'll always be a deputy parked out front?"

"That's the scenario. Be sure you're comfortable with it. Just because I am doesn't mean you have to be. He's your son."

"Unless I wait until the DA's office opens tomorrow to have the restraining order removed, I can't think of any other way to do it. Dad's going under the knife at eight-thirty. I hate even to consider it, but several serious things could go wrong. If I weren't there with Momma, heaven knows how she'd react if something went awry. Her health is more fragile than Dad's. And if Web were there with us, and she went to pieces . . . "

She thought some more, convincing herself. "I can't think of a better way. Or even another way than not to allow Jason to take Web to lunch. Besides, there's no guarantee I'll get back in time to pick Web up from preschool, which means you'd have to. That would put me right back to square one. Let's do it."

"You sure?"

"Hell no, I'm not sure. There's simply no other way. But don't pick him up any sooner than necessary; that way he won't be at your house for long."

"I have an appointment with Fanner at eleven-thirty. I'll ask Dad to pick Web up shortly before that, on his way over."

134

"Okay then." Short pause. "Ty, I really am sorry. Not only about your dog, but about all this mess you've gotten sucked into."

"It'll be over soon."

"I hope so."

"I intend to make it so."

★ ★ ★

Muted sunlight in my eyes, the taste of sheep-dip on my tongue. Sandpaper feel to my palms from digging. I heard movement downstairs, footfalls. Dad and Dave.

A small knock at the door, hesitant "Daddy?"

Next to me Nubbin lay, ears pricked, gazing at the door. He recognized Cullen's voice, maybe his smell drifting under the door. His tail was still, though. No eagerness to play. He was remembering.

Last night.

Me too.

I called, "Just a minute, son," pushed away the heavy chest of drawers, and unlocked the door.

There he stood, all thirty-five pounds of him, low-down and miserable. Softly crying, holding a collar in one small hand. I knelt in front of him, gathered him up. He clung tightly. I clung tightly. Nubbin hopped down and came over, and leaned against us.

We three.

Yesterday, four.

The sun moved. The moment passed. Feelings shared were put away, in the secret place, where

135

dwelt my mom, and his mom, and others past.

We went down to see what Dave and Dad had wrought.

A lot. Damaged furniture was being piled in the yard, a new front door leaned near the doorway, heavy-duty hinges, its inside surface festooned with Kevlar bulletproof vests hung in ordered, overlapping sequence, covering every square inch.

I looked a question at Dave. He responded, "Thought about a sheet of quarter-inch steel, but Cullen would have trouble opening and closing the door. This was the best I could come up with on short notice."

I looked more closely at him. He looked back, a bit sheepishly. Under a baggy, colorful Hawaiian shirt was the unmistakable outline of a Kevlar vest.

"You're as well protected as the door," I said.

"Got used to wearing a flak vest in Nam. Fine habit to get into where bullets are flying. Saved my life once. In chow line! Mortar shell landed ten meters away. I was standing in a group of eight guys, the only one with a vest. Ones on each side of me bought it. The other five had to be evacked. I was knocked on my duff and my ears rang like church bells for a couple days. No other damage. 'Cept to the vest. Couldn't use that one again."

"You expect bullets to be flying around here?"

"They did last night."

"Say no more," I replied, and went to hunt up my father.

136

★ ★ ★

In the kitchen, on his arthritic knees, grimacing, mouth full of nails, preparing to construct a window casing, I found my immediate male forebear. Around him were a T-square, several brown paper bags, two hammers, other evidence of imminent frenetic carpentry. He glanced up and started to offer an oral salutation.

I held up a hand. "Don't try to speak, you might swallow a nail."

He mumbled something that sounded like "summeluvich," but I refused to let it hurt my feelings.

Web was sitting at the kitchen counter — the dining room table having been relegated to the yard — with a bowl of Rice Krispies under his nose and a steady trickle of two percent milk running from his chin to the bowl. Recycling.

Cullen asked him if he was finished yet, which I thought imperceptive; the child was obviously not done with his brunch. Web moved his head side to side, indicating the negative. Cullen told him he'd be in the living room helping Uncle Dave, if he ever quit eating.

Smart aleck. Where'd he get that from?

I patted Web's curly pate and said, "Take your time. Enjoy your cereal."

His head bobbed affirmatively as he chewed. He smiled damply, a drop of milk dangling precariously from the point of his chin.

Entranced, I waited and watched, to see it fall into the bowl.

It didn't. He wiped it off with the back of a

hand, then shoveled in another spoonful.

I shook my head as if to dislodge an especially annoying horsefly, and told my dad, "I'm going to see Fanner."

"Better call first, might save you a trip," he said, without looking up.

"No need. He'll be there. Anyway, y'all be careful. I doubt anything will happen with that sheriff's deputy out front, but who knows? Keep the boys in the house, please."

He favored me with one of his dark looks, the one that makes me feel like a butterfly specimen pinned to a corkboard. "Teach yer granmaw to suck eggs," he said. If he had chewed tobacco, that would have been when he'd have spit, *patouie.*

I left before I had to bear further brunt.

A kiss and a hug from Cullen and I backed the Supra out of the driveway, wanting the bad guys to know I wasn't at home. I told the deputy where I was going and when I expected to return. He told me his replacement would be on duty then. I nodded and drove away.

15

I'D spoken with Fanner the night before, after my house had been shot to dollrags. We'd made an appointment for eleven-thirty, ante meridiem. So there I sat in the substantial chair, centered in front of his desk, while he informed me of the gruesome details surrounding the demise and discovery of the hapless bank teller, Felita Hutchins.

She'd been shot in the head, once, and laid on the backseat of her car, which had subsequently been hidden in a cluster of trees adjacent to an abandoned farmhouse, just this side of the Rockingham County line. Two good ol' boys intent on a carefree day noodling in a Haw River tributary had spotted the car and investigated. Well, *tried* to investigate. After approaching the car, from which radiated a most noisome odor, they'd retreated to their Bronco and cellular-phoned a come-hither to the authorities.

And thus were discovered Ms. Hutchins's remains. Already Fanner had told me more than I'd any desire to know, but he continued.

"The lady was not robbed," he said. "The contents of her purse were intact and seemingly undisturbed. There were no signs of abuse, physical or sexual. No traces of semen, no swelling of the — "

"I get the picture."

"The autopsy was thorough."

"Thanks for sharing that with me."

"I brought it up not for its lurid aspects, but as illustration for two points. One: These men kill with no compunction whatever if they fear they might be identified. Two: They are interested in little at this moment except erasing you. And avoiding capture, of course."

"You're suggesting that their blasting away at a restaurant full of patrons doesn't indicate that they'll kill anyone and everyone?" I asked.

"Not necessarily. They had a reason to open up on the restaurant. You were inside. And while I doubt they were overly troubled by conscience after the shooting, they nonetheless do not seem to kill simply for its own sake."

"No?"

"No indeed. They did not kill the owner of the Chevrolet Camaro, and they could have as easily as they bashed him on the head. However, the man told me that he was just getting out of his car when he was struck from behind, thus did not see a thing. They knew it, therefore had no reason to kill him."

"Hope you're not giving these fellows too much credit as humanitarians based on their sparing one guy."

"I think not. In fact, quite the contrary. The large man was overheard discussing the probable fate of Ms. Hutchins by an adjacent teller. In his opinion, the robbers intended to kill her as soon as they made good their escape. This conversation occurred minutes before you arrived to put a damper on their

140

scheme, so the less than vague allegation in the newspaper relative to your possible initiation of the kidnapping was hogwash, as is much of that woman's material.

"Here." He reached for a file folder, bright green, not manila. "Let me offer you the fruits of our investigation so far.

"Mr. Irving J. Hooker — one of the men you shot, as you may recall, remorsefully, no doubt — worked out of Washington. He had — "

"D.C.?"

"No, state. He had an associate, John Phillip Bynum, with whom he worked almost exclusively. They trusted one another, rare among such lowlifes as these. They did not specialize, but participated in anything from petty theft to bank robberies, carjackings to kidnappings, some leg breaking for loan sharks. Often the long arm of the law plucked them from their lair, incarcerated them under very high bail, developed well-conceived cases, only to have witnesses relocate or refuse to testify for questionable reasons."

He nodded sadly, then resumed. "Commonly, the Messrs. Bynum and Hooker preferred to practice their professions far from their own bailiwick, so as not to foul their nest, so to speak. At the time of his death, Hooker was not wanted anywhere for anything, not even driving without a seat belt.

"Bynum, on the other hand, is wanted in several states, and is currently under bond on an assault charge in Seattle. The victim in the case, a prostitute known on the street as Ryda

Trane — due to her predilection for multiple partners one after another in rapid succession — is half Sicilian and all pluck. She has put out the word that she will not only testify against her former client, but geld him should he beat the rap. Her family, which is not without influence in the Seattle underbelly, supports her."

I interrupted with, "I suppose the gist of this is that Bynum is scared shitless, and his misfortunes are none of our own. So, applying a little leverage, the Seattle police have brought out the canary in him. He sings and they keep him in a safe cage until the heat is off from the Sicilian contingent."

"Not exactly the way I would put it, but accurate. Our detective on the scene claims that Mr. Bynum has been the very model of truth and cooperation. All of his statements that could be confirmed have been." He paused dramatically.

"And this is what we've found out . . . " I said, by way of encouragement.

He straightened up and looked at me nasally.

Was I being pushy?

"Bynum and Hooker were approached a month ago in Seattle by a pair of European gentlemen, one of whom possessed barely sufficient English to request directions to the bathroom. The other spoke fluent though lightly accented English. Another man — a Mexican, we suspect, Hispanic for certain, and reported to be quite large — was along apparently as a bodyguard for the pair, who were thought to be brothers, although one was much older than the other.

"Bynum pulled out of the deal after a week of association with these foreign gentlemen, claiming them to be" — he looked at his notes — "'pit bull-mean, tight-ass, white motherfuckers with no sense of humor.' His words, of course."

"No kidding?"

"Bynum went to Las Vegas — which is where we ran him to ground — to run numbers for an acquaintance dating from his Vietnam tour. That way he could avoid his new but unpleasant friends while still earning a living."

"Not to mention ducking the assault charge, jumping bail, staying out of jail, and avoiding ol' Ryda Trane — what a *nom de rue* — and her half-Sicilian family."

"All Sicilian, except for her father, now deceased."

I thought about it. "Your detective got all this from the delectable Ms. Trane and the prolix Mr. Bynum?"

"A cooperative pair."

"I'll say."

We observed each other for a while, I expecting him to go on, he obviously undecided. The building creaked; policefolk trod the hollow halls, their oppressive conversations muffled by the walls of Fanner's den. In the snack bar, someone was likely sampling the vendor's wares. Cookies, anyone? Almond joy? Coconut pie, potato chips, cheese crackers? Coffee — fresh, hot, black? My mouth began to water.

Reality check. Fanner, droning on: " . . . best that Bynum could provide was that they needed a pair of men to assist with two separate jobs. The first was a bank robbery somewhere back east. The brothers claimed information from an inside man in Zurich who knew the ultimate destination for a bundle of illicit money, newly laundered, and the exact date of arrival at the targeted financial institution. They would simply walk into the bank and make a withdrawal."

"Which is where I blundered into the picture."

"For a fact. But you merely halved their team, unfortunately for you taking out one of the siblings. You did not interrupt the transfer into undesirable hands of what we have been told — in strictest confidence, of course, by the FBI — is a sizable sum of money."

"When you say sizable, do you mean *sizable*?"

"Yes."

"How sizable?"

"Two million, one hundred thousand dollars."

"Ah. That sizable."

"I had no intention of telling you the exact amount."

"I wormed it out of you," I said. "I apologize."

"Accepted."

"When money is transferred from one account to another, especially internationally, isn't it usually only on paper, or on disk, or something?"

"Most often that is correct."

"But not this time," I said.

"Right."

"Why not?"

He hesitated. "My understanding is that a request for a cash withdrawal was forwarded to

144

the bank, along with the proper documentation from the IRS to show that that worthy organization had been duly notified of the exact amount and circumstances surrounding its withdrawal. Bank officials knew that they would have the cash on site for only one day, and since the IRS had been notified of the impending transaction in advance, they had no choice but to ready the money."

"If these gents could simply withdraw the dough, why did they rob the bank?"

"The gentlemen to whom the money belonged did not rob the bank."

"You mean the FBI let illegal money come into the States from Europe, bound for identifiable parties?"

"What they knew and what they could prove were two different things."

"Ah."

"Indeed."

"What was the second job Bynum, Hooker, and Associates had lined up?" I queried.

"A gun buy."

"Lot of guns?"

"Sizable quantity."

"When you say sizable, do you mean — "

"Do not start."

"Okay." I grinned puckishly. "Might it be safe to say that they planned to spend the bulk of the bread on bazookas?"

"Yes."

"And similar heavy-duty stuff? Mortars, grenades, rocket launchers, machine guns, Hershey bars?"

"I disapprove of your levity."

"Shucks. I thought you admired it."

He smiled briefly, like a depleted firefly signaling to his mate for one last tryst in the grass.

Then he said, "The subject under discussion is too grave not to be serious. If these gentlemen locate a seller, and the word is that they found one in Seattle while the bank job was in its planning stage, then someone, somewhere — probably Europe — is in for grim difficulties."

I digested what he'd told me, then said, "I remember witnesses at the bank mentioning the unusually large thief. They all agree that he was Latino?"

"Yes. Consensus was that he had a most threatening presence. They referred to him variably as formidable, threatening, scary."

"Well, he sure scared the hell out of me at The Sweetery," said I.

"He never spoke, wore a ski mask, rubber gloves, a long-sleeved sweatshirt. A few mentioned his dark eye color. All commented on the fact that he was the only one to touch anything. And when they left the bank, he carried the bag of money under one arm, the unfortunate Ms. Hutchins under the other."

"No gun?"

"He never brandished one, although several people mentioned that he had a shotgun slung across his back. One man, a hunter, said the gun was a Mossberg twelve gauge."

That information stopped me for a second. "Then you were pretty sure," I went on, "that the Mossberg riot gun found in the Camaro was used both in the drive-by shooting *and* at the bank, even before your forensic technicians matched the shells to the gun."

"Yes."

"Funny, you didn't mention it to me."

"I cannot tell you everything."

"Suppose not," I said. "Well, you're in my debt."

"I beg your pardon."

"Sure. If I hadn't sidetracked this group, they'd likely be examining all that military hardware as we speak. And planning their escape route from the U. S. of A. If they haven't already."

"Yes, but while your sidetracking them may well have created a delay in hostilities somewhere, it has been a continuing source of annoyance for me."

"Like a shot-up ice cream eatery?"

He nodded.

"And my home attacked, my dog killed?"

He nodded again, adding, "And a quiet suburban neighborhood in a lather about a high-speed chase through their secluded streets."

I dipped my chin, contritely. Tried to look like Cullen when he's flushed a Power Ranger down the toilet.

"What are you saying about that, officially, to the residents, the press?"

"Little, except that we are following every lead. No mention of you."

"Thanks. At least I won't be subjected to more reckless-endangerment tripe about myself in a Rita Snipes column."

"Do not be so sure. She will surely be apprised of the attack on your home. Then she will put two and two together and go straight for your jugular."

"She'll say I invited it."

"Most certainly."

"By existing."

"I doubt that is what she will write, but it is what she will imply."

"Can I have her arrested?"

"On what charge?"

"Visual pollution? Abuse of undergarments? Impersonating a human?"

Again the hint of a smile. "All misdemeanors. We could never hold her. She knows the chief."

"Now there's a pair. Rita Snipes and Tugboat McBayne. The Grand Tetons in the flesh."

"Never use the word 'Tugboat' in this office. Any word from your, ah, other sources?"

"Too soon, I suppose. But I'll call them with this new information. Give them a starting point if they haven't got one already."

Changing the subject, I said, "You or the sheriff plan to leave an officer at my place for a while?"

"I can get away with it for a day or two."

I nodded my thanks. "I'll try to have a plan in motion by then."

He frowned. "A plan? What kind of plan?"

"I cannot tell you everything," I said, and left.

★ ★ ★

I drove a few blocks to the gym where I
sometimes pump iron, to use the phone. Dad
answered. All was quiet; the kids were watching
Aladdin; Dave had rented some furniture from
a friend in that business to replace temporarily
my own bullet-riddled stuff; McElroy had called
thrice; one of my editors had phoned, wanting
to know where my piece on home-defence
handguns was.

"Somewhere over Topeka," I told Dad. "I
mailed it yesterday."

He said I'd better call and tell the man, who
seemed a bit high-strung. I concurred with that
assessment, assured him that I'd give the guy a
buzz when I found a spare minute, then asked
for Dave. Pop went to get him.

"Y'ello."

"Got the banister up yet?"

"No."

"What's taking so long?"

"Kiss my ass."

"No offence."

"The hell there ain't."

Ritual raillery concluded, I said, "From what
Fanner told me, we're up against some bad
dudes, as the parlance goes. Real bad." I filled
him in.

"In other words," he said, "watch out for men
bearing shotguns. Or anything else. Who knows,
maybe next will be a bomb."

"Bite your tongue."

"Right. Hard to guard against explosives."

"Leave the mail out in the box beside the street," I said. "Accept no packages. Eat only what's already in the house."

"Paranoia's an ugly thing."

"Yeah, but it makes for longevity."

"Umm."

"And keep the boys in the house."

"Couple hours of boy play, it'll look worse than after the shooting."

"I don't doubt that. Where's Nubbin?"

"Last I looked, upstairs in your bed."

"Keep him in too. Please."

"Sure."

"I'm going to call McElroy soon as we hang up. If there are further developments, I'll call you right back. If not, I'll just come on home."

"Can I go now?"

"Yep."

★ ★ ★

As I dialed McElroy at Fort Bragg, I watched a comely lass do bent-over rows. Her hindquarters were heart-shaped, inadequately covered, cellulite-free. Splendid.

"McElroy," came out of the phone.

"Hello, Colonel, Tyler Vance," I said, a hitch in my voice.

"You okay?"

"Can't seem to catch my breath. Been watching a scantily clad young lady exercising."

"Know the feeling. Look the other way. I have news, not much of it good."

150

I waited, but he didn't continue. I said, "Well?"

"Not over the phone."

"When? How?"

He paused. "Can you slip down to Bragg today?"

"No. Things here are getting out of hand." I told him about the assault on my house.

"Lucky you weren't there, with your son."

"I know."

"Well, it jibes with what I've heard, little enough though it is. You get any more out of GPD?"

I reiterated what Fanner had told me.

"Hmm. Let me toss what you just told me into the stove, see if there's a coal in there that'll stoke up the fire. Any intel is welcome. We're in a race here.

"Meanwhile, I'm sending you four Delta guys, in mufti of course. Two to watch your digs, two for your dad's. Introduce them to the cops as old fishing buddies volunteering to help out a pal. If the cops insist they're in the way, give me a call and I'll pull somebody's lanyard."

"I really appreciate this."

He brushed it off. "No problem. Things get worse, you might come uncorked and unleash some of that army training, assuming you can find out who to unleash it on. That'd make things tough for me, and the Pentagon. Some snoopy reporter might sniff something out, or figure it out."

"Not anyone at our local newspaper. Most of them can't figure out what day it is."

151

"Old son, if *you* cut loose, this thing'll go national in a heartbeat. I know what you're capable of, remember?"

"I remember."

"So keep a tight rein on. Just form a perimeter, with your family inside, and keep it secure. No sorties, okay? Just for twenty-four hours? By then, I'll be back in touch. You got my word.

"Remember, the police are covering you, and a pair of our nation's finest, covertly. Hell, we might just step on those slugs if they try another trip into the garden."

"All right. Twenty-four hours. Starting now."

"Bingo," he said, and hung up.

★ ★ ★

At that exact moment — I would learn later, after the police had pieced together the precise sequence of events — a marked police cruiser pulled into the driveway of my home. The uniformed officer riding shotgun got out of the car, walked around to its rear, and opened the trunk. Meanwhile, the driver, a slender blonde of average height and structure, sauntered over to the deputy's car, told him he was being relieved, and offered the hope that they'd arrived in time for him to make his son's soccer game.

The deputy thanked him and pulled off, in a hurry to see the opening kick.

By the time the driver had returned to his cruiser, adjusted his Sam Browne belt, and tipped his hat to keep the sun from his opalescent eyes, his partner had slipped

152

a slender leather thong through an eyelet in the stock of a Franchi combat shotgun, then looped one end of it around his neck, hanging the 12-bore autoloader down his back out of sight from the front.

The driver slammed the trunk lid, hitched his belt once more; then the two of them walked down the short sidewalk to my front door. Dave Michaels waited just inside the door as they approached. He did not spot the thong around the taller officer's neck, nor the way it pulled at the man's collar, nor yet the slightly ungainly way he walked. There was no reason to. These were uniformed cops, come to serve and protect.

When the pair stepped onto the front porch, only the blond policeman was visible through the narrow window beside the solid wooden door. As Dave watched through that window, the smaller officer looked at his partner, waited a few seconds, then rang the doorbell.

Unsuspecting, Dave opened the door wide.

And was shotgunned twice in the chest from two feet away.

16

THE double dose of buckshot — coupled with his own nervous system's reaction to the sudden trauma — sent Dave reeling backward. His head slammed into the heavy oak knickknack shelf affixed to the wall behind him, splitting his scalp like a ripe muskmelon. He spun partway around, slumped limply to the floor, and lay twisted, an unfeeling bloodied lump. Stepping over Dave's inert body, the shotgun wielder scanned the room. On his heels came the shorter "cop," pistol drawn, who glanced around, said, "I'll take the upstairs," and moved to the bottom stairstep.

Hearing the gunshots from his seat in the second-floor bathroom, my dad stood, hitched up his trousers and secured his belt, and ran quickly to Cullen's room. The two boys had come to the bedroom door, wide-eyed. Dad grabbed them both by their shirtbacks, hustled them down the hall into the master bedroom, and sent them over to the window that overlooked the garage, whispering to Cullen to raise the sash while he checked things out.

Somberly, Cullen asked, "Has Dave been shot?"

Dad, equally somber, answered, "Maybe."

Dad recrossed the room, grabbing his M1 carbine from the top of the chest of drawers, and stood in the bedroom doorway listening. He chambered a cartridge by sharply manipulating the operating-rod handle — *snick!* The guy coming up the stairs must have heard the sound and felt a mite exposed; he suddenly decided to retrace his steps and rethink his advance. Dad hosed down the stairwell to hasten his departure, succeeding admirably. He told me later that "the blond feller jumped faster'n a mongoose at a rattlesnake convention."

As soon as his adversary had dived out of sight downstairs, Dad went back into the master bedroom, closed and locked the door. He thought about sliding the chest of drawers against the door and attempting to secure the room, but decided that carrying the fight outside would not only give him more space to maneuver but provide the boys with an escape route should he meet with grief.

He held each boy by an arm and dangled them from the window, then dropped them the short distance to the garage roof. Several 9 mm bullets zipped through the bedroom door, thwacking into the wall not far from where he stood. This encouraged him to follow the kids out the window and onto the roof below. From there it was but a short climb down through the spreading limbs of a dogwood tree. Once on the ground, he sent the boys loping to the Cranford house three doors away, admonishing Cullen to have Mrs. Cranford call 911 "right damn now."

Dad found a hiding place in the shadows inside the garage. He stood, one tennis-shod foot on the lawn mower, the other covering a small paint spot on the concrete floor. A pair of pinking shears hung from the wall beside his left shoulder, a coiled steel plumber's snake near the other. Suburban camouflage. His maroon shirt and navy slacks enabled him to blend with the dim interior of the garage, nearly invisible. There he waited, World War II relic .30 carbine at the ready, just as he had at Guadalcanal. Taste of copper, palms damp, beads of perspiration along the hairline.

Waiting.

For the fur to fly.

Not long now.

★ ★

While his buddy was being fired at from above, the shotgun-toting police impersonator hurriedly searched the ground floor. He then returned to discuss the situation with his partner, who was rubbing a bruised hip and working up an attitude.

"I'm gonna blow out that bastard's liver," growled the blond, jaw working, fillings scraping against one another.

"Keep your cool. Run around with a mad on and that old dude just might punch your ticket."

"Fuck him! He's dead."

"We were going to kill him anyway, Lyle."

"Yeah, well now I'm gonna make it *hurt*."

They conferred another moment; then Blondy went back upstairs and fired a volley through the bedroom door and kicked it in.

156

While all this activity was taking place upstairs, the shotgunner ran to the back of the house, espied the boys dropping from the tree, followed by the geezer, on their heels and carrying a short rifle of some kind. He watched the old guy tell the kids something, then bustle them off out of sight, heading east.

Sending them to a nearby house for help, he reasoned. Or to use the phone. Better get 'em quick, before this neighborhood was crawling with *real* cops.

Out the front door he went, aiming to head them off or wipe them out, whichever was easier.

★ ★ ★

Blondy came onto the driveway in a hurry, hot on the scent, having also dropped from the upstairs window. Dad had heard his feet scrambling on the garage roof, and monitored his limb-snapping descent through the dogwood branches. The guy seemed to have targeted the garage as a likely hidey-hole for scared little boys, though his primary concern at this point should have been the whereabouts of an old veteran and his much used, fast-firing rifle. Maybe the buff-haired, pale-eyed gunman was just a killer, not a tactician. Perhaps he had little patience. Whatever his shortcoming at that moment, he was in for an expensive lesson.

Profiting from it was not in the cards.

A bullet to his rib cage was.

Then another to the shoulder, causing him

157

to spin away from the hit as he brought up his police-issue Beretta 9 mm and cranked three rounds into the shadows of the garage, brilliant sunlight in his eyes, blinding him to all but a veil of pain and anger and surprise.

One of his 9 mm slugs found flesh, taking my father's wind but not his resolve. Dad triggered the rest of his load, twelve rounds in all, four going home. They didn't expand, being full-metal-jacket projectiles almost as large in diameter as they were long, but one of them struck Blondy's breastbone — crushing it, driving razor-sharp splinters into nearby lung tissue — then keyholed, buzz-sawing its destructive path through the superior vena cava and aorta, atop the heart. It coursed on, coming to rest in the left bicep muscle, hard against the inside of the humerus.

The resulting rapid drop in blood pressure put Blondy on his side in the driveway, where he lay in the spreading pool of his own fluid and feces.

My dad, his back to the garage wall, slid down it to a squatting position, hugging a broken rib and bloody gash along his side, unfortunately not numb to the pain. His breath came in ragged gasps as he sat wondering if he was having a heart attack, if Blondy was part of a tag team, if Cullen had raised the police.

He tried to get up. His legs just wouldn't respond. So he rested. Listening. For sirens in the distance.

★ ★ ★

158

Unfortunately for all concerned, while Cullen and Web had indeed reached the Cranford house without incident, no one was home. All outside doors were locked — Cullen checked each one — so he couldn't call the police, or anyone else. Realizing that he was responsible for Web, and having heard the shooting behind him but no word from Dave or his grandfather that all was well, my young son stood at the Cranfords' back doorstep, shivering from the effects of abject terror and isolation, and did his very, very best to choke back tears and come up with a plan. He remembered that everyone else in the immediate neighborhood was at work or school; only Mrs. Cranford was usually at home during the day. He thought and thought, looked and looked, but no matter how he examined the situation, there appeared to be only one place to go. So he took Web's quivering hand into his own, squeezed it tightly for reassurance — Web was crying quietly — and went there.

17

JASON PATTERSON pulled into the Vance driveway, stopped behind a police cruiser, and looked at his Rolex, squinting against the sun's glare: 1:13. He'd called just after noon, telling the elder Mr. Vance that he was running a little late.

As usual.

As he opened the car door and lifted a leg out, he heard a barrage of gunfire from somewhere behind the house that so unnerved him he cracked his head against the doorframe.

"Shit!" he grunted, biting his lip against the sudden throb at his temple.

Pow! Pow! Pow! Pow! The shooting went on, seemingly never ending.

Then . . . silence.

Rubbing his tender spot, he said aloud, "I know the man's a gun fanatic, but this is ridiculous." However, with the pain in his head fading, he reasoned more clearly. *This is inside the city limits. He can't shoot guns here, not legally.* Then, remembering the police car, he wondered if the cops were shooting.

If so . . . at what?

He eased quietly down the drive and peered around the corner where it curved, widening into an apron capable of holding several vehicles. Only one car, though, an ancient Chrysler New Yorker. What caught Jason's eye was not the

Chrysler but the uniformed policeman nearby, slumped askew in an unpleasant, odiferous puddle.

He proceeded with great reluctance, calling, "Web?" and giving wide berth to the leaking, prostrate body.

There came a weak, "Patterson?"

"Hello?" answered Jason, growing more apprehensive by the second.

"In here," came a disembodied voice from deep within the shadowy garage.

Jason approached slowly, slowly, until a hoarse but surprisingly strong, "Hurry the hell up!" assaulted his ears.

He hurried the hell up.

Entering the garage, his eyes adjusting to the relative dimness, he saw the old man squatting against one side wall, holding himself, blood dribbling between his fingers. Jason hurried over, dropping to one knee.

The old fellow was having trouble breathing, let alone talking, but he managed, "Other cop's not a cop neither . . . after the boys . . . Dave's dead . . . go help 'em." He couldn't continue.

"Let me help you first," Jason said, reaching out a hand.

Odie shoved it away, wheezed, "No time! Cop with shotgun . . . " Stopped again, head sagging to his chest.

Jason, urgently: "Where are the kids?"

Odie jerked a thumb over his shoulder, indicating the direction. "Three doors down . . . yellow frame house. Told 'em to

161

call . . . police . . . from there," he gasped.

Jason said okay and stood up. Odie grabbed his pants leg and pointed to the dead man's service automatic lying in the grass beside the drive. Jason, who knew little about firearms and less about handguns and next to nothing about autoloading pistols, picked up the Beretta as if it were a tainted addict's needle.

"Won't bite" — from the old man, voice rasping. "Shake a leg now . . . go find the boys."

So Jason went.

★ ★ ★

Inside the house, Dave Michaels groaned, rolled over, pushed up onto his knees and vomited all over the carpet, his tattered bulletproof vest, and the remains of his Hawaiian shirt. His head strummed like a cheap banjo; he literally saw stars before his eyes. Aching and feeling constricted beyond endurance, his chest heaved from the combined efforts of breathing and barfing.

Not easy being Dave Michaels at that moment.

Or for days after.

But Dave being Dave, he bore the momentary pain and ignominy, and achieved an upright, if unsteady, posture. Then he leaned heavily against the wall, panting.

In the pain-racked, half-conscious recesses of his agile brain dwelt an urgency — if he could only lasso it and look it in the eye. He knew he had to do something, think of something, tend to something . . .

Now if he could just remember what it was.

But before doing so, he could try to walk a little. Maybe. If his head would stop swimming. Hand on the wall for support, he took a tentative step, fixing his gaze on the elk antlers above the fireplace across the room.

About those antlers . . . Dave remembered the bull as boasting six points to a side; it now appeared to have twelve. He found that odd, and was trying to come to grips with it when his legs turned to rubber and buckled under their load.

It was his last conscious thought for two hours.

* * *

The shotgun-carrying gunman, currently answering to the name Bobby McGee (being a longtime fan of Janis Joplin), held the shotgun at port arms and peered in the front windows of the yellow frame house. *Nada.* He listened hard for sounds of habitation — TV set, radio, folks talking, whistling, vacuum cleaner sucking up grit. More *nada.*

Same as the last two houses. No cars, no people, and especially no kids phoning the cops.

Just plain old *nada.*

He liked that word, *nada.* And *cabrón*, and *pendejo*, and the half-dozen other Spanish words in his vocabulary. (Which was about half of his

163

English vocabulary.) Maybe next job he'd go Hispanic, maybe Pedro or Juan.

Juan McGee? Naw, need some beaner name to stick on the end. Ortega. Or Garcia, like that guy Warren Oates was supposed to bring back the head of in that Peckinpah movie. What was the guy's first name? Armando? Augusto? Alfredo!

Alfredo Juan Garcia. Is that me, or what?

Well, I surely do look Latino. The old man's Indian blood, he mused, walking around to the side of the house to smoke over the rear. No car around back, no sound, no signs of life at all. *Ain't nobody around here in the daytime?*

If not, where'd them kids go?

Thinking of his old man again (the bastard) always put him in a foul mood, as if he wasn't usually in one anyway. He looked around, then ahead, could see the phalanx of middle-class backyards marching away from him, down the street. No fresh wash hanging from clotheslines, billowing white pillowcases refracting sunrays helter-skelter. No backyard smells of motor oil, stale beer, sun-cracked vinyl from an ancient, dying lounge chair, dank walls of the tree house he and his brother had built in the stunted cottonwood tree, with their own hands, no help from the old man, who was usually at work or stinking drunk and beating up on their ma, till she died on him and left him no one to beat up on but them. Their only refuge was the tree house, where they'd hide when he was on a binge, though he'd finally remember where they were and come out after them, hands curled into

164

fists. But he could never climb the tree, scrawny though it was, would fall back time after time until he either passed out or was reduced to shaking his fist and blaspheming.

As he walked, he sang sibilantly, the lyrics barely audible. "Oh, Lord . . . "

Stopped to glance at the screened-in back porch, bending over to peer under the divan, moved on.

" . . . won't you buy me . . . "

Poked the muzzle of his shotgun into a thick mimosa bush, looked in back of it where it abutted the house.

" . . . a Mercedes-Benz . . . "

Yep, that old tree house had saved his skinny butt many a time, him and his brother's. He'd reached the far edge of the yard — barely mindful in his self-absorption that he was still moving — when he stopped suddenly, as if his father's vengeful fist had come forth from the grave to pinion him where he stood.

He trembled from the combined effects of elation and the vestiges of his desperate and ugly childhood, the sodden chill of triumph and despair at the memory of his father's death, of the old man's skull resisting, then caving, then dissolving to mush under his strength, his wrath, the solid heft of the bloody tie-rod as he chopped it up and down, up and down, a metronome of catharsis, his wild-eyed, rictal countenance surveyed by his little brother from a distance, from the eerie, from the haven of their tree house.

Tree house.

The slender, swarthy head swiveled on its reptilian neck — eyes still white with remembrance, appearing unlidded — and stared out toward the backyard. Took in the high board privacy fence, the sturdy elms and oaks, the abandoned bicycle, on its side, no kickstand, and the yellow beach ball under a tree.

An oak tree.

And up in that tree, twelve feet off the ground . . .

. . . was a tree house.

★ ★ ★

Jason Patterson ran as fast as he could. So fast he tripped and fell once, but arrived at the second house just in time to see a tall, dark policeman slither around the left rear corner of the next in line, a handsome yellow frame number just like Mr. Vance had said.

While the cop was out of sight, Jason hotfooted it to the left front of the house, peeped around the corner, then negotiated the driveway toward the rear as carefully as if he were treading a wire over Niagara.

He held the Beretta straight out in front of him, like he'd seen in movies and TV, so tightly that his hands and arms began to ache. Approaching the rear quadrant, he belatedly wondered whether the gun's safety was off. If it wasn't, and he had to shoot in a hurry, the situation might run amuck. He thought he'd better stop and check.

Having once fired a military .45 — a beat-up

166

Ithaca brought home from Inchon by a long-dead cognate, inherited by his Aunt Sophie, who kept it in her tatting box, unoiled so as not to discolor the lace — he remembered where its safety was. The strange-feeling pistol in his hand had one in a similar location, but on the slide instead of the frame. Since the hammer of the gun was to the rear, in ready-to-fire mode, and the safety lever was in its uppermost position — which on the military .45 was "safe" — Patterson depressed the safety lever.

The hammer dropped with a mild click — but not so mild that Jason didn't clear the ground by a good three inches — and the trigger lurched forward in the trigger guard. Alarmingly, it stayed in the forward position.

I broke something, thought Jason, unsettled in the extreme. *Did the cop hear it?*

The safety lever was down and theoretically in the "fire" position, but when Jason pulled the trigger nothing happened. He cocked the hammer, but it wouldn't stay cocked, simply dropped back against the rear of the slide, into its recess.

Shit, I did break it, he thought. *Now what? There's a homicide specialist roving the neighborhood, intent on who-knows-what, and here I am with a broken gun. Great.*

Maybe I can sneak up and hit him over the head with this useless handgun.

Sure I can.

Jason peered cautiously around the corner of the house. The tall, thin cop was advancing

167

to the rear of the yard, hunched lizardlike, eyes fixed on a tree house as if nothing else existed.

Jason looked toward the tree house. Through the cracks between the boards, a flash of red, seen and then gone. Reflected sunlight? No, too vivid. Perhaps a shirt.

And then a dread realization, with all its horrible implications, hit him in the pit of his stomach.

The boys were in that tree house!

* * *

As soon as Cullen boosted Web up into the tree house, he pulled the rope in behind them. Barry Cranford's father had affixed the hemp tether to a two-by-six that served as a brace for the roof, placing it so that the boys could use the line both for climbing into the house and swinging Tarzanlike with their feet secured through a loop tied in its groundward end. He and Barry had swung so often from that sturdy rope that its length had increased noticeably.

Cullen told Web to lie down in the center of the floor and stay still. He watched to see if anyone was following them. Directly, a policeman came into view, sneaking around the corner of the house. Not a nice-looking man. Why was he sneaking around as if playing a game of hide-and-seek?

Maybe he was.

They were hiding and *he* was seeking. What was Cullen going to do if he found them?

168

He looked around the little shack. A few Power Rangers stood forlornly in the corner. How he wished the *real* Zack were here now — a woolly mammoth could sit on this guy and squash him like a snake! Or Kimberly — she could simply whisk them away, her great wings spreading, blotting the sun from the sky . . . But no, this was real. No *Rescuers Down Under* here. Whatever had to be done he had to do.

He looked some more: a decrepit two-cell flashlight, innards exposed, one leaky battery lying in a knothole; the green two-burner propane camping stove, beyond repair, purloined from his dad's camper and brought up here by Cullen, on which he and Barry had cooked many a pretend meal of venison and sourdough and pork 'n' beans; an orange kazoo, still functional; two Limited Edition Air Pressure Super Soaker 50 water guns, with . . .

The stove.

Cullen scuttled over and hefted it. Pretty heavy. What if the policeman came over to the tree house and tried to climb up? Maybe he could drop the stove on his head, *whap!*

But what if the man didn't try to climb up? Just stood outside and called to them?

They wouldn't have to come out. He wasn't their daddy.

But what if he got mad and shot his long gun up into the tree?

Cullen looked at the rope. Then the Coleman stove. Carried the stove over to the doorway, staying in the shadows so the mean policeman

169

couldn't see him. He hoped.

Pulled the looped end of the rope over and around the empty propane canister. A tight fit, but he managed, and was pretty sure the rope wouldn't come off when he most needed it not to.

Next, he sat cross-legged near the door opening, still remembering to stay in the shadows, and held the stove — heavy as it was — on his lap. If the man would just come close enough, he might could swing this old stove at him and bonk him on the head good. The thought made him wince.

That would *really* hurt.

So would getting shot.

He almost started to cry, but didn't. Web might see.

Where's Daddy? he thought.

Not here. He snuffed once, not loud.

What would he tell me to do?

Be brave. Be calm. Think my way out.

So he thought.

Maybe if that man thinks there's a kitty in here, he'll want to see it. Come real close.

"I would," he said under his breath.

Cullen, always an excellent mimic, cut loose with his best cat imitation.

★ ★ ★

Zebulon "Bobby McGee" Carey stood close to the tree house, shading his sensitive serpent's eyes from the sun, trying to see between the cracks into the little shack above and before

170

him, where he was now certain the two boys were hiding, when a cat meowed nearby.

Loudly.

Scared the pudding out of him.

"Look at you jumping out of your skin. What the hell's the matter with you, Zeb?" — using, as he did on those occasions when he made himself the object of direct address, his given name. "Just a couple of scared-shitless little boys and a horny tomcat somewhere close."

Looking up at the tree house, squinting against the sun's relentless blaze, he saw movement. Through a smile expansive enough to expose his fangs, he said, "Well, now. Let's get it over with, fellas."

And raised the shotgun.

★ ★ ★

Twelve feet off the ground, Cullen whispered, "Lie back down!" to Web, then returned his attention to the man below. Saw the malignant grin, the shotgun coming up. His little fingers tightened on the stove. It had to be now and it had to work, or he'd never see his daddy again. Except in heaven. He heaved the stove out the doorway.

★ ★ ★

Jason had closed the gap between himself and the rogue cop by two thirds, leaving about ten yards separating them — the man was still staring intently at the tree house — when

171

the squall of an ailing cat halted him in his tracks. Jason saw the policeman jump, heard him mumble something, then watched as he tossed the shotgun to his shoulder.

Oh God, he's going to shoot! thought Jason, in a panic. He looked dispiritedly at the useless pistol in his hand, held by the slide and barrel as if it were a hammer, then dropped it at his feet. There was nothing else to do but distract, so he yelled "STOP!" so loudly it strained his larynx. He didn't even notice.

What Jason did notice were two things: the gunman spinning in his direction like a matador, not dismounting the shotgun but aiming it straight at his face; and a dappled — green, rectangular object — flashing now, blindingly, as it caught the sunlight — swinging downward from the tree house doorway . . .

Straight at his opponent.

Jason stood like a deer caught in a spotlight, mesmerized, watching as the unusual pendulum descended in an agonizingly slow arc.

Down, down, down it swung, seemingly too slow to make any difference. He closed his eyes, braced himself to hear the hollow boom that would end his life.

And it came. *Boom!* Just like that.

★ ★ ★

As Zebulon Pike Carey — alias Bobby McGee at the impending moment of his death — thought to himself, *Big mistake, pal, now I'm gonna cut you in two!* and began the trigger squeeze intended to achieve that goal, an unpleasant thing happened to his right scapula. It was struck with such mind-rending force that he was propelled forward, firing his Franchi into six potted plants instead of the man who'd just yelled at him from behind. Zeb lit on his face, in excruciating pain, a furrow the size of a peanut hull having been notched into his back, not to mention a fissure in the bone directly beneath the wound.

Staggering to his feet, facing the wrong way and somehow bereft of his shotgun, he reoriented himself in time to see the crazy man running straight at him, not far away. With the speed of a striking cobra, he drew his service automatic and triggered five rounds at his insane attacker, receiving the satisfaction of watching blood fly as two bullets found tissue.

But not only did the man fail to fall . . .

He failed to *stop.*

This couldn't be happening. Zeb, accustomed to a shotgun as he was, knew that when you socked a man with a load of number one buck, the son of a bitch fell down right *now*, thank you very much, like that dude back in the house. *Boom, boom,* two shots and the guy literally slammed into the wall behind the door. *That's* what a shotgun did for you.

He'd used a handgun on a job just once, a .357 Magnum Python — nice gun — and the woman he shot with it had keeled over, no fuss, lots of muss.

So what's with this guy, takes two slugs

173

and keeps on coming? Maybe two more'll do the job.

But there was no *time* . . .

* * *

Jason felt the bullets strike, felt his breath leave, didn't care, kept churning his muscular legs — in shape from handball and jogging — arms outstretched, reaching, saw the pistol trained on him once more, batted it aside and grabbed for what he could reach . . . the man's oily, sweaty ears, securing one in each hand, fingernails digging for purchase as his arms encircled, knowing the gun — knocked aside momentarily — would again come into play . . . did the only thing he could think of, having no hands free to strike with . . . jerked his head back, way back, and then — pulling with his arms as hard as he could, hands still clinging tightly to those ears, the man struggling against him, battering his ribs with a fist, striving to get the gun back into action — Jason rammed his head forward, chin tucked in, butting his assailant smack on the nose with all the adrenaline-charged strength he could muster, which was considerable.

* * *

Upon impact with Jason's forehead, Zebulon Pike Carey's nose geysered blood from both nostrils. Instantly, he lost all interest in shooting this nutty bastard, wanting nothing so much as to get him OFF! He dropped the 9 mm, brought

174

his hands up against the man's chest — no mean feat, since the lunatic was still trying to rip off his FUCKING EARS! — and gave a mighty heave.

It worked!

The maniac was cleft from his body, although he took with him several ounces of ear meat and did not fall back but sprang to the attack once more, arms again reaching for Zeb's head, thumbs extended, clawlike.

And then those thumbs, those horrible menacing appendages, were at his eyes, *in* his eyes, probing the sockets, encroaching, piercing . . .

He screamed.

★ ★ ★

Jason Patterson was weakening fast. Blood left his body from four separate exits, and from his weakness came despair. Despite his best efforts, this wiry, slippery, vicious man had flung him off as if he were nothing, although the guy *had* dropped his gun. The problem was that Jason was flagging precipitously, and if he lost the bout, so did his son. Girding for one last all-out effort, he launched his attack.

Found the man's head again, too long a reach for the ears this time, went for the eyes instead. On target, poked with the thumbs, kept pushing, deeper, deeper, felt the warm liquids gush, heard the screams, then felt himself being thrown to the ground.

Too tired to get up. Tried anyway. Hand

touched something hard, smooth. Gun stock. A shotgun stock.

Jason wasn't well schooled in pistolcraft, but he'd grown up quail hunting with his uncles outside Charleston. He knew what to do with a shotgun, and how to do it.

So he got his feet under him, one of them at least, and did it, removing most of what was left of Zebulon Pike Carey's head.

Then he passed out.

* * *

Cullen had been watching the duel from above. After Jason inserted his thumbs into Zeb's sockets, eliciting mind-numbing shrieks, he had averted his eyes, covering Web's body with his, protectively.

Thus did neither boy witness Mr. Carey's unseemly departure.

After a few minutes of silence from below, Cullen told Web, "Stay put, and I mean it," then crawled over to the doorway, and looked out. He spied Jason's supine form, still bleeding profusely, and decided to deal himself in.

Once again ordering Web to stay put, he came down the rope, approached Jason with both trepidation and haste, and ascertained that he was breathing. He then ran to the Cranfords' screened porch (unlocked) and moved to the back door (still locked) and its four sections of glass. Using a bust of Wolfgang Amadeus Mozart — the Cranfords' Labrador retriever, long dead but immortalized in plaster by an

176

artist friend of the family — Cullen broke every pane of glass in the door, as well as the wood partitions, then prudently draped an afghan across the frame before climbing in.

Police cars, ambulances, and fire trucks arrived six minutes after his call.

In time to save Jason.

★ ★ ★

Web had, surprisingly, obeyed Cullen and stayed where he was, although he was withdrawn upon Cullen's return, didn't understand why Cullen wouldn't stay with him, wondered where his dad was (Cullen had refrained from telling him about his father's situation), and wouldn't come down from the tree house for an hour.

A policeperson named Terry ingressed the tree house and stayed with Web while Cullen went to check on Paw-paw, whom he found giving the paramedics hell. And advice. And instruction. Said samaritans suffered more than his grandfather did on the way to the hospital.

Dave had been attended to, though he was still out like a light. The adults in charge assured Cullen that although his grown-up friend had taken a bad blow to the head, not to mention the equivalent of two mule kicks to the midriff, he would almost certainly be all right.

Cullen thanked them very much, asked had they reached his daddy yet. Not yet, they replied, but did he want a donut? *What I want is my daddy*, he thought, but being too polite to say so, merely answered, "No thanks, I'm not very hungry. But thank you for asking."

Then he went to his room, got one of his pair of little blue plastic chairs, carried it through the array of emergency equipment that littered the house, and out into the front yard.

Where he sat.

Alone.

Shivering violently.

And waited for his daddy.

18

THE blue light loomed in my mirror so suddenly that I knew he'd come out of a side street. I hadn't been speeding — well, not much — and was wearing my seat belt like a good boy, it being the governor's fetish and all, so I wondered what beef this deputy had with me. Signaling, I pulled over, cut the engine, and started to get out. He stopped me by running up to my car.

"Mr. Vance? Tyler Vance?"

The hair on my neck again, prescient, crawling around.

"That's me."

"Sir, there's been a shooting at your home. Not thirty minutes ago. Of your family, only your father was hurt, and I understand his wound is superficial. A Mr. David Michaels is down with unspecified injuries."

"My son?"

"Unharmed," he said reassuringly. "In fact, he made the 911 call.

"There's an APB out on this car. We wanted to bring you in as soon as possible. If you'll follow me, I'll clear the way."

"Lead on," I demanded, and cranked up my motor.

★ ★ ★

179

There was no place to park when I pulled up in front of my house, it was so crowded with all manner of police and emergency vehicles. So I left the Supra in the middle of the street, jumped out and hoofed it to my yard.

I spotted Cullen, sitting in one of his little blue chairs, off by himself, looking white as a sheet even from where I stood. He saw me too, but didn't come over, just sat and looked vacantly at me.

Uh-oh.

I went straight to him, and looked down. He didn't look up. I knelt beside him, said, "Son? You okay?"

He flung himself into my arms, sobbing, shaking, shivering. Clinging tightly. Me too.

Eyes roamed our way but no one interfered.

Torrential tears, father and son.

Abating somewhat; enough just to rest in each other's embrace, cheek to crown.

Vehicles came and went, horns blaring as trucks reversed. They brought Dave out on a stretcher. My escort, a young black deputy, mouthed, "He'll be okay."

I nodded a thank-you.

He gave a little half-salute and a smile, got in his car and drove off.

Ethyl arrived, quit her car, and started over. I gave a quick headshake, halting her, and tossed her a thumbs-up. She pursed her lips disapprovingly, but went inside.

Cullen moved in my arms. He looked up, pale but dry-eyed, at least momentarily.

Progress.

"I didn't *want* to hurt that policeman," he said.

Not knowing what he was talking about, I said, "But you felt like you had to?"

He nodded. "At first I wasn't sure about him. He looked mean. But you always tell me not to go by a person's looks. Then he snuck over, kind of weaselly, and pointed this long gun at me. And I saw Web's daddy coming up behind him. So I figured out he must be a bad guy, even if he was a policeman."

"Web's dad was sneaking up on the policeman?"

"Yeah." He wiped his nose, then again, smearing both his cheeks.

"Then the policeman turned around and pointed the long gun at *him*. That's when I threw that ol' stove at him."

"What old stove?"

"The one in Barry's tree house? That I got from your camper?"

Confused but gaining, I said, "So you threw that old propane stove at the policeman?"

Little face earnest, deeply disturbed, he cried, "He was going to shoot Web's daddy! He was! Promise!"

Clutching my shoulders, tears returning. "I had to," he finished, dropping his head.

I tilted his chin up with a forefinger, looked straight into those troubled eyes. "Of course you did. And it was exactly the right thing to do."

He brightened. Slightly.

"It was?"

"Absolutely."

"You sure?"

181

"No question about it."

"Will I be in trouble with the other police?"

"No."

"You sure?"

"Absolutely."

With a sigh, hopefully of relief, he collapsed against me. His breathing was shallow but regular. I held him.

And held him.

And held him.

Until my legs went to sleep and two men had to help me up.

19

CULLEN, now sound asleep, was better guarded than Fort Knox, Jean-Bertrand Aristide, and three Colombian drug lords, combined. Not only had the quartet of Delta elites arrived, courtesy of Colonel McElroy, but two sheriff's deputies and one off-duty GPD SWAT man, volunteering on his own.

One of the deputies was Ben Adcox, the man tricked by the bogus cops into leaving his post early. Extremely remorseful and contrite, he told me that he had three days off, starting now, and would be grateful if I'd let him watch over my boy, as he should have done to begin with. What could I say? I'd have felt the same way in his shoes.

And Fanner; by golly, you never saw such a change. Obviously so ashamed of the way he'd shrugged off my earlier request for protection (perhaps mindful of the ancient bromide about poop rolling downhill, should I choose to enlighten his superiors, or — heaven forfend — the *press*), he offered the use of his own ample self as guardian of my household. Disinclined to hold a grudge, but not above rubbing someone's nose in the residue of his own folly, I — reluctantly, of course — agreed.

After seeing to the distribution of forces — Delta team outside, forming a perimeter;

Adcox and his partner upstairs; Fanner and the SWAT guy on the ground floor — I heated up enough coffee for a siege, put out cups and plates, and bagels sufficient to engorge a Romanian track-and-field team, then repaired to my office.

There I phoned Dr. Lea Derrien, the child psychologist who had helped Cullen through the crisis of losing his mom, and apprised her of the situation. She absorbed my narrative with absolute attention, as always, her harried grey matter recording each and every syllable and syntactic nuance, for sorting out later. If I had to endure the tales of woe she heard every day, I'd bludgeon myself insensible with a jousting mace.

"Will it be okay to leave Cullen with Ethyl while I go visit the wounded at the hospital?" I queried.

In an accent reeking of vichyssoise, she answered, "He is asleep now, yes?"

"As we speak."

"Will Grandmama stay wis him?"

"Yes. And he's well guarded, so it's doubtful anything else will happen tonight."

"Zen I think so. You can go. To hospital. Do not stay all night. He will need you. When he wakes. He will sleep long."

Talk about syntax. Not to mention cadence.

"Then I'll go. To see my father. And come home early."

Now she had *me* doing it.

"Will you bring Cullen to me tomorrow? Early?"

184

"Sure."

"Good. *Au revoir.*"

I went into Cullen's room, where he lay small, burdened. But not helpless. I sat on the bed beside him, rubbing his arm, watching him sleep.

Ethyl came in. She stood beside me, watching too. After a moment, she said, "Tough day for the little man."

I nodded, whispering, "I hope not *too* tough. No nightmares like after Tess died."

"Was killed," she corrected. "My daughter didn't die. She was killed."

I looked up at her. "I know, Ethyl."

"Today *he* was almost killed" — pointing with her chin at Cullen, deep under the covers — "from what that Lieutenant Fanner told me."

"I know that, too, Ethyl."

"What you gonna do about it?" Defiant, eyes flashing. "Same's you did about his momma?"

"The guy was drunk. What did you want me to do?"

"What a *man* would've done, put him under the ground, like he did your wife."

"Then where would Cullen be, with no mom *and* no dad?"

She shook her head, lips tightened into a thin grim line. I knew what she was thinking: *With me, where he belongs.* Ethyl believed, as did many people, not all of them females, that only a woman can rear a child properly.

She was wrong.

I said, "I shouldn't be more than a few hours.

185

I think it's important that you or I be here, in case he wakes up. Agreed?"

She nodded, curtly, one bob of the head.

Tucking the covers under his chin, I bussed Cullen on the bridge of his nose. He didn't stir. When I turned to leave, I kissed Ethyl on the cheek. She pursed her lips deprecatingly, but didn't pull away.

One giant leap for mankind.

★ ★ ★

It was late afternoon when I arrived at the hospital. The going-home-from-work traffic had been hectic, but at least I had trouble finding a parking space. As I approached the entrance, a squirrel ran up a tree trunk nearby, dropping the nut he was carrying. It wasn't my fault, but he decided to take it out on me anyway, assaulting my ears with strident rodent invective. If I'd had a Moon Pie, I'd have thrown it at him. Might've improved my mood. And taught him some manners.

I took one parting glance as he upbraided me from his leafy lectern, laying his misfortunes at my feet. He reminded me of a professional athlete complaining about his meager salary. Except the squirrel made a better case.

At the reception desk a very nice lady wearing a tunic and a red dot on her forehead told me where they had stashed my papa, my friend, and the man who had saved my son's life. Their rooms were all on the same floor, for which I was grateful. I hate elevators, and staircases are often haunted by clandestine cigarette smokers.

Dad first.

As I entered the room, there he sat, bed cranked up to forty-five degrees or better, thermometer in his mouth and a twinkle in his eye. A cute little candy striper stood beside his bed, all bosom and frizzy hair, waiting to see if his temperature was elevated.

He saw me enter and said, thermometer bouncing as he spoke, "Howdy, son. How's Cullen?"

"Fine. He's asleep. Just left him."

"The troll lookin' after him?"

"Now, now."

A breathy giggle from the candy striper, who punctuated her contribution by withdrawing the thermometer and peering at it myopically. She said, in a voice two octaves higher than a Metropolitan soprano, "Ninety-nine point four. Guess you'll live," then patted his knee and left the room as if Tom Cruise were watching.

"Cute little thing" — from my lecherous male parent.

I tsked-tsked him, adding, "Aren't you ashamed? She's younger'n a hen's egg."

"Hey, I didn't pat *her* knee."

"Your aim isn't that bad."

"It ain't, for a fact." He chuckled, then winced as it hurt him. "An old man can remember, can't he?"

"Yeah, well, keep an eye on your blood pressure."

"What fun would that be?"

"You need a keeper."

"My vote goes to that little gal."

We grinned at each other.

He was my dad, and he was going to be okay.

"How bad is that, really?" I pointed to his bandaged side.

"I'll be out of here soon's they're sure there won't be no infection. Bullet glanced off a rib, then ripped hell outta me. Broke the rib, o' course, and the cut bled to beat the band. They said I was a pint low when I got here, but they stuck an IV in and filled me back up."

He stabbed a thumb in the direction Florence Nightingale had taken. "She told me they might let me take a little stroll here directly, if I feel up to it. Thought I might check on Dave. Understand he was one lucky feller, so far as gettin' shot goes. But he does have a nasty concussion, and nigh as bad a rent in his scalp as I got in my side."

"After I make certain you aren't going to die on me, I plan to go see him," I said.

"Go ahead. Tell him I'll be down in a while. That little gal's fetchin' me some juice."

"I'll tell him. And you keep your hands to yourself," I said, then ducked out the door.

Wouldn't want to get hit by a bedpan.

★ ★ ★

Dave was sitting in a wheelchair watching CNN when I walked in. As soon as he saw me, he smote it with the remote. His head was capped in white gauze from the eyebrows up, down

188

to the hairline in back. He pointed to what appeared to be a couple of C-shaped ashtrays lying on the windowsill, silver grey in color. I picked them up.

They were not ashtrays.

I glanced at him. He raised his brows in a *What do you have to say about that?* gesture.

"Thank God you were wearing your vest," I said.

"I'll never visit your home without it."

The globs in my hand were two clusters of buckshot — each one consisting of twelve lead pellets larger than many fishing sinkers — fused together by the heat of firing and sudden impact with an impenetrable object. A bulletproof vest. The one Dave had been wearing. Shivering, I put them back.

"Fanner gave me those. Plan to keep 'em as a reminder of how dangerous it is being pals with the likes of you."

"I know. I'm sorry."

"Hey, I'm just kidding."

"I know that. I also know that if you hadn't been there, you wouldn't be here."

"You don't *know* that. I could have been in a wreck on my way to the hardware store. Maybe it's just my day to be in the hospital. You know, like what the Presbyterians believe?"

"Predestination?"

"Yeah."

I sat on his bed, engulfed by a sensory miasma: ether, rubbing alcohol, misery, hope, despair, excrete, lousy food. And shots. Always hated shots, since I was a kid going to get my typhoid puncture every summer. Ugh. Hospitals.

To Dave: "Anything you want they aren't providing?"

"No. My head hurts too bad to want anything."

"Haven't they given you something for the pain?"

He pointed to a little paper cup containing pills large enough to choke Godzilla.

"Those suppositories?" I quizzed innocently.

"Don't make me laugh. Hurts too much."

"Then why are those pills still in their container and not in your body?"

"Nurse said they'd make me woozy."

"And then you couldn't make a move on her?"

"She looks like a groundhog."

"You should see the caregiver Dad has." I waggled my hand and made a blowing motion with my lips, the universal gesture we men of few words use when describing a nubile female.

"Figures."

"So why not" — I reached for the pills — "take one of these right now?"

He shook his head, then closed his eyes against the pain. "Want to see your dad first. La Rodent promised me a ride later."

"Tsk, tsk," I clucked, "you disparage her so. Undoubtedly her sole interest in life is your welfare. She can't help it if she's unpleasant to look upon."

"Unpleasant to look upon? She's a blight."

"Well, anyway, Dad said to tell you he'd be along in half a tick."

He frowned in thought. "That's a W. C. Fields line, isn't it?"

I nodded. "Borrowed it."

"Stole it, you mean. Like all your material."

"Not all. I made up 'You're ugly and your mother dresses you funny' all by myself."

"No you didn't. I saw that on a T-shirt."

"Oh."

"Get the hell out of here. Go see Patterson. He's the worst for wear out of this fracas."

"Okay, if you can get along without me."

"Go!"

"All right, don't yell."

"*Go!*"

I left smiling. He was my friend, and he was going to be okay.

★ ★ ★

Jason Patterson was indeed the worst for wear. He lay in the center of his bed, tubes running to and from goodness knows where, looking wan. Fresh flowers decorated his window, three vases' worth, all yellow and red and bright and redolent. Despite their olfactory efforts, the room still smelled frowzy where I stood.

Although his eyes were open, I wasn't sure if Jason saw me. He did. "Come in," he said weakly.

I walked over, stood beside his bed. "I'm sorry," I began, "that all this . . . "

Shook his head minutely, said, "Doesn't matter. All over now. The kids are safe." His voice was very hoarse.

I nodded. "And how are you?"

"Okay," he whispered. I could barely hear him.

"May I sit?" There was a chair right beside me, touching the bed.

"Sure," he breathed.

I sat, inhaling the floral aromas, pleasantly blended when you drew close to them, overriding to some extent the harsh hospital effluvium. Indicating the arrangements, I said, "Nice."

"My live-in, and a couple of friends. The gay community is quick to rally, and very supportive."

"Appears so."

We sat quietly for a while. Then I asked, "Can you tell me the extent of your injuries?"

"I was wounded twice. No bones struck, and only one organ injured. One, I was told, that I can get along quite well without."

"An organ you can do without?"

"The attending physician, a gentleman with a somewhat macabre sense of humor, said he'd heard of venting one's spleen, but this was ridiculous. Ha-ha."

"Little medical play on words."

"If I hadn't been in such pain, I'd have laughed out loud."

"Real knee-slapper all right."

The conversation kind of dried up.

"How can I ever thank you?" I said, after a moment.

"No need. To tell you the truth, I gave little thought to your son, mostly just Web." He looked a bit guilty. "Do you understand?"

"You bet. I'd've done the same. The point is, you did save him, and I owe you for that. Without you, he would likely be . . . " Couldn't bring myself to say it. Couldn't swallow well either.

After a spell, I said, "And you did it all with your bare hands, or most of it anyway."

Whatever color he had drained away. "Don't remind me. It was horrible."

"Always is, taking a life. But sometimes, no matter what theorists claim, it has to be done. Has to, period. This was one of those times. You had no other choice. If you'd merely tried to subdue him after being shot twice, you probably would have passed out from shock or loss of blood. I've seen it. Not read about it, *seen* it. Where would our kids be now if you had passed out?"

He nodded.

"That was one of the bravest things I've ever heard of. Charging a killer who had a shotgun pointed straight at you." I shook my head in awe. "It's incredible."

He grimaced, obviously hurting inside. Beckoning me closer, he whispered, "If your son hadn't hit that guy with something, we would all three be dead. He's only a child, but he did what was necessary for all of us to make it through. He's the hero."

"His mental switch was on fight-or-flight. To his credit, he didn't panic or give up. He used his head and fought back, luckily doing the right thing. But he didn't charge into a shotgun, my friend. You did."

193

Jason stiffened suddenly, as if the pain was too much to bear, perspiration beading his face. Eyes closed, fighting it. He put out his hand, palm up. I took it.

"Can't they give you something?"

"Already have. Morphine. Couldn't stand it if they hadn't, be screaming my lungs out." He squeezed my hand, tightly.

I squeezed back. Ever so slowly, he relaxed.

I sat there holding his hand for nearly an hour, while he fought the pain.

★ ★ ★

Jason was asleep when I left, hopefully for quite a while. Heading for Dave's room for a last goodbye, I trod the long, bright, spotless corridor, uncomfortable being there. Dodged a gurney. Avoided looking into open doors, not only respecting folks' privacy but, to be truthful, not desirous of witnessing despondency and affliction.

Coward.

I *hate* hospitals.

When I approached Dave's room, I overheard the following conversation:

Dad: Why the hell didn't you come see *me*?

Dave: I can hardly walk, my head hurts so bad. Besides, Ty told me you were on your way here.

Dad: My ribs hurt just as bad as your head, likely worse, but I come to see *you*. Shoot,

194

we wouldn't even be here if you'd been payin' attention to —

Dave: What do you mean if *I'd* been paying attention? If you hadn't been upstairs taking a dump —

Dad: Oh, I can't even shit now, is that it? Listen, if I hadn't been upstairs to drop those children out the window, who knows —

Dave: You wouldn't have had to drop them out the window if you'd been downstairs where you belonged. We could have nailed those cops right there in the living room.

Dad: *We* could have nailed 'em? That was *your* job. And why in the hell did you let 'em in, anyway? You should've known they weren't cops.

Dave: How was I supposed to know that? I'm sure that if *you'd* been looking out the window . . .

They were having too much fun to interrupt. I tiptoed down the hall and went home.

20

TWO hours later, McElroy leaned across my kitchen table with two photos, dropping them in front of me. One of a guy with a lean, mean face, mustache, wide-set eyes, high forehead, salt-and-pepper Elvis Presley sideburns, low threshold for tolerance, from the look in his eyes. The other a softer, younger version; more sybarite, less menace. Definitely the same bloodline, though.

"Older guy's Valentin Resovic. And that's his younger brother Mikhail on the right, with whom you exchanged lead outside the bank, and on whom Valentin doted. *Doted*. Says that right here in the Interpol fax." He pointed. "See? Means to bestow excessive love on — "

"I know what it means."

"No need to be surly. Big brother here is one bad son of a bitch. Born 1950, city of Banja Luka, in a country now called Bosnia-Herzegovina. Ever hear of it?"

"Sounds vaguely familiar."

"In Europe, which is full of opportunistic assholes, this guy is a standout in assholery. Want to hear his résumé?"

"Go ahead."

"Thanks, I will. No known political ties or religious affiliations, except In God We Trust. Will do, and has done, most anything for money. Sold Chinese AKs to the Libyans, Korean

.50-caliber ammunition to the Sandinistas, Stingers to the Serbs, Cuban cigars to a wealthy group of Republican industrialists in southern Illinois. Food en route to Somalia was, ah, redirected to Rwanda, then sold on the black market. Weapons-grade plutonium disappeared from the Ukraine, showed up in Pakistan. One hundred and three Mexican nationals — all female, pretty, and pregnant, heading for California to have their babies on American soil and attach themselves to the public dole — wound up as prostitutes in Shanghai, their babies sold off for adoption to barren American ladies.

"Money. Always money. Valentin only goes where the green stuff flows. Hey, I made a poem."

"A rhyme anyway."

"Don't hurt my feelings. Anyway, Resovic protects his interests with uncommon zeal and ruthlessness. Last year he bombed the home of a competitor in Lisbon, wiping out the entire family. He drowned a Scottish spirits merchant in his own whiskey vat, over some small amount of vigorish on a loan."

"'Drowned in a vat of whiskey. Death, where is thy sting?'"

"Say again?"

"Nothing," I said. "Just a few words from my role model. Now, where might I find this Bosnian gentleman who's such a thorn in my side?"

"At this time, he's in the United States on a travel visa, visiting the Seattle space needle and arranging for a shipment of arms to South

Africa — legal hunting stuff from a Miami importer with an office out west. Problem is, no one has seen him for about a week."

"You mean surveillance on a guy with a dossier like this was so lax they lost him?"

"Seems he just evaporated. He was videotaped in the company of your other pal from the bank, the one whose face you perforated, and this J. P. Bynum the cops told you about. Local small-timers, nothing noteworthy to the international spook community. The FBI might've been interested, but somehow they were left out of the loop. Since the Resovics ended up pulling a bank job, I'll bet the Fibbies are real happy about that. Inter-agency rivalry. Ugly thing."

"What about the other man Fanner mentioned, the big Hispanic? Anyone know who he is?"

"Oh, yeah. Seems the elder Resovic met him in Mexico City while setting up this rerouting of California-bound baby factories, and the two hit it off. After the deal went through, enriching both parties, they formed an alliance of some sort, with the big Mexican fulfilling the muscle role. His name, by the way, is Hector Hernandez Diaz, and he ain't no pussycat. If you ever find yourself close to this bastard, shoot the son of a bitch. And quick. They say he's hell on wheels with a pistol too."

"Lovely. All this is lovely."

"Hey," said the colonel, "don't shoot the messenger."

"So," I asked, "where does this leave us? We know, through Fanner's network, that a gun buy

198

is in the offing, and not some hunting-rifle red herring bound for Cape Province. Who had the guns, and why does Resovic want them? Who's his end user?"

McElroy shrugged elaborately.

"Great," said I.

"Not so bad, actually. We know that Resovic and his gorilla are hanging around the Triad, trying to get to you."

"So?"

"So find them."

"How am I supposed to do that? The entire Greensboro Police Department can't locate them."

"Yeah, but they've got a lot on their plate. What else have you got? Besides, you have a bit of experience in this field — I should know."

McElroy frowned. "Resovic's a slick, elusive bastard. He could hide nearby all year, and laugh. He has plenty of money. All he needs is a hole to crawl in and someone to fetch the groceries. No problem for an operator like him. He bought those two locals to knock you off, didn't he?"

"His resources can't be unlimited."

"The two-plus million he stole from the bank is pretty close, and time's on his side so long as he has a safe house."

"So what do I do?"

"Same as when you were turned loose in the Korean DMZ in '74. Seek and destroy."

"This isn't combat."

He slammed his fist on the table, making the condiment shakers jump theatrically. "The hell it's not! Vance, this guy isn't going away. He wants you, bad. *And* your family. You nailed his brother, and he won't forget it. Ever."

I mulled it over. "Let me talk to Fanner. See what he's come up with on the police impersonators. Maybe there'll be a lead there someplace."

"Maybe. Don't bet on it."

"If not, then I'll decide what to do. Can you keep your men here for a few more days, until Dave and my dad get out of the hospital?"

"You got 'em as long as you went 'em. But don't," he warned, "let this get out of hand. Find the motherfucker and erase him. And his greaser pal, too."

He quaffed the dregs of his coffee, tightened the knot on his tie, and left.

I sat alone at the kitchen table for a very long time. Tired body, overactive brain.

But I came up with a plan.

21

FANNER was in the living room reading my copy of *Tourist Season*, by Carl Hiassen. Laughing. No one can read *Tourist Season* without laughing.

The SWAT guy had gone outside for a smoke. Good for him. Going outside, I mean.

I said, "Lieutenant, what can you tell me about those two artificial cops today?"

He carefully marked his place with a three-dollar bill bearing the President's unctuous likeness and imprinted with the words "The Disgruntled States of America," which he had obviously lifted from a stack I had on the coffee table, then sat back, rested big hands on big knees, and began his recital:

"Hoods out of Jersey, freelance mob enforcers. Both had records of assault, assault to murder, and other activities they did not learn in Catholic school, which they both attended. They grew up together in Trenton, one from a broken home, the other from one in which the mother died early on. When he was eight, I think. That one had a brother, Leplin, whereabouts uncertain but actively being sought. He has a record, too, having worked often in alliance with his big brother. Their surname is Carey. The deceased sibling was named Zebulon, although he had been using an alias of late, Bobby McGee. The other defunct gentleman was Jerry Smith. That was his real name, not an alias."

"I'd have chosen an alias. How does Jerry Smith sound for a tough guy, especially in his line of work?"

"A valid point, I think, but obviously not one that concerned Mr. Smith. Nor will it."

"Maybe if his name had been Lance Turbicle, my dad couldn't have taken him so easily."

"Pardon me for mentioning it, but your father ambushed Mr. Smith, who still managed to get off three shots, one of which struck oil."

"That's because my dad refuses to give up his World War Two peashooter, or even use expanding bullets in it. He believes that what was good enough for Mr. Roosevelt's officers then is still good enough."

"That little carbine serve him well in the war?"

"I suppose. He's here, and he wasn't a deskbound soldier by any means."

"Well then."

"Maybe he was just lucky in the war."

"Maybe now as well. But it could be that he is simply brave and skillful, or views his carbine as a talisman. Perhaps both."

"Hell, Fanner. Maybe it *is* a talisman."

"Then he will not need expanding bullets."

"I give up. You sound like him."

He smiled benignly.

"Any more information you have that might prove helpful?" I queried.

"I doubt it."

"Have you tried to go backward down the chain, find out who made contact with Zebulon and Jerry, and maybe his brother, who could be

202

lurking in the weeds?"

"Yes."

"Any luck?"

"No."

"Can you go on protecting my family?"

"Not indefinitely."

"How long?"

"Until Tugbo — the chief tells me otherwise."

"Maybe just a few days, huh? Until the urgency is gone, or perceived to be so. At least by the public."

"That is about it, in a nutshell, yes. Meanwhile, we will be hunting these men earnestly."

"That's not good enough."

"Meaning?"

"Meaning that I can't continue to sit back and wait for them to come to me, or hope that somebody else will stumble onto them. I'll have to handle it myself."

Fanner narrowed his eyes. "How will you go about that?"

"You cover your ass, I'll cover mine and my family's."

"Then I must tell you this," he said. "Be careful that you stay within the boundaries of the law. No concealed weapons, no booby traps, no initiating hostilities in public places, with or without weapons. I want you to understand: If you are caught breaking the law, you will be prosecuted without regard to what has happened to you and your family in the recent past. I will *not* countenance vigilante justice within my jurisdiction, especially from one so lethal as your

203

background suggests you to be. Is that clear?"

"Sure. You're telling me on the one hand that you can't protect me and mine, that you've had absolutely zero luck finding the mugs who are after me, so you can't arrest them. On the other, that I better be real careful how I go about trying to defend myself and my son, because while you can't nab the bad guys, you know where I live all right."

I bent over the coffee table, jerked the bookmark out of Fanner's reading material, and said, "Get out. Tell your SWAT friend that we'll take it from here. Don't come to my house again without a warrant for my arrest or a delivery from Domino's Pizza."

"I suppose you know what you are doing."

"Yeah," I said, "ridding my house of a sheep in wolf's clothing."

★ ★ ★

Following Fanner's departure, I went to each Delta member individually and told them I'd cut our defense team by one fourth. Oddly, not one of them fainted from fear.

I then asked the on-duty deputy to assume security for the ground floor, placing Adcox outside Cullen's door. Spreading a pallet beside my son's bed, and putting my Benelli twelve-bore out of sight but not out of reach, I tucked a Glock 10 mm beneath my pillow and retreated willingly into the arms of Morpheus.

I slept lightly, though, so as to listen for Fanner. 'Case he brought back a pizza.

22

"HI, I'm Alec Baldwin."

"No you're not."

"I don't look like Alec Baldwin? How about a youthful Marlon Brando?"

"How youthful?"

"*On the Waterfront.*"

"You wish."

"*One-Eyed Jacks?*"

"Forget it."

"*The Godfather.*"

"Right on."

"That hurts."

"Come in and sit down, Don Corleone."

She was radiant in bathrobe and shower cap; water, water everywhere. I decided against commenting on her dewy disarray; she'd say it would teach me to phone before stopping by. Besides, I liked the unmade look.

"Coffee?" she asked, over one slender, terry-clothed shoulder.

"Sure, but first fill me in on your dad."

She did, speaking from the kitchen as she prepared the java. The operation had been a success: he was up and around, complaining about daytime TV; would be out of the hospital in a few days, assuming no complications. While she talked, I sought the rocker in the corner. It creaked pleasantly as I sank into it.

Rocking chairs. Me and Dad and JFK.

She brought in a handsome coffeepot, accompanied by a cut-glass bowl of sugar cubes on a gilt-edged ebony tray. Two Calvin and Hobbes ceramic cups. She handed me one.

I said, "Glad you got out the nice china. Makes me feel like company." After a sip, I asked, "How's Web?"

"He's asleep now, for about an hour. When he's awake, he won't let me leave the room without him."

"Nightmares?"

"Um-hmm."

"He talking much?"

"He never was a chatterbox, but no, not much as usual. Mostly he sucks his thumb and watches TV, or follows me around when I have chores to do."

"I'm sorry."

She looked at me over the rim of her cup. "Ty, this is not your fault. For heaven's sake, your son was up in that tree house too. You didn't invite those bastards to shoot up your house, your father, your friend, and try to kill our children. You did all you could to protect them before the fact."

"I tell myself that at least five times an hour."

"Then believe it. Don't torture yourself over this. It could have been much, much worse.

"I know. *How* I know."

"Then let it be. If you can't change things, it's foolish to worry about them. How's Cullen?"

"Seems okay to me. A bit subdued, but maybe he's just tired. On my way here, I dropped him off at a doctor's office, the child psychologist who saw him when his mama died. She's first-rate. If you'd like her to talk with Web, I'll try to arrange it, but I can't promise anything."

"Thanks, I'll think about it." She sucked her upper lip between her teeth. "Cullen allowed you to leave him?"

"Yes, which I understand is a good sign."

"A very good sign," she said. "So what do you plan to do next? About this situation?"

"Get the guy responsible."

She sat up straight, nearly spilling her coffee. "You know who he is?"

I nodded.

With narrowed eyes, she responded, "I want in."

"What?"

"I said I want in. Whatever you decide, I want to help. Obviously, the police aren't doing you much good. Are they the ones who found out who the man is?"

"No, that information came from contacts I have in the military."

"Tell me about this deviant who tried to destroy my son."

I told her what I knew about Valentin Resovic, or at least what I'd learned from McElroy. She absorbed the information like a sponge.

"So you think that Resovic and this Diaz are laying low around here, playing cat and mouse, looking for any opportunity to kill you? And can hire whatever assistance they need to accomplish the task?"

"That's what McElroy thinks, and it fits

Resovic's modus operandi."

"What does Lieutenant Fanner say?"

"That he can offer protection for only so long, maybe a few days, a week. Then I'm on my own again, until something else happens."

"The police department really isn't much help, is it?"

"Not much."

"Then how are you going to find Resovic?"

"I have a plan. I'm going to the hospital after I leave here, to discuss it with Dave Michaels. Cullen's coming along to see Paw-paw."

"Will the doctor think it's okay, his going to the hospital, seeing his grandfather all bandaged up?"

"He saw him at my house right after he'd been shot, gore all over everything. He needs to know his granddad's really all right, see it with his own eyes, not have me tell him so. I suspect the doc will support that. If not, I'll certainly listen to what she has to say."

"But if you don't agree with her, you'll make the decision."

"Sure I will. Heather, I'm with Cullen every day. Dr. Derrien has talked with him maybe a half-dozen times."

"Of course. By the way, tell everyone hello, especially Jason. Tell him I'd visit if I could, but I don't think it's a good idea to bring Web, and right now I can't leave him with anyone else."

"Sure. He'll understand."

"You like Jason, don't you?"

"I'd like Genghis Khan if he saved my son's life."

"You liked him before that, when you first met him."

"Yeah, well. He's a nice guy. But I'm not falling for him, if that's got you worried."

She got up and came over, fleeting glimpse of thigh as she walked. Not blatant, most likely unintentional. No matter; the result was the same. Blood in my system began suffusing a portion of my anatomy that normally remained relatively arid. She leaned down to kiss me. Then, nose to nose, she said, "Good."

"No groping," I said.

"Want to bet?"

23

WHEN I picked up my little bundle of Y chromosomes, the good doctor told me he seemed to be handling his recent trauma quite well, was not suppressing to any significant extent, and wasn't especially reluctant to discuss any aspect of the situation.

"It is good zat he will talk so," she opined.

"I'm glad," I responded, thanked her and paid her, made one follow-up appointment for Cullen, and one initial interview for Heather and Web. She made note of the referral, her nurse handed me a receipt, and the Vance duo departed.

Cullen talked all the way to the hospital about his visit with Dr. "Darry-un." They'd played good guy/bad guy games; he'd engaged in monologues with stuffed animals; he'd drawn her pictures and played word games. After one particularly lengthy soliloquy, he ground to a stop, glancing obliquely at me, looking kind of guilty.

"What?" I asked.

He glanced at me again, but didn't answer.

"*What?*" I repeated.

Resignedly: "She gave me ice cream."

"And so soon after breakfast," I commented parentally. "What flavor?"

"She let me pick."

"And you chose . . . "

"The green kind, with the chips."

"Mint chocolate chip?"

He nodded.

"Your favorite. And now you're ready for a good, healthy lunch."

Shook his head. "I'm full."

"After only one dish of ice cream? Hard to imagine."

Looking miserable, he said, "She made me eat two bowls."

"*Made* you eat them. What a witch."

"Not really *made* me. She asked if I was still hungry."

"Ah. And you said yes."

Another small nod.

"Hard to imagine."

Sidelong look again, followed by, "You mad?"

"Steaming."

A little light behind his eyes, tiny smile. "You are not."

"Are, too."

More light.

"Are not."

Couldn't help but smile.

"I love you." Aurora borealis.

"I love you, too."

We motored on, being together.

★ ★ ★

Paw-paw, sitting on the edge of his bed when we arrived, greeted his grandson with open arms. Cullen responded with unease and gingerly handling of his granddad's bandaged area.

211

"Does it hurt bad, Paw-paw?"

"No worse than if Jaws had bit me."

Cullen, not entirely derailed by Dad's levity, looked skeptical. "Where were you shot?" he asked.

"In the side, here." He pointed to the offending spot.

"Where Thomas put his hands?"

"Thomas?"

"Doubting Thomas."

Dad looked up quizzically, saying, *Help me here*, with his eyes.

I said, "Remember the apostle Thomas, the Twin, who doubted the word of the other disciples about Jesus' resurrection. Said he wanted to feel the Master's wounds for himself. Jesus visited a group of them, told Thomas to thrust his hands into the sword cuts, which were in Jesus' side."

Dad turned back to Cullen and said, "Yeah. That's right, in the ribs."

"Will you be okay?" my son asked.

"Sure. I'm coming home tomorrow."

Delight and relief vied for equal time on Cullen's face. He practically danced with excitement. Me too.

I took him to see Dave, promising Paw-paw we'd be back in a few minutes. Cullen was pretty relaxed around Dave, his anxiety obviously having been centered on his grandfather.

"That a new Terminator shirt you got there?" Dave asked.

Looking down at his chest, Cullen replied in the affirmative.

212

"Can I get one just like it?" said Dave.

Cullen allowed as how one big enough to fit Dave might be hard to find at Toys "Я" Us.

"You're saying I'm fat?"

"No. Large."

"Guess you're right," Dave concluded, tousling the boy's hair.

Then off to pay our respects to Jason.

★ ★ ★

Jason's room was filled with bouquets, which worried me a little. Cullen had been exposed to copious quantities of the florists' art only once before, at his mother's funeral. I watched him carefully.

Although appearing slightly uneasy, he walked straight over to Jason's bedside and put his hand on the man's arm, still connected to an IV line. Cullen didn't seem to notice the tube, or care.

"You okay?" he asked, in a small but firm voice.

Jason said, "Well, I'm not ready to play soccer just yet, but the doctors tell me I will be soon. How are *you*?"

"Fine."

They looked at each other for a moment.

"I was really scared," Cullen said.

"Me too."

"When I saw you bleeding. Lying so still. I thought you were dead." Tear forming, just one so far. Likely no deluge in the offing. One or two was okay, healthy.

"You saved my life, Cullen. Without you, I

would be dead now, no question about it. You did what many grownups couldn't have done. And you saved Web, as well. You're quite a little man."

Another tear, other eye, but accompanied by a look of pride and self-esteem. It wasn't bloated and self-congratulatory; more like, *I did good, didn't I*.

Jason took Cullen's hand in his and shook it, man to man. He said, "Thank you for saving my life. And my son's."

Solemnly, Cullen answered, "No problemo."

Jason took in Cullen's *T2* shirt, Schwarzenegger's stern visage on the front, and understood.

Cullen said, "Thank you for saving mine."

With equal solemnity, Jason said, "No problemo."

You should have been there.

★ ★ ★

Cullen having been left in Dad's room, the two of them playing poker with a deck of USAir cards, I joined Dave in his temporary quarters for a mind meld. There were no flowers in *his* room.

He began with, "Why haven't you sent me flowers? Jason has a roomful. And candy. His digestive system isn't up to snuff, so I ate half his box of chocolates. Felt like Forrest Gump."

"*I* didn't send him those flowers."

"Yeah, well, you could have sent *me* some candy."

"It'd rot your teeth," I said, then told

him about my conversations with Fanner and McElroy.

"Anything bother you about McElroy's insistence that you tackle Resovic and his beef burrito yourself?"

I nodded.

"That he might have ulterior motives?"

"Um-hmm," I um-hmmed.

"Like using you as a convenient, well-trained tool to rid the free world of a particularly virulent virus?"

"You're so cynical."

"But wise," he said.

"A veritable sage."

"So what are you going to do?"

"Rid the world of a particularly what-you-said virus."

"And how, the man asks, head aching unbearably, are you going to do that?"

"I have a plan."

"Oh."

"What do you mean, oh?"

"Like the plan you had when we were sixteen, renting Captain Harry's old boat and guiding well-heeled sportsmen to buckets full of flounder in the Inland Waterway?"

"We made sixty bucks a day, each."

"How much did the good cap'n charge us for a day's charter of his boat?"

"Seventy-five bucks apiece."

"Didn't clear much, did we there, Butch?"

"Ingrate."

"Or the time — we were ten, I believe — when Lindy Packer stole all those apples

215

from her uncle's orchard. You thought it would be a great idea to take 'em off her hands at a nickel apiece, and — "

"I was younger then."

He grinned at me. "Tell me your plan. I'll pretend to be interested."

"Good, because you're involved."

"Why am I not surprised?"

I told him my plan. And my contingency plan, and who I had in mind to help with that one.

"Sounds okay to me," said Dave. "But aren't the police pursuing those avenues?"

"Probably. But halfheartedly."

"And we can do it better, right? Just the two of us."

"We're smarter, and we have motivation. They don't."

"They have badges, leverage, manpower."

"And many other cases to pursue."

"When do we start?"

"When're you getting out of here?"

"Tomorrow, if the groundhog doesn't scotch my plans."

"I'll speak to someone in accounting."

"Accounting? How will that help?"

"You're in here under my insurance coverage. Claimed you were my older cousin. My much older cousin."

"Gullible, aren't they? Who'd believe you're younger than me?" he said. "Fine. I'll set things up with Thurman. Tell him not to take in any more repair work."

"Okay." I got up to leave. "You need anything?"

"New nurse."

"Leave her alone. From the likes of her flow the milk of human kindness."

"Curdled."

"You're incorrigible," I said, crossing the room. Stopping at the door, I glanced back at my old friend, sitting there in a hospital bed, bandaged, damaged, still willing to go along with whatever I decided.

Simply because it was me.

He'd been doing it since third grade.

I said, "We made money on that apple cobbler deal."

"It was supposed to be apple *pie*."

"Some people are never happy."

He grinned again. I went to get Cullen.

24

THE following few days slogged by. I divided my daytime hours between my martial arts/physical training regimen, fixing up my bullet-scarred house, and Cullen, who helped with the refurbishing. All the bullet holes in the stairway wall he covered with dinosaur stickers, except one which had a butterfly on it. The splintered places in the unvarnished, newly installed banister Cullen sanded down and filled in with Play-Doh of a closely matching color.

Involving him in make-work projects for a couple of days kept him from getting bored, but his having been banned from going outside was becoming to him an untenable situation. Unfortunately, a necessary one; I couldn't take a chance on a drive-by attempt, or worse yet, that Resovic might set a sniper in place. The sheriff's department and GPD had roving patrols in the area, and the neighbors were alerted to watch for strangers or strange goings-on. I could have taken Cullen elsewhere, and I intended to, soon, but didn't want his uprooting to be connected in his mind with what had happened to him, or what he'd had to do to protect himself. It could induce guilt feelings, plus the possibility of his being uncomfortable living in his own home.

Two deputies were stationed at our house, and the four Delta lads were around, sometimes seen, often not. Even when they were not in evidence, I could feel their presence.

One day Cullen came into the kitchen while I was sitting at the counter drinking coffee and reading the paper. He got out a plastic plate with Ernie on it, covered its surface with saltine crackers from a box on a lower shelf, placed the plate on the dining room table, and affixed to said table a sign, to wit:

> craKKers 4 sell
> won niKKel
> to For a pinnY
> thayr Fresh

He sat down at the table, beside his plate of merchandise, and began crayoning in a Batman coloring book.

Directly, one of the officers came in for a glass of the iced tea I kept in a large thermos beside the sink for their convenience. He'd turned to go, his large plastic cup replenished, when he spotted Cullen's hand-lettered sign. Went over. Looked at the array of comestibles, limited in selection but laudably profuse. Chose four and laid a quarter down beside the platter.

Cullen looked at it. Then up at the man. Said, "I'm sorry, but I don't have change."

"Keep it," said the deputy, munching a craKKer.

"Okay. Thank you."

I kept reading the paper, an editorial by Rita Snipes about the potential harm of single-sex classrooms at the elementary education level.

The woman was consistent; she never let facts murk up her thinking.

Twenty minutes went by. The other deputy came in, obviously having received the word from his partner. Straight to the table he strode. "Got any peanut butter?"

"Plain or crunchy?"

"Crunchy."

"The crunchy's Dad's," said Cullen, then looked over at me. I nodded. He ran to the cabinet, opened the lower doors, extracted the requested item, dug a butter knife from the flatware drawer — wiping it carefully with his shirttail — then spread the peanut butter liberally onto four crackers.

"How much extra for the peanut butter?" asked the officer.

"Fifty cents for the whole shootin' match," answered my son.

The deputy put down four dimes and two nickels, and waited. Cullen counted, not as fast as a carney barker, but quick enough for a soon-to-be-five-year-old. "Thank you," he said, looking up. "Please come back."

The little capitalist.

★ ★ ★

Having been chauffeured to his home from the hospital by Ethyl, believe it or not, Dad was currently involved in rocking, hammocking, watching CNN, and consuming copious quantities of chicken soup. He was healing nicely.

I called him every day, and would have gone

to see him except for the risks involved. I didn't want to request a police escort every day to go visit my pop. So we conferred by phone.

"Ethyl's drivin' me crazy."

"What's she doing?"

"Shovin' soup down my throat."

"How's that so bad?"

"I want eggs, and steak, and barbecue. Slaw, spuds, goobers . . . "

"Send her home."

"Won't go. Says I need tendin'. Makes me sound like a cabbage patch."

I asked, "Sheriff's men in evidence?"

"Yep. One parked out front, t'other out back. Two of McElroy's bunch come and go, check to see if I'm needin' anything. Always ask 'em to shoot Ethyl, but they just laugh and go back out.

"Don't that beat all. Ask me do I want anything, then won't do it for me."

"Tell her hello for me."

"Tell her yourself. Here she is . . . "

I hung up quick.

★ ★ ★

After Cullen went to bed at night, I'd spend several hours at the word processor processing words. I was cleaning up some assignments I'd accepted before the Mexico-Bosnian Bank-Fund Liberation Coalition made my life a mare's nest. Money was not my motivation in finishing the articles I was assigned. Keeping my word was; I'd promised various editors that I would deliver

221

pieces on this and that. So I would.

For fourteen years I'd written a book a year, all published by a major house or produced under my own imprint. More than half of those books remained in print, providing me a six-digit annual income in royalties derived therefrom. Even the out-of-print books still earned me dollars, since my wife had so wisely invested the money while the tomes were still available and bringing it in.

Tess had had her own career, as a professor of American history. I'd been writing magazine articles for a lucrative living since 1978, so we had needed to use none of my "book money," as she referred to it, for living expenses. Thus, all of my royalty earnings had been tucked away, turned into real estate, or brokered by a friend of Ethyl's. None of my investments had ever lost a dime; none of my properties had failed to appreciate; none of my books had failed to net at least fifty thousand dollars over their publishing life span (some of them had earned much more). And my tiny publishing "business," run by Ethyl in conjunction with a retired brick mason from Hendersonville, grossed nearly a hundred thousand per annum, *after* deducting their salaries.

As I said, money was not a problem. In fact, all the current revenue from my magazine articles went directly to Cullen in either of two ways, a blind trust or a college fund. My periodicals' earnings alone ran to thirty-five thousand plus each year, so my son's financial future looked pretty sound. When he was grown, maybe he'd lend me a couple of dollars.

But then the immediate problem for Cullen was not fiscal but physical. I'd been thinking about that, too.

★ ★ ★

One morning Dave came over, minimal cranial bandaging in evidence. Cullen examined that wound site closely, then we oohed and aahed over the horrendous bruises on the big guy's body — the solar plexus vicinity for you anatomists, or you ladies who envision Dave as having a handsome chest, which he does but mine is better. After submitting to all this scrutiny, Dave and Cullen settled in on the couch to watch our newest video, John Wayne's *McLintock*, one of the last of the Duke's movies to be released on videotape. I could hear the two of them laughing as I slipped up the stairs, then on to the attic, where I kept my workout paraphernalia.

I did my twenty minutes of stretching (the older I got, the less stretchy I felt and the longer the warm-up I required), then launched into an experimental kata for an hour. By the time the movie was over and the boys had joined me, I was finishing up four sets of handstand press-ups on the parallel bars. It was propitious that they'd arrived when they did; Dave couldn't do as many press-ups as I could, and I needled him whenever the opportunity presented itself. Like then.

"Give me another couple of days for my head

223

to get right and I'll take you on in a squatting contest," he said.

The hell he would. I had only five hundred pounds of barbell plates; Dave could squat more than that after falling out of an airplane. Which meant that he had high reps in mind. Forget it.

"Uh . . . my knee's been acting up," I offered, rubbing one to support my alibi.

"Aw, that's tough. How about we arm-wrestle?"

"Trying to embarrass me in front of my boy?"

"Don't worry, Dad," Cullen chimed in, "I won't tell anybody that he beat you."

"*That* he beat me? What about *if* he beats me?"

"Sorry, Daddy. There's no way you can out-arm-rassle Dave."

Dave looked smug.

"But it doesn't matter," said Cullen, coming over to hug my leg. "I love you anyway. Besides, he can't kick high like you, even if he is taller."

I looked smug.

Then Dave and I went to work on the heavy bag, rattling its moorings with our punches. Sweat rolled off our backs as we grunted from the effort. Kicks next, taking turns holding the pads, me careful of Dave's midriff, taking no chance of even a light tap or a slight miscalculation.

Cullen watched, raptly attentive, as the sun took its leave and tree frogs greeted the night.

224

Heather made the trek to Charlotte regularly, phoning often with medical updates. Her dad was doing quite well, though he was tired a lot. That seemed to work out, as he didn't have the energy to bully Web.

Mother and son visited only once, home from Charlotte for a day. They stayed a few hours, then headed back. Cullen was in a blue funk after they left. He came into my office, lay down on the floor beside my green swivel chair, put his feet up on the seat, and commenced to swivel.

Back and forth. Back and forth.

Writing a piece, I was currently at an impasse trying to remember the Smith & Wesson Escort's year of introduction, to give it its due as the progenitor of the currently successful line of Smith small-bore autoloaders. Try as I might, the year escaped me.

Back and forth. Back and forth.

I went over to the reference shelf, and pulled out several copies of *Gun Digest*, guessing at the most likely years.

Back and forth.

"Cullen. Please don't do that. It distracts me."

No answer except more back and forth.

"Son?"

Back and forth.

"*Cullen.*"

"All right! I just wanted to be near you!" he shouted, and fled the room. Part of that was probably true. Most of it was that for some reason, he simply wanted my attention. Something was bothering him. I put down my stack of books.

On his bed, in his room, index and middle fingers of his right hand firmly in his mouth, lips working. Clearly upset. I sat on his bed. He wouldn't look at me.

"Cullen?"

No response.

"What's bothering you, pal?"

No response.

"You and Web have an argument?"

Visibly less suction on the fingers.

"He hurt your feelings?"

Mouth stopped working altogether.

"He eat one of your raptors?"

"No, but I don't understand why he doesn't want to play anything I want to. No matter what it is. All he does is watch my TV, and every once in a while go out to the top of the stairs to look if his mom's still down there with you. I don't think he likes me anymore."

"That's not it. Web is suffering from a problem called post-traumatic stress syndrome."

"What's that?"

"When someone goes through a very scary experience, like you and Web did, they often suffer the aftereffect of being afraid all the time, even when there is nothing to be afraid of. Sometimes they have nightmares, which makes it hard for them to sleep."

"Like when I see a scary movie."

"Yes, very much like that. Only worse."

"Wow. Worse. No wonder he likes to know

where his mom is all the time. And won't play under my bed, even with a flashlight."

"Your grasp of things never ceases to impress me, son," I said, quite truthfully.

"Thank you."

"You're welcome."

"Is that, whatchacallit, madic syndrome, can I catch it? Like flu? If Web sneezes on me?"

"No, babe. It's not a disease but a condition. You can't catch it from Web."

"Good. I'm glad I can't catch it."

"Me too." And I was.

25

ONE rainy spring evening not long after Cullen had imparted his own twist to the colloquialism "His back is stove up," the Vance/Michaels/Patterson/Cullowee Strategy Council held its first meeting. Present at my dining room table were Dad, Dave Michaels, Heather Patterson, Ethyl Cullowee, and Jason Patterson, who was reclining uncomfortably in a rented hospital bed with a crank at one end, like a Tin Lizzie.

I opened the meeting with a prayer, thanking God for sparing as He had most of those at the table, especially Web and Cullen, not present but upstairs playing Candyland. Since everyone there except Ethyl had either been shot, shot at, or both within the past couple of weeks, the prayer was amen'd by all.

Next, I informed the assembled of my plans for Resovic's future, something for which Dave and I had been laying the groundwork all week. Silence coursed unimpeded amongst the little cluster of divergent but intertwined souls as they absorbed my words. Ethyl spoke for the group, asking, "What do you plan to do with Cullen while you and Dave are out gallivanting?"

I laid that out for them too in general terms, not dwelling on specifics. There were approving nods from some, mild head shaking from others.

Ethyl: "Cullen will be bored to tears."

Jason: "I need something to do."

Dad: "Cullen'll be fine, he'll just need to be watched and entertained."

Heather: "Web will be with me in Charlotte, or with my parents if I'm working. I want to be involved in this."

Dave: "Ty and I have worked out a way for you all to be involved. Really involved."

I joined in. "Before we get around to who does what and how, we need to make our getaway plans."

Several heads turned, training interested and inquisitive eyes on me. "Getaway?" said Jason.

"Right," I responded. "We need to coordinate the getaway, liaison, and defense of Cullen."

"Exactly where is he going?" asked Heather.

"Need to know," I answered, and waited for the storm.

"What?"

"Only those who need to know will know," Dave answered for me.

Heather's green eyes filled instantly with heat and animosity, resembling sparklers at a Fourth of July picnic. This woman's temper was so close to the surface you could prick your finger on it.

"You mean to tell me," she began, "that I can't be trusted to know the whereabouts of — "

"Heather," said Dave quietly.

"Don't interrupt me."

"Heather," he said again.

"What!"

"Do you think Resovic knows who you are?"

"Maybe. Probably. So what?"

"Then," Dave went on, "he might know where you live. Work."

She paused briefly, trying to bring it under control. "Yeah, maybe he does. Again, so what?"

"He just might grab you."

Her eyes grew large.

"To find out where Ty is."

Larger.

"Or Cullen."

Big as saucers, as she digested the implications, the enormity of our enterprise, our dilemma. "My God," she said.

"And Ty won't be there to protect him."

"My *God*. Then I have to go also. With Web. Because they could grab him, too, to make *me* talk." She turned to me. "About you, and Cullen."

"You have a good handle on the situation," I said. "It's obvious that Resovic will stop at nothing to get at me and my family. None of us is safe unless I get to him first. And I will. My immediate problem is to ensure Cullen's safety. Here's how I plan to do that."

For the next hour, I talked and they listened. Except Dave, who came and went from the table as he pleased.

He'd heard it before.

★ ★ ★

My next meeting was with Fanner, who agreed quite readily to his minor role in the subterfuge, as well he should. My remedy relocated several

230

of his immediate concerns, and with luck, just might dump the solution to this entire situation in his lap, leaving the FBI out of the spotlight and Fanner with all the glory.

Then a closed-door session with McElroy at Bragg, laying the foundation for him.

"I like it," he said. "Cullen will be safe as catnip at a dog show, my boys'll see to it. You got my word. When's the shift of command post?"

"Tomorrow. We'll meet at the police annex a half hour before first light. The cars will all be there six hours earlier, checked for electronic devices by your experts and such as the GPD can provide. No one there knows anything about our destination, or future intentions, just that they are to sweep the vehicles, make sure no one goes near them once the drivers drop them off and the sweeping is completed, and to secure the underground parking area from anyone and everyone not handpicked by Fanner.

"Dave will spend the night there too, and I expect your guys to double-check the police. Ever since that fiasco at my house, with the two pretend cops, I'm less than one hundred percent trusting of the GPD."

"Fanner ever figure where the uniforms and equipment came from?" McElroy asked.

"Two cops, roommates, had their apartment broken into while they were on a week-long trip to Atlanta."

"Simple."

"The best plans usually are," I said. "The question is, how did Resovic's goons know who was going to be out of town?"

231

"The old-fashioned way, I suspect," said the colonel. "Pieces of silver changed hands. I'm curious why they didn't steal sheriff's department uniforms."

"I thought about that, mentioned it to Fanner. He and the sheriff surmise that our gunnies thought that — Guilford not being the largest county in the United States — the deputy on duty at my house might know all his fellow officers, be able to spot a couple of imposters right off. But it was a good bet that the deputy mightn't know every cop on the city force."

"Resovic's no dummy."

"His résumé will tell you that."

"Well, okay." McElroy stood up, stretching his arms and groaning pleasurably. "I'll be there tomorrow too. Make damn sure your retreat goes as planned."

I held out my hand. "Figured you might," I said.

"How long before you plan to go after Resovic actively?"

I told him.

"Word has it that the big gun buy has not taken place, yet. We're trying to pin down the location. I'll have more inter for you when you return from the new CP," he said.

"Don't think of it as a command post but as a perimeter. A secured perimeter."

"But you'll be making decisions while you're there."

"My decisions have already been made. I merely have to implement them."

"Bingo," he said, and shoved off.

26

WHEN I walked into the parking basement of the police annex, four white limos stood in the center of the huge windowless space. Each had fully blacked-out windows, three doors to a side, cellular phone antennae. None had mud flaps. Money can't get you *everything*.

Since it was still dark outside, I had forgone sunglasses, likely spoiling my chances of being mistaken for Al Pacino. Probably all for the better; some of the cops loitering in the dimness might have seen *Serpico*.

Eight Delta Force men — in full gear — encircled the cars, looking as if they could take Cuba. Before lunch. Directly in front of the limousines, seated on Barcaloungers, were Dave and Colonel McElroy, neither in battle dress but both wearing their kick-ass faces. Those two probably couldn't take Cuba. Not alone.

Maybe Haiti.

I had on my kick-ass face too. Not to mention a Model 97 Winchester riot pump slung over one shoulder, a Ruger .45 auto on my right hip, a Browning 9 mm P-35 cocked and locked in a horizontal rig under my left armpit, and a Smith Airweight Bodyguard strapped to my calf, out of sight. (There were a Swiss Army knife and a pair of nail clippers in a pants pocket, but I don't want to belabor the hardware.)

Cullen walked behind me, taking in everything, bleary but wide-eyed from excitement. Dad walked behind him, carrying his ever present .30 carbine. In one back pocket rode an ancient Smith & Wesson Hand Ejector .32 Long. I supposed it was loaded; with the .32 Long, it didn't really make much difference. In a shooter's lexicon, ".32 Long" and "anemic" were synonymous.

If we were charged by a rat, Dad's little revolver might be up to taw.

Make that a mouse.

As I approached them, Dave and McElroy got to their feet. I said, "Gentlemen."

Dave said, "Watch your language."

The colonel just nodded curtly, putting on a show of macho, or military competency, or aloofness — or indifference, so far as I knew — for the gendarmes. If the cops were impressed, I saw no sign of it. They just looked bored, sleepy, anxious to be rid of us.

Fanner stood at the head of the entrance ramp. I turned to him and waved a hand, my manly manicure marred by a blackened nail, the result of last night's sparring session with one of my martial arts cronies. I'd been practicing my defense against attackers armed with club or stick. My partner, a kendo expert and former British hand-to-hand instructor in what used to be called Burma, had a better attack than I had a defence. Hence the mashed nail. Nonetheless, at the end of the session I'd managed to take his stick away — and reduce him to pounding the mat in submission — by means of a jujitsu takedown and hold. And a modicum of pressure applied to his arm, using his elbow as the fulcrum, which initiates pain not unlike that of childbirth, only worse. Or so I've been told by female acquaintances familiar with both conditions.

Well, he shouldn't have slammed my finger so hard.

We'd parted still friends, however, with me offering assurances that his arm would be out of the sling in no time.

At least his elbow hadn't turned black, like my fingernail.

When I waved to Fanner, he pivoted, motioning out into the darkness. Directly, in drove Ethyl, behind the wheel of her Olds 88, its cavernous trunk filled to overflowing (literally; the lid was tied down with a cord) with Cullen's clothes, toys, TV, VCR, movies, books, games. The back seat was taken up with foodstuffs, liquids, washing powders. Such prerequisites to ablution as soap, shampoo, toothpaste and toothbrushes. Towels. Linen. Ammunition.

The essentials.

We were putting civilization behind us.

We — Dave, Dad, Ethyl, and I — transferred the cargo from Ethyl's car to the four limos, distributing the matériel with no special rhyme nor reason, just transferring items from one conveyance to four others. Later we'd sort things out.

Cullen's wont was to run and play, and I had a little trouble squelching his exuberance.

235

Ultimately, Ethyl had to put him in a limo and dig out a deck of cards.

I queried McElroy about the bug sweep.

"Those four cars are as void of unwanted electronic devices as modern technology can determine. As are ours." He pointed to an array of eight cars parked to one side, in which the Delta troops had arrived, one to a car, except for the Ford in which McElroy had bummed a ride.

Dave agreed. "And since they were swept, none of us has so much as gone to the bathroom."

"Glad I'm not riding with you," I said, then went to thank Fanner for his help.

We were just beginning to get light from the east when we exited the underground garage. The quartet of limousines, each with a lead car and a follower driven by Delta men, sped into the early-morning gray, none going in the same direction. But all bound for the same rural rendezvous, one hour hence, after each trio of cars had aimlessly circumnavigated Greensboro, ensuring that they had no armed and malevolent bad guys in tow.

I drove one of the limos, with Ethyl and Cullen in back. Dave piloted another, my dad a third. McElroy handled the fourth rented car. The three of them were concerned only with detecting any following vehicles. I had to attend to that chore while also watching for any overt action in case, despite my best efforts, Resovic or his consorts had anticipated my moves, bypassed them, or simply had enough men to attack all four convoys simultaneously.

We came back together in northeastern Guilford County. Pulled into the yard of an abandoned farm, out of sight of the main road, running the risk of being cited for trespass.

Once again we transferred food, toys, luggage, and stuff, this time from the limos to a big Chevy Suburban which had been purchased used by the second cousin of one of our Delta lads, in Aiken, South Carolina. Still had South Carolina plates, and a South Carolina title — in the cousin's name — on the dash, along with insurance information and an epistle from the cousin — whose name was Bradford Ashley — "To Whom It May Concern," granting permission for the bearer of the letter to do whatever he or she pleased in the Suburban, "'cept run dope and dip snuff."

Them South Carolina boys have a right keen sense of humor.

McElroy and his least competent-looking commando started to climb into a Ford Thunderbird. I motioned the colonel to one side and asked, "Is he the best of the bunch? What about that tall one with the scar below his eye? He sure looks tough."

"Oh, he's tough all right. But the gent in the Thunderbird there" — he pointed with his chin — "*gave* him the scar."

"No kidding."

"They were drunk, horsing around, going at it with steak knives. For fun." He smiled fondly. "Those South Texans love booze, broads, and brawls. No kidding, though, that one there's

237

meaner'n a wolverine with a hemorrhoid when he wants to be. And he has a boy of his own. He'll look after Cullen, best of any I got. And that's the best there ever was, except maybe you in your prime."

"I haven't even reached my prime."

McElroy smiled, walked over to the Ford and climbed in.

We loaded everyone into the Suburban, which had plenty of room inside since much of our cargo was secured to its roof rack. Dave sat up front with me as we pulled out of the farm road and headed for I–85 North. McElroy rode directly behind, sticking to our bumper like tar. His men followed as well, but every ten miles or so, one of them peeled off. Finally, only the two of us were left, the colonel and the Suburban.

We turned west just south of Richmond, Virginia, and took to the back roads. No chance of detection or pursuit. Just lazy, laid-back cruising, with Cullen and my dad singing, "May I sleep in your barn tonight, mister . . . " in back. Ethyl had dozed off against one back door, probably a defense mechanism against Pop's singing. But I liked his voice, and his songs. He'd sung the same ones to me when I was little.

I joined in as we motored on, following the sun to our Blue Ridge hideaway.

27

AS a teenager, I'd worked one summer on a dairy farm in the mountains near West Jefferson, North Carolina, for no pay except the privilege of hunting whitetail deer there in the fall. The job encompassed early rising, large breakfasts, enough teat squeezing to give you forearms like Popeye, and fresh cow patties everywhere you looked, stepped, or — sometimes — sat. It was worth all the trials and tribulations.

Not that I didn't have access to good deer hunting in the eastern part of the state, you understand. It's just that the bucks found in those coastal quarters ran to runty and piebald, nature's payback for overpopulation and overcopulation, resulting in rampant inbreeding.

Occasionally, Dave or I — sometimes both in one season — would drop a well-horned buck with eight, nine, once even thirteen points. Our hunting peers, not to mention their elders, were suitably impressed with our skill, tenacity, and especially the quality of our inventiveness when it came to skipping school without suffering the usual ramifications. For example, Dave lost four uncles and a cousin to various diseases one year, more's the pity, especially considering the fact that neither of his parents had male siblings. Oh, the funerals he attended.

Nonetheless, and despite our considerable

239

success, we were vexed beyond comforting much of the time. The reason? Both of us read Warren Page (of *Field & Stream*, to which Dave subscribed) and Jack O'Connor (shooting editor for *Outdoor Life*, which I received by mail) religiously, repeatedly, and resignedly. Those stalwart nimrods coursed hither and yon, reporting their adventures monthly in the most insightful of prose, stirring us to envy and awe, in equal parts, followed closely by emulation.

When our heroes wrote of the huge deer they'd slain in Alberta or Arizona with their trusty 6 mm Page Super Pooper or .270 Winchester, their articles replete with photos, Dave and I would be gripped by the fantods for a fortnight. Never mind that as often as not the monster buck depicted next to an ad for Red Man — or Bausch & Lomb binoculars, or Red Ryder BB guns — was a *mule* deer, a larger, heavier breed than the whitetail. Never mind that mule deer did not live east of the Mississippi except in adolescent imaginations and the Bronx Zoo. Never mind that Page and O'Connor — being big-name scribes backed by the overflowing coffers of large-circulation national magazines — generally had professional guides to ferret out the big ones, or were privy to secret buck hidey-holes known only to local landowners who sought to curry favor and publicity. Never mind that the duo pretty much had unlimited time to spend in the outback seeking game, and were paid handsomely to do so.

Never mind *any* of that. Michaels and Vance faunched for the *big* one, the scale breaker, the

240

buck with a neck you couldn't get your arms around, antlers wrist-thick at the base, brow tines long as a caping knife.

North Carolina mountain bucks were as close to that as we were likely to come, assuming we could locate one or two to fix our sights on. So, every fall for several years, much of our weekend time (Sundays too, illegal though it was, there in the heart of the Bible Belt) was spent in pursuit of Blue Ridge bucks. We found a few, none a monster like in the magazines, but respectable. And in doing so — spending the time, shank's mare up slope and down, fording bitterly cold mountain streams, ofttimes with snow pelting down, later hunkered over a fire, s'mores on the end of a laurel stick, night all around, and stars, more than we'd ever seen in the city — Dave and I grew to love those mountains, the dairy farm we hunted on, and the dairy farmer himself, Lawrence Goodall.

Who stood in front of me now, short and bent and bristle-faced, tobacco stains on his plaid shirt, holes cut in his shoes where his corns hurt, smiling, exposing the darkened remnants of what was once a mouthful of teeth. I hugged him; the hell with shaking hands.

"God bless you, Lawrence Goodall," I said as we embraced.

"And you," he replied, "and all who travel in your shadow."

I hadn't seen him since the year of his stroke, when he'd called to tell me that he had a stand of corn the crows were eating, a field of tobacco that needed bringing in if he was to pay his bills,

241

a few cows in want of milking. No mention of his illness. Dave and I left our homes the next day, had everything finished in two weeks. Filled his larder. Stacked wood high and close to the house. Padded his bank account a bit more than his crop allowed for.

He deserved it.

"Where's your boy?" he said now. "Wanna meet him."

"Cullen!" I said loudly, turning my head.

"Yes?" he replied, just getting out of the car, helping Ethyl.

"Come meet someone."

"Okay." He walked over, took in the stoop, the stiff left arm, cut-out shoes, and beard, then smiled, bright as a copper penny, held out his hand, and said, "Pleased to meetcha."

Lawrence Goodall chuckled, shook the proffered hand. "You look just like your mama."

"I do?"

"Nobody never tol' you that?"

"Just Granma."

The old man looked over at Ethyl, who smiled primly and disapprovingly back. He said, "She looks like your mama too."

Cullen said, "I reckon so. Can I go see your barn?"

"You can go see anything you want, boy."

Cullen looked up at me. I nodded. Off he went, Ethyl calling after him, "Mind where you step."

"Fine boy," Lawrence Goodall commented.

"Yes, he is. Thank you."

"Kin'ly like you was."

"I could never hold a candle to him."

He nodded. "Way it's s'posed to be. Not always the way it is, though."

We looked into each other's eyes a moment longer. I said, "How are you?"

"Alive," he answered; then: "There's David." And shuffled off.

Reunions of the heart.

I began to unload the Suburban.

★ ★ ★

Heather and Web left her father's home in Charlotte the following day, having been taken there from Greensboro by four of McElroy's soldiers. She drove herself to the airport, first proceeding aimlessly around the city for an hour prior to her early-morning departure to Columbia, South Carolina. She bought their tickets at the window instead of in advance. In Columbia, she rented a Ford Escort and proceeded to Augusta, Georgia, where mother and son boarded an Amtrak headed north. Although her ticketed destination was Greenville, South Carolina, she detrained in the little town of McCormick, hopped a bus to Union, then another train to Spartanburg. She waited on the platform at each stop to scrutinize other passengers as they quit the conveyance.

That same morning, I flew out of Bristol, Tennessee, arriving in Spartanburg long before the Pattersons. I was in place to observe their fellow travelers' comings and, especially, goings when they arrived. No one remotely suspicious.

243

No slavering hulks brandishing cudgels, nary a machine gun-carrying cretin, no 280-pound jumping beans in sight. Just a lazy southern day, flies buzzing around a garbage can, a grizzled old feist snoozing in the shade.

Heather hailed a cab in front of the depot, heading for our prearranged destination, while I watched unobtrusively from under my hat brim. Nobody followed the taxi.

Back in my rental five-liter Mustang — five-speed box, limited-slip differential, six-speaker stereo/CD, 12-gauge shotgun twixt the seats — I aimed for the Blessed Bread Bakery, where Heather awaited.

★ ★ ★

The smell of pastry set my gastric juices flowing when I walked through the door. Heather and Web were seated at a tiny table, milk in front of Heather and a mug of steaming coffee in front of Web. Just kidding.

Heather smiled fetchingly. I grinned back at her, ruffled Web's hair, and said, "Hiya, sport," to which he responded with a shy smile.

After I ordered pie and coffee, Heather got right down to business. "What did your friend tell you?"

The friend she was referring to was Axel Mershon. Formerly of the NYPD, and the GPD, and the Department of Corrections, Axel — called Ax by everyone who knew him, had dealings with him, had been arrested by him, or was afraid of him — honchoed a private security

244

firm. He stood just under six feet and tipped the beam at maybe 225, unless he was on one of his perennial fasts, at which time he faded away to 217 or 218, a shadow of his fighting heft. His Long Island accent you couldn't erase with a maul. He was fair and honest and decent and invariably drew to an inside straight. What more could you ask of a man? I related to Heather verbatim what the Ax had told me:

"My sources on the department tell me that officers have canvassed every rental and real estate firm in the Triad. They sent four badges to question the curb markets, grocery stores, mom-and-pop beer-and-cigarette establishments in the county. No luck.

"Furthermore, they sent some vice guys into the shelters, under the bridges, in general wherever the skells gather. Looking for anyone new, out of place, and especially anyone really big and really south-of-the-border. Less luck.

"Furthermore, no one on the street — hookers, narcotics vendors, users, pimps, or crackheads — has seen or heard a thing about anyone fitting the descriptions you gave me. I offered them some serious green, just like you told me. If I got no takers among that collection of maggots, then there ain't nobody like that moving around.

"Furthermore, what with no progress and the stiff they found on Church Street yesterday, and that jewelry store heist getting the chief's attention, your situation is no

245

longer priority number one like it was, especially with you out of town and all.

"What they're waiting for is some uniform to give one of these creeps a citation for a seat belt violation, or expired inspection sticker, have it show up on the computer. Then, whammo, they send five carfuls of blue uniforms out to nab the cocksuckers."

And so spake the Ax.

After hearing this heartening report, Heather said, "Those guys are really on their toes, aren't they?"

"Other fish to fry."

"And you are going to . . . ?" She paused on the rising inflection, making a question of it.

"Fry some fish of my own." I reached for the check.

★ ★ ★

Dave picked us up outside of Lenoir, North Carolina, following at a distance for twelve miles, checking our backsides. Nothing.

I turned the Mustang in at Avis, patting its flank as I left; what a fine automobile. The shotgun was wrapped in Heather's coat, my own jacket being needed to conceal the .45 on my belt. Dave was there when I turned in the keys. He reached for Heather's luggage, which was sparse, since we'd brought along most of her things in the Suburban the day before. Her lone suitcase held mostly items for entertaining Web on the long journey they'd just undertaken.

246

We piled into the Suburban, performed a few tricks to cover our tracks, and headed northwest. We ate supper at the farm.

Next morning, Cullen and Heather were first up, except for Lawrence Goodall, of course. I found them at table, soaking up a mess of "grips," flapjacks, pork sausage patties, and milk fresh from the udder. Well, almost.

Coffee smell from the stove. I homed in on it, snatching a cup from the drainboard en route. Settling into a chair tableside, I listened to the early-morning gab.

Lawrence Goodall was saying, "What'd you think of the horses?" to Cullen.

"I like 'em, 'specially the red one with the light-colored hair on his neck and tail."

"Called a sorrel," said the old man.

"Oh," said Cullen, absorbing. Quiet for a spell, then he said, musefully, "I'd like to be a horse, or a cow, or a goat. But not a pig, no way!"

"You don't like pigs?" I asked.

"Yeah, I like 'em, but I wouldn't wanna get baked up!"

Well, me neither.

Dave walked in, then Web. More flapjacks disappeared. I joined in after my first cup of coffee, putting away my share "and half o' Bolivia's," according to Lawrence Goodall. "You allus was a big eater. Like to broke me when you worked up here as a teenager."

"You worked here, Daddy?" — from the only person in the world who can call me Daddy.

"Long time ago."

247

"You milk cows?"

A snort from the ancient's end of the table.

"Yes, I did," I responded, "in spite of what some present might claim."

Dave chimed in. "Tell him about the time Boss's sire nipped you on the butt while you were milking, causing you to holler so loud that old brindle cow stepped in the milk bucket, dumping fifteen minutes' work into the straw."

"I mind the time he fell asleep astride the board fence whilst pourin' feed to the chickens, and went fanny over teacup backwards into the hog waller," added Lawrence Goodall, nearly choking with laughter.

"What's a sire?" asked Cullen.

"And a waller?" queried Web.

"Never mind. I don't have to take this kind of abuse," said I, feigning pique.

"What kind do you have to take?" asked Heather, tears streaming down.

Now everyone was laughing, Dave so hard he was red in the face. I stomped out angrily.

Cullen came after me, to assuage my seemingly hurt feelings. I ambushed him from behind the hall door, grabbing him and taking him to the floor, tickling him unmercifully. He laughed until he was gasping; I let up, so he could breathe.

"You aren't really mad?" he asked.

"Course not. But Dave and Mr. Goodall wouldn't enjoy it nearly so much if I didn't act like I was."

"Let's wrestle!" he hollered, launching his wiry little body.

We did, there on the cool hallway linoleum, the smell of kerosene rank in our nostrils from the nearby stove.

My son.

Intact.

Happy.

Up to me to keep him that way.

★ ★ ★

Late one evening, Heather and I sat in the bed of the farm truck, a double-axle number as old as my Aunt Flo but more personable. I'd driven the old Chevy to the top of the highest pasture, and parked it facing away from the farm buildings far below so we could sit in the bed and lean against the back of the cab, looking down on the picture book setting. In the pasture immediately below our perch, two groundhogs played in the lengthening grass. A fawn-colored doe browsed within fifty yards of the cavorting chucks, stocking her several stomachs with fodder. Her sides swelled, but not from food. From the size of her, she'd drop soon, and maybe twins.

Heather had a pair of Zeiss ten-power binoculars to her eyes, zeroed in on the woodchucks. "Aren't they cute?" she gushed.

"As a quilted bunny."

"Hardass."

"New. Sensitive, that's me."

"Women are sensitive."

"But men aren't?"

"Unfortunately not. Men are into sex, power,

control, sex, competition, waging war — at one level or another — and sex. 'Sensitive' is antonymous to 'male.'"

"How about male bonding?"

"You don't have to be sensitive to bond, for heaven's sake! A football team *bonds*. Do you think that makes them sensitive?"

"That's the most egregious ipse dixit I've heard since a drunk cornered me at a party and opined that Raoul Cedras was simply exercising population control."

"What's an ipse dixit?"

"An allegation without supporting evidence."

"For supporting evidence, simply observe your fellow males."

"I have for years. You're full of turkey stuffing."

"Such an enlightened, cogent rebuttal," she said.

"I knew you'd see it my way."

Emerald smile. I felt its punch behind my sternum.

The sun sat in the trees, orange-hued, then dipped lower, winking playfully through the branches. Hid, finally, behind the mountains to our left.

Dusk.

Magic time.

Any moment I expected a leprechaun to peer out from behind a bush.

Cupid instead; Heather took my hand.

★ ★ ★

"Tell me about your wife," she said quietly, after a while.

It was completely dark now, Venus and Mars dazzling us with their sparkle, a few stars venturing forth. Lights were on down at the house. Dad and Dave were probably stirring up grub. Mashed potatoes and gravy, country-style steak, pinto beans . . .

"You aren't answering."

She was right. I did more of the same.

Not to be put off, she said, "Is it painful? Speaking of her?"

"Sometimes. Most of the time. With others. I talk to Cullen about her, when he seems to need to. Keeps her alive, close to his heart."

She squeezed my hand. I wanted to squeeze back, but didn't. She'd invoked the pain, not me. Erasing it wasn't easy, or quick.

"I'd really like to hear about her."

"Why?"

"I want to get to know her, through you. It's a way to get to know you, what you like, admire, look for in a woman."

"*She* was what I look for in a woman," I said, more harshly than I intended. She started at my vehemence, but held on to my hand. Easing me along, letting me know I wasn't on a therapist's couch, or out listening to night sounds all alone.

I took a deep breath, and related the following:

We'd met in the summer of 1982. Tess Cullowee, still at Greensboro College, third year. She was tall and lean and intelligent, with the keenest sense of humor I'd ever known, little laugh lines like parentheses bordering her

251

lovely mouth. Light green/brown eyes, hair the color of straw, thick and naturally curled and worn shoulder length to lessen the visual effect of a long, graceful neck. Perfect teeth. Lithe, muscular arms, from tennis and weight lifting.

I'd first run into her at the gym, literally, bumping her as I slipped past the let machine without watching where I was going. I said, Excuse me; she said, Next time honk your horn. We both laughed.

"Did you ask her out right away?" inquired Heather.

"No. I was dating a couple of other ladies at the time, one of them kind of seriously. I enjoyed raquetball and dancing, so meeting women was not a problem."

"You dated around a lot?"

"Had since returning from Korea in '74."

"Did you sleep with many?"

"Kinda nosy, aren't you?"

"So were you, the other day. But talking to you about it, pulling it out and looking at it, changed my outlook. Permanently."

"I know the feeling. Four months after I met Tess, a man said something to me that cut short my lustful and incessant wandering from flower to flower."

"What'd he say?"

"'I now pronounce you man and wife.'"

* * *

We drove back the long way, crossing the creek on the east side of the property, catching a couple of bucks — antlers forming, sheathed in velvet — in the headlamps as we went. They stared into the lights for a moment, then bounced away into the night.

Web and Cullen were delighted to see us; taking us by the hand, they escorted us into the kitchen to view the sideboard. No pintos, but snap beans cooked with chunks of ham hocks. A mound of warm corn bread, flanked by recently churned butter, lumpy and yellow, and a jar of mountain honey from Lawrence Goodall's beehive. Two pecan pies, baked with nuts from Lawrence Goodall's own trees, using lard rendered from one of his own pigs. A pitcher of milk for the young'uns, scalding coffee for us old folks, with maybe a touch of chicory if I knew Lawrence Goodall.

We said grace standing, Cullen doing the honors, then heaped our plates, found seats at the long table, and filled our bellies with food and our hearts with bonhomie.

And I sorely needed the goodwill, the pastoral pleasure, the close company of my son, because tomorrow I would be leaving. And despite my assurances to Cullen after the bank robbery, there was a chance I wouldn't be coming back.

A very good chance.

★ ★ ★

"Is it after midnight?"

"Not yet, son."

"So I'm not five yet?"

"Not quite. Couple more hours."

253

"Reckon I'll feel different tomorrow, being five and all?"

"Maybe so. You tell me, at breakfast."

Five years old. Hard to believe. The years had slipped away like the waters at low tide. How many tomorrows did we have together, he and I? In the morning he'd be five; next month, if I lived, I'd run head on into forty. Each day was precious.

And here I was, leaving him under the protection of two old men, one old woman, one young woman, and a soldier I didn't even know. No choice. Resovic could bide his time, strike when our defences slackened. Have someone else do it for him while he traveled the world in his illicit pursuits.

Not an option. Had to take the fight to him, and I knew how to do that. Lord, I surely did. Sitting on Cullen's bed as he fell asleep, I absentmindedly stroked his silken hair with my fingertips, pondering how I had come to know such things.

28

SLIGHT stirring beside me, brush of lips against mine. "I love you. Is it midnight?" I one-eyed the clock: 4:31.

"Happy birthday."

"I'm five?"

"You're five."

"Yay!"

Knees in my stomach. "Ouch!"

"Oh, sorry. Can I have my present now?"

"No. Not till everyone is up. It would hurt everybody's feelings, especially Web's."

"Can I get 'em . . . "

"No! It's only four-thirty in the morning, son. Way too early to get up, except for Mr. Goodall. Go back to sleep."

"I can't. I want to know what I got for my birthday."

"A hay baler."

"Did not."

"No?"

"No. Mr. Goodall already baled the hay. Besides, I'm too little to drive one. Yet."

"I guess that's true, even if you are five. What was it you wanted?"

"The lellow fire truck."

"Not the red one?"

"No, the lellow one, with the siren and the horn that goes *boop boop boop boop* when you back it up."

"You be quiet as a gerbil and don't wake anyone and we'll see, after everyone gets up."

"Soon as?"

"Soon as what?"

"Everyone gets up."

"Provided you don't encourage them to wake up."

"'Courage them?"

"By blowing a bugle or setting the kitchen on fire."

"Don't have a bugle."

"It's why you don't."

"Can I watch TV?"

"Nothing on this early. Mr. Goodall doesn't have cable."

"*Beauty and the Beast?* I just watched half of it last night."

"Keep the sound low."

"Okay."

"Real low."

"Okaayy."

"If you get hungry — "

"Daddy."

"What?"

"I'm five."

"Oh, sorry."

While he went to enjoy his fifth-birthday sunrise, I went back to sleep.

29

TWO hours later, still in pajamas, I stood at the foot of the stairs smelling Irish Cream coffee, a fresh cup of which rested on a table beside Dave, warm humidity rising enticingly from its surface. Dave sat in an enormous armchair under the 150-watt glare of a brass floor lamp.

"What are you doing?" I asked.

"Minding my own business. Ever try it?"

"What are you doing?" I repeated.

"Shoveling snow," said Dave.

"What *are* you doing?"

Cullen was over in the corner, rocking in Lawrence Goodall's big rocker, eating a cherry Pop-Tart, taking this all in, knowing something was coming, smiling, a crust crumb adhering to his lower lip.

"Must you know everything?" Dave said.

"No. Just this."

"Then will you leave me alone? Go milk a cow or something?"

"We'll see. So, what are you doing?"

Dave looked up at me. Perched near the end of his more than adequate nose was a three-power pince-nez, or what amounted to a pince-nez since he'd removed the arms. The lenses were virtually rectangular, with rounded corners and gold wire frames only an inch from top to bottom. He looked somewhat like a bookish owl. He said, "If I tell you, no nasty comments."

"From me?"

He just glared.

"Okay, but first tell me why you're wearing those glasses."

"To see with."

"Thanks. But why that, ah, style?"

"You don't like them?"

"Of course I don't like them. On Grandma Moses, maybe, but — "

"There you go. Forget it. Go away."

"Sorry. Well, what *are* you doing?"

"Little stress reliever."

"Yes?"

"I'm making a miniature sampler, on silk gauze, fifty-four-count, number ten crewel — "

"Number ten what?"

"Crewel. Tapestry needle. Don't interrupt. Anyway, this is a miniature of the kind of samplers schoolgirls of the mid-1700s to early 1800s used to make."

On his lap was a cardboard panel about four and a half inches square, with a two-and-a-half-inch window in the center. It looked like a mat for a painting. Affixed to the mat with tiny staples — covered with cellophane tape to prevent snagging, I suppose — was a section of gauze that resembled very fine wire screen. In the lower center was a two-story brick-red church, two-dimensional angle, with thirteen tiny white windows, two white doors with beige staircases leading up to them, all surrounded by green grass (complete with tombstones), blue sky, and bordered on the left by a stark, defoliated tree, its branches spreading at roof level. Above the church was the obligatory alphabet, done in burnt orange, and beneath the grass was a greyish-brown line into which was stitched the date, 1769.

"That a real church or a product of your fertile and artistic mind?" I asked.

"Don't start."

"I really want to know. Honest."

Cullen came over, stood beside Dave, peeking over his shoulder.

"It's the Falls Church, of the town in Virginia by that name. The original building burned, and this one was built in — "

"Seventeen sixty-nine."

"How observant."

"Kind of small, isn't it?"

"The church?"

"Your sampler."

"Why it's called a miniature."

"How many stitches?"

"It's eighty-five by ninety-five."

I did a quick computation in my head. "That's over eight thousand."

"Not only observant but a whiz at math, too."

"Take you long to do one?"

"Couple weeks, if people let me work without a lot of busybody questions."

"What do you do with them?"

"Frame them . . . "

"In itty-bitty frames."

"Then give them away, sell them at flea markets."

259

"For how much?"

"Four, five hundred."

"Dollars?"

"No, yen."

"You sell many?"

"All I find time to make."

"What do people do with them, use 'em for coasters?"

"Dartboards."

"Seriously."

"Put them in dollhouses, or on their walls in groupings. All sorts of things."

"What'd you say the wire mesh is made of?"

"Silk, and it's tough as hell to get. Nobody makes it anymore. Anywhere. The thread is silk too. Vegetable-dyed, like the originals of the period. No chemically colored stuff for us dyed-in-the-silk miniature people."

Cullen asked, "Doesn't miniature mean small?" Dave answered in the affirmative.

Putting a little hand on Dave's bulging, muscular, needlepointing right arm, he said, "Are you the only big person who does this?"

Dave smiled, said, "When I say 'miniature people' I mean people who do miniature samplers, not small folks."

"So not just midgets, elves, and leprechauns?"

"Right."

I said, putting my hand on Dave's bulging, muscular, left arm, "Aren't you afraid I might tell people you do this stuff?"

"Why would I care what you told them?" he responded, returning to his tatting, or whatever.

"Mightn't someone call you a sissy?"

He looked up at me. "Only once."

"Oh."

Cullen hugged his arm. "I don't think it's sissy at all. It's pretty." He looked up at me admonishingly. "Why would you call Dave a sissy?"

I winked at him to make certain he didn't mistake our joshing as serious. His face relaxed and he winked back.

"Because I don't believe for a minute he sells his work. I suspect he sews them onto his underwear."

Dave snorted.

"Don't worry about it, Dave," Cullen said. "I've got Batman on mine."

★ ★ ★

After breakfast I went out to speak with our centurion. His name was Stephen Sandford, rank staff sergeant, roughly five nine and 150 pounds. Not very imposing. Well, I was no Incredible Hulk myself.

Cullen and Web were in the front yard playing with Cullen's birthday presents: a fire truck (yellow); a bike with training wheels (burgundy); a "bow-an-arrol" with rubber suction-cup tips on the "arrols" and Robin Hood on the bow's limbs. "I'll be an Indinee," shouted Cullen, tying a washcloth around his head. "And I'll be John Wayne," countered Web, who had never heard of the Duke until he'd started playing with my son.

Good for Cullen.

Nice to keep in touch with your heritage.

I climbed the hill to where Sergeant Sandford sat watching the only road to and from the farm. He spent a lot of his time in this one spot, elevated and secluded, offering a view of most of the property directly surrounding the farmhouse and to which the boys were restricted unless accompanied by two adults.

"Howdy, Sarge," I said, as I approached the patch of weeds in which Sandford sat cross-legged, M-16 in his lap.

"Hello, sir," he responded, springing more or less to attention, rifle now slung over his shoulder.

"No need to 'sir' me, Sandford. I'm as far removed from a military officer as anyone could be."

He grinned. "So I hear. However, I call you sir not out of military protocol, but respect. The colonel has told me a little of your background."

"Oh."

"Yes sir. I want you to know, sir, that I won't let anything happen to your little boy."

I extended a hand. "Good."

He took it, saying, "Even if I do feel like the sentry guarding Catherine the Great's rosebush."

"Beg pardon?"

"Old Cath planted a rosebush in 1776 — why does that year ring a bell? — and ordered a guard to protect it. Of course the bush eventually died, but a sentry was always posted at the spot. In 1903 the czar noticed a soldier standing near a patch of weeds, and decided to find out why. The CO claimed he was following standing orders in placing a guard in that spot. No one could remember why."

"Well, I can understand your reasoning. Chances are you will never have to do anything but stand guard in this patch of weeds, and that's exactly the way I want it. If I thought there was much chance Cullen could be traced here, I would've requested ten men from McElroy. But remember this, no one ever died overestimating his enemy. Always try to figure what your opposition *can* do, not what he will do."

"Yes sir."

"Just take care of my boy."

"Count on it, sir."

"I will," I said, taking my leave.

★ ★ ★

"Is Web comfortable here?" I asked Heather half an hour later.

"Seems to be. He's spending more and more time with Cullen and Lawrence, out from under my skirt."

"That's good."

"I hope that in three or four days, he'll be able to handle being without me for a while." She looked up earnestly. "I really want to help with this."

"Not to mention being with me."

"There's that, of course."

"And who could blame you?"

"Such arrogance."

"But fun-loving."

Her eyes twinkled. "I'll say."

"Quit. You'll embarrass me."

"It wouldn't embarrass you if I went on Letterman and sang 'Merrily We Roll Along' while dancing the polka."

"It would if you were wearing that outfit."

Heather did a slow spin, pink polyester robe billowing, fluffy bunny slippers on her feet. "You don't approve of my flannel nightie?"

"Well . . ."

She stepped close, entwining my shirt in her supple fingers. "Someday, when we've come to know each other better . . ." She let the promise hang limply in the air.

That was all that hung limply.

Clearing the frog from my throat, I said, "I need to say goodbye to Cullen, get on the road. Dave's waiting."

Green glare of promise. "Take care of yourself."

I followed her advice.

★ ★ ★

"We leaving sometime this year?" Dave said.

"Just get in the car."

Cullen bounded over, in cowboy garb. "You John Wayne?" I asked.

Shaking his head, "Kirk Russell."

"Kurt."

"Kurt?"

"*Kurt* Russell."

"Yeah, him."

"When did you see Kurt Russell play a cowboy?"

"At Barry's one time."

"What movie?"

His brow wrinkled in thought. "Don't remember. He played this sher'ff named Wyatt Earp."

"*Tombstone?*"

Smile erased the wrinkle. "That's it!"

My brow wrinkled. "Son, *Tombstone* is rated R."

His face said, *Uh-oh.*

"I've showed you how to look for the upper-case 'R' on a tape box."

"There wasn't one. They rented the movie."

"Barry's mom let you watch it? Or did you and Barry sneak it in?"

His face said, *UH-OH.*

"Uh-hmm," I said.

"But Barry said — "

"Never mind. Next time, if it isn't obviously a children's movie, you ask the grownup in charge if it's okay for you to watch."

His face said, *Whew.*

"You sure you're okay with my leaving for a while?" I asked.

"Well, I'll miss you. Real bad." He hugged me, very firmly.

"Me too, pal. Now remember, if you look up at that rise and Sergeant Sandford isn't there, you get back in the house quick and tell Paw-paw or Mr. Goodall. And never, never leave this yard without Paw-paw or Mr. Goodall and Sergeant Sandford. You promise?"

"Promise."

"I'll call you in a couple of days."

"Okay," he responded, eyes on the ground. He hugged me again, even tighter. "I love you, Daddy."

"I love you, sweetheart. You take care."

"You too." Quick kiss, then he was off to play, leaving a hole in my being large enough to hangar a plane.

I blew Heather a buss and climbed in the rental beside Dave, headed back to Greensboro. Seeking villains.

30

DAVE and I were at Jason Patterson's small, neat apartment, the three of us plotting our next moves while munching popcorn and enjoying the canorous lilt of Michael Jones's piano from a high-quality six-speaker sound system. We sat at the dining room table, an exquisite mahogany number polished to a sheen that looked inches deep. I could see my face in it.

I looked tired, drawn, irritable.

I was.

For four days Dave and I had been canvassing curb markets, questioning greengrocers, darkening the stoops of every bait shop-cum-Gatorade emporium in Guilford and Rockingham counties. The results of our efforts were the consumption of enough soft drinks and acidic coffee to swamp the *Queen Mary*, plus six half-eaten Moon Pies and a large bag of pistachio nuts for Jason, who was recuperating nicely though slowly.

He had requested involvement, so we were getting him involved. Dave was saying, "What we want you to do is call No-Place-Like-Home Rentals, which is the largest, and whatever other places you find listed in the yellow pages. See what's been rented within the past two weeks or so. Ty and I're going out to make another run at the curb markets, case these guys have been sending out for pizzas all this time and are simply dying for a six-pack and a Little Debbie oatmeal cake."

"Do the rental outfits hand out such information?" Jason asked.

"Use your ingenuity."

"You mean lie and pretend to be a cop?"

"Whatever works," Dave said.

I rose from the table and sank into a big leather armchair, leaving them to work it out. The music swirled, engulfing me, easing accumulated tension. Jason's slender silver Persian joined me, jumping up, circling, settling, her warm heft amorphous, a formless gravity melting in my lap. Burring *purrrrr-purrrrr*, twitch of an ear, both of us relaxing . . .

★ ★ ★

A big hand on my shoulder — Dave's. "You ready, breeze, or do you plan to spend the night?"

Michael Jones was gone, replaced by Nigel Kennedy doing Vivaldi's *Four Seasons.* That stirred me to movement. "Y'all work out the details?" I asked, rising, kitty in my arms. Put her back in the chair, still curled shrimplike, one eye partially open.

"Yep" — from David. "More legwork tomorrow."

"Terrific." I waved to Jason, still sitting at the table, yellow legal pad in front of him covered with notes. He said goodbye. I stroked the cat once, pale hair soft under my palm.

"Good cat," I said.

"You like cats?" Jason asked.

"Broiled," I answered, making for the door.

"He does but he'll never admit it," Dave proclaimed.

"I'm a dog person," I insisted, waiting with my hand on the knob.

"What about the time that kitten got run over in front of your house? You scooped it up, took it to a vet, paid the bill, broke the news to its owner . . . "

"A seven-year-old girl who — "

"Right . . . don't interrupt. But you rescued the cat. After kitty came home, you offered to . . . " And so forth, all the way to the car.

★ ★ ★

I covered the curb markets and convenience stores on the east side of town, Dave took the west. No luck. Next day we tried again, south and north this time. Same result. Jason used varying ploys to extract a list of houses recently rented or leased and had been running a check on those. Zip. Of course, private owners often simply stuck a sign in front of their rentals, or relied on word of mouth. It would be tough indeed to ferret all those out.

We were back at Jason's apartment the next evening, fresh out of prospects. "Maybe you two missed a store here and there" — from Mr. Patterson.

"We were systematic, but it's possible we didn't check them all," I responded.

"Should we all go out tomorrow and look for

ones that may have been missed?" Jason asked. "I need to get out of the house."

"I suppose. Don't know what else to do."

Dave said, "You talked to the Ax lately?"

"This morning. Nothing from nowhere. Seems like the earth just swallowed these guys up."

"Think they might have gone? To do their gun deal, come back later to pop you, or maybe hire it done. He did that, we wouldn't know who to look for."

"True, but I sure hope not. Don't know when I'd be able to bring Cullen home."

"Let's cross our fingers and keep at it. Might get lucky," said Dave. And we went home to bed.

★ ★ ★

Jason decided to work the south side of Guilford, with me and Dave spreading over into adjacent counties to the north and east. We met at the Dunkin' Donuts on Battleground at four-thirty in the afternoon to compare notes.

"I hate to be negative, but this isn't producing much in the way of results," Jason offered.

"Don't know what else to do," I said. "I haven't heard a peep out of McElroy, Fanner, or Axel. We'll just have to keep plugging."

Dave said, "It's like hunting deer. You hunt for weeks from your best stands, work the wind, station yourself according to bedding areas or feed plots, memorize the solunar tables, but don't see a thing. Then one evening, on the way back to your truck, a buck steps into the road and stares at you. If your gun is slung over your shoulder, he makes a fool of you. You have to be ready all the time."

"And if you were home watching CNN instead of out hunting, you wouldn't even get to see the deer," I said.

"Today's lesson is never quit?" Jason asked.

"Right," I said. "Saddle up."

★ ★ ★

It was nearly dark when I headed out Lake Brandt Road to hit a couple places Dave had checked but not me. On the right sat Bobby Tew's Bait and Tackle Shop, a squat cinder block structure that peddled Citgo gas, Mountain Dew, and cellophaned beef jerky. In the far left corner were fishing poles, artificial bait, baseball caps, most blister-packed and displayed on pegboard. Canned goods on their shelves, cold drinks to my front, wieners revolving on a wire rotisserie beside the microwave at my right. There was a smell of mustard and relish in the air. Overhead hung an inflated child's float shaped like a blimp, red and white with "Bud Lite" on its side.

Class place.

The counter clerk said, "What for you, bub?"

Love being called bub.

Be nice. You seek information here.

"How about a half-dozen of those cucumbers?"

"He'p yourse'f."

I did, filling a brown paper poke to its rim.

"Seventy-nine cent a pound," he said,

271

reaching for the bag, taking it, weighing on a stainless scale suspended from the ceiling above the cash register with bailing wire. He'd pronounce it *war.*

He rang the amount into the register. "Anythin' else?"

"Little information," I said, sliding a fiver onto the counter.

He snorted. "Little's right. What kinda information you askin' after?" Reached for the five.

I held on to it.

He grabbed a corner of the bill, giving me his ass-whuppin' glare. Clint Eastwood he was not. He and McDuffy must practice in front of the same mirror.

"Any new customers lately?" I queried, maintaining my grip on the money.

"New. Same ol' crowd. Once in a great while some Yankee bonehead comes in, been fishin' at the lake, needs a Cricket or a Slim Jim." He tugged on the five.

"You're sure? No new faces stocking up on Cokes maybe, eight or ten bags of chips? Dozen of those delicious dogs?" I held on. Lincoln was starting to look strained.

"Nope. Same ol' boys."

I let the five go so abruptly he lost his balance and had to step backward. He was a little embarrassed, but recovered his composure and pocketed the dough. "Keep the change, right?" he said.

"Don't forget to take out for the cucumbers."

"On the house," he replied, showing a

mouthful of teeth that would give an orthodontist a gastric attack.

I took my vegetables and turned to go, but spotted an enticing loaf of bread on top of a case of canned goods. I'm a nut for bread, so I looked it over. It was semita bread, thick and dark and round, baked in an Asheboro bakery that specialized, according to the label, in Mexican bread.

My nape hair, again.

I examined the case of canned goods: San Marcos-brand serrano peppers. Next to the peppers in a cardboard box were several bags of what appeared to be pork rinds. Only their labels didn't say pork rinds, they said: "La Banderita Chicharrones." I bent to scrutinize the two cardboard boxes supporting the peppers. A full case of Corona beer, the other Chihuahua.

The clerk watched me, teeth no longer on display. Suspicious.

Why?

"You expanding into gourmet Mexican chow?"

"Naw," he answered. "One of my regulars ordered that stuff. He damn sure better come get it too. I had to run clear over to I–Forty for the beer, and to that greaser store off Market for the other stuff. He don't buy it, I gotta eat it myse'f."

"Who's the customer?"

"Guy named Feron Simmons."

"When you expecting him?"

"Tomorrow. Around lunchtime, he said. He's prob'ly guidin' some wetbacks to a messa bluegills out on the lake. He sure as hell don't

273

drink that Mex beer, taste like horse piss. Give you a buzz, though, you can choke it down."

"Reckon he could show me some prime fishing?"

"Could, you got a boat. He ain't cheap, though. Ten bucks a hour and you clean your own catch."

"Sounds fair."

"Come look him up. Lemme sell you the bait."

"That sounds fair too."

More teeth. Friends again. Going to do business together.

Bait business.

Damn right we were.

31

AT my house, flipping venison burgers — low fat, no cholesterol — Dave said, "Sounds to me like Mr. Diaz has developed a powerful hankering for snacks from his homeland."

Jason was preparing an Indonesian vegetable salad, mixing Chinese celery cabbage with some lightly steamed green beans, a sliced raw carrot, couple of tomatoes, and one of the cucumbers I'd bought at Bobby Tew's. His opinion: "It might be for a group of migrant workers, or perhaps even as the clerk said, some fishermen."

"True, it could be either of those," I agreed, using a very long, very sharp knife with a serrated edge to slice a loaf of onion-dill rye fresh from Carolina Country Breads. "But then again, it might not. So far, it's our only lead. Besides, there's a mitigating factor."

They waited breathlessly.

Well, maybe not breathlessly, but I made them wait anyway.

"I talked to the Ax. Feron Simmons has a sheet. Nothing heavy, just lengthy, since he was twelve, thirteen. Petty larceny, grand theft auto, assault on a pickerel . . . "

"What?" said Jason.

"He thinks he's funny" — from Dave.

"Anyway, Simmons is a punk. Mean punk, but still a punk. He's on probation right now."

"That pickerel thing?" said Jason.

I smiled, to show I appreciated his appreciation of my wry wit. Finished cutting the bread, then arranged the thick slices on an oval platter, overlapping. Julia Child. "Toss the potatoes in the microwave," I told Dave.

"Aye-aye, Cap'n. You want your Bambi-burger done medium, right?"

"Don't *say* that," said Jason, wincing. "I'm having trouble enough convincing myself to eat one as it is."

"You'll eat a pig or a cow or a turkey, you'll eat a deer. No difference," Dave argued.

"But a deer's so . . . "

"Cute?" said Dave.

"I've heard this argument so many times," I butted in, "it makes me nauseous. 'It's okay to kill something if it's ugly, but not if it's cute.'" I said, falsetto.

"I know it sounds silly, but that's the way I feel," Jason said.

From Dave: "It doesn't just sound silly, Jason. It *is* silly." He spatulaed up an eight-ounce patty, nicely browned, and laid it on a nest of paper towels to soak up what little grease there was. Then another, and another.

"Besides, don't you think a calf is cute? Or a woolly sheep? You'll eat veal, or mutton, won't you?"

Jason put the salad and its tangy sauce on the table, in two Tupperware bowls, side by side, one small, one large. I placed the bread platter beside them and sat down.

Jason said, "Point taken," then leaned over

slightly, hugging his side, and took a deep breath.

"You okay?" I asked.

"Pain mostly comes and goes."

"But now it's mostly come?"

He nodded. Dave came up behind him and helped him to a seat. "You aren't so light on your feet," he jibed.

"Ha-ha," said Jason.

Then we ate Bambi.

★ ★ ★

"How you planning to work this tomorrow?" Dave asked.

"Since Fanner is on my case about Marquis of Queensberry, I'll carry no hardware on my person."

"You're the bait. What if someone tries to shoot you?"

"You won't let them," I said.

"I'll have a gun?"

"You bet."

"Oh."

"Fanner didn't warn you, threaten you with jail, Davo."

"He wouldn't mind my carrying, then?"

"He'd clap you in irons."

"Better me than you, huh?"

"You have no recently-turned-five-year old."

"Far as you know."

"So" — from Jason, sitting on the couch chewing aspirin — "what if you snare this gentleman, and he's the right fellow, but he

277

won't tell you anything?"

Dave and I smiled at each other.

Jason raised a conciliatory hand. "Stupid question."

"Don't worry," I reassured him. "We probably won't have to hurt him."

"Then how . . . ?"

"Little trick I learned in-country," said Dave, reaching into his shirt pocket to withdraw a cartridge, then tossing it over to Jason, who caught it deftly, one-handed. He examined it.

"It's a bullet. A big bullet. You're going to shoot him with a big bullet to get him to come clean?"

I said, "It's a cartridge, the copper-and-lead thing there on one end is the bullet. But the answer is no, Dave isn't going to shoot him with that cartridge. Look at the head of it, where the letters and numbers are."

He did.

"See that deep cavity?"

"Yes."

"That's the primer pocket. Normally there would be a primer there, facing downward toward the inside of the case, with a silver cup filling the cavity. When the trigger of the gun is pulled, the firing pin strikes the primer, igniting the powder within the cartridge, which then burns very rapidly and kicks the bullet down the barrel."

"But there's nothing in the hole. No primer, no little silver cup or whatever," he protested.

"Right."

He thought a minute. "So if there's no primer,

what sets off the powder?"

"You tell me?"

"Nothing. It won't fire," he said, looking over at me for confirmation.

"Right," I agreed. "It's a dummy round."

"What's it for?"

"Intimidating a dummy," said Dave.

32

IT was warm, sunny, and noon when I again pulled into Bobby Tew's place. Dave was already there, sitting on a picnic table over in the shade next to a row of U-Hauls. He had on a yellow windbreaker, despite the heat, to cover a Smith & Wesson .44 Magnum, six-inch barrel; blued steel, not the faddish stainless version.

Dave's a traditionalist.

He was imbibing Dr Pepper from a can, his sunglasses trained on a close-cropped brunette with long limbs, an aqua halter top, and a navel that would hold an olive. A casual observer would think he was ogling the pulchritude as she filled the tank of her Dodge Ram truck. Not so; he was watching me closely out of the corner of his eye as I entered the shop.

"Well, hey there, bub" — from my pal behind the counter.

Smiling a greeting, I noticed immediately that the Mexican beer and provender were not in sight.

"Feron been here already?" I asked.

He took a fifty out of his shirt pocket, waved it at me, saying, "An' he pays a helluva lot better than you do," then stood there smirking. I wrestled down the impulse to reach over and slap the smirk off his face.

"When did he come in?" I said, in lieu of violence.

"Early this mornin'. He was real interested in exactly what you look like. After I told him, he allowed as how he'd come back to see for hisself."

He looked out the window. "Here he comes now."

I walked out into the harsh light. A man bearing an uncanny resemblance to a common vegetable stood off to my right, tapping a tire iron against his leg. Before me approached a more abbreviated specimen, a bit taller than me but no muscle tone, broader through the hips than the shoulders.

"Mr. Simmons?" said I, friendly as a pup.

"Hey, spooge lips," was his return salutation.

Short on manners, but colorful.

"Are you aware that you're shaped like a zucchini?" I asked.

"Up yours, scumwad."

Obviously into reproductive metaphors.

"And he" — I indicated his partner with a tilt of my head — "resembles a parsnip."

"Mr. Resovic wants to see you" — from the parsnip.

I looked over at him. "Great. Where is he?"

"We're gonna take you to him," said Simmons.

"Let's go then" — from me, Mr. Agreeable.

"First we're gonna soften you up a little."

I smiled at him. "Just the two of you?"

Not liking that, he drew himself up, but adding a half-inch to his height and sucking in his soft belly did not transform him into a threatening presence. He didn't know from

281

threatening, so he tried for mean. "After we beat the shit outta you, pissweed, we might go see your little boy."

Wrong thing to say.

From deep within me a flash of red, fleeting, molten, intense.

I hit him so hard and so fast he didn't have time to blink, his head snapping clockwise from the blow, twisting, body following, falling facedown onto the blacktop. The parsnip raised his tire tool and took two steps, putting himself within range. I side-kicked him at the base of his throat. He said "Ack" and slammed backward into a garbage can, the back of his head impacting the side of the building, oil from his hair making a slick as he slid downward.

I took a deep breath.

The red haze disappeared.

"Yo, Anglo."

To my left, from behind the store, a Latino stepped into view. Not Diaz; too short, only five nine or so, but thick, maybe one-ninety. This one was no pussycat, like the two at my feet. More like *el tigre*. His left eye was milky, no visible iris, and a deep scar traversed it diagonally.

He waggled a finger at me, as in "Come with me."

I glanced at Dave, gave a barely perceptible headshake, then went to commune with my new Hispanic friend.

Make that friends. Four more, similar in ethnic background and malicious intent. Some were taller with less meat relative to their length, some shorter and bulkier amidships. Fighters these, conscience-free, scars worn like medallions in various locations.

As I rounded the corner, they spread out into a rough semicircle, with Milk Eye closing the open end as I stepped into it. The back lot was graveled but hard-packed, solid under foot. Over against the building a stack of discarded shelves, an ancient popcorn dispenser, couple stacks of cinder blocks left over from an "improvement" project, some paint cans, pile of rotting two-by-sixes. No back door visible. I fixed my focus on the task before me.

The nearest man stepped up to the plate with a twelve-inch length of lead pipe that appeared from nowhere, intending to dent my cranium. I blocked the blow with a jodan-uke — outside forearm block — and countered with an extended-knuckle punch to his solar plexus, rolling away a little when he doubled over to deliver a roundhouse kick to his temple. It landed with a sound not unlike that of an adz sinking into soft pine, and piled him in a heap at my feet, the side of his neck exposed. To avoid further trouble from this gentleman, I dropped to one knee and applied a hammer-hand to the aforementioned area, feeling ligaments and tendons yield beyond their normal elasticity, *crunch!*

One down.

Here came the others, all grim and martial-artsy, rotating their heads to loosen up, work out the kinks before reducing this gringo to whimpering mush. Milk Eye stayed back, shrugging his massive shoulders like a constipated crab. Stocky. Strong. Stolid.

Implacable.

The scar through his eye had turned white as his face deepened a shade from excitement, anticipation.

Here was The Man of this group.

El jefe.

A lean, swarthy specimen moved in from my left, attempted a thrust kick with his back leg, aiming for my kidney. Too slow. I blocked it with my left arm. His mae-geri having been turned aside easily, he tried a spinning back kick with the opposing leg, executing nicely. Still slow, though. I again blocked with my left, then reverse-punched him in a kidney — drawing a grunt of painful appreciation — following with a leg sweep that dumped him on the gravel, hard. My ax kick to the bridge of his nose finished things so far as he was concerned.

As I recoiled into an on-guard stance, one of my new pals sucker punched me, aiming for my temple but finding an ear, snapping his wrist sharply on impact. This rang my chimes and knocked me off balance. I had no choice but to duck low, swivel toward this dirty dealer, and strike upward to his ribs, driving with my legs as I punched. As he staggered back from the blow, I leaned right and smashed a hooking back kick to his jaw. He dropped like a brick, so I immediately turned to greet my next challenger, now advancing in a swirl of rapid punches, Bruce Lee style.

Two can play that game.

Negating his furious attack with combinations of low-cross, forearm, and palm blocks, plus a few basic dodges and weaves, I let only one of his punches get through; it landed solidly on my chin. Chimes again, but instead of moving away like he expected, I closed the gap, a little surprise in store.

One of the most difficult but impressive demonstrations of jeet kune do mastery is the one-inch punch, developed by my immediate opponent's obvious idol, Mr. Lee himself. The strike is not trickery, as Bruce demonstrated very effectively more than once, in real life. I'd worked hard on the blow for years, but had never used it against an adversary. Now was as good a time as any. I held my right fist vertical, cocked at the wrist, then socked the man's floating ribs while I was still in close, twisting my hips for added thrust, snapping my wrist upward on impact. The effects were not only impressive but instantaneous. My attacker's mouth flew open, causing the abandonment of his vigorous attack in order to suck air for a second before resetting his defence. A second was all I needed. I grabbed his left wrist with my left hand, jerking him toward me while simultaneously striking sharply with a back fist, my right hand whipping up and across to bust him on the snoot. His head bounced. Then I jerked him forward again — still holding the wrist — this time driving my forehead into his unprotected nose, hearing bone give, a scream bubble. Backing away slightly, his wrist still locked tightly in my left hand, I used a palm-heel strike to put him to sleep.

Four on the ground, but one woozily trying to get up, still potentially dangerous. I danced a quick shuffling sidestep to my right, then launched a side kick, my left knee bent slightly, leaning backward for balance, pivoting on the ball of my left foot, twisting my hips an instant before full extension to gain power through the twisting movement, snapping my foot just before impact for a whipping effect. The kick impacted the rising man's spheroid bone, between the ear and the eye. Lights out.

Applause.

Applause?

Yes. Milk Eye, aloof from the action, stood clapping, wide grin on his swarthy face. He genuflected, as if he'd sincerely enjoyed my performance . . . admired it . . . found someone worth his effort, a suitable adversary.

Well now.

He bowed once again, formally, Orientally, then with a guttural exhalation snapped into a horse stance, legs wide apart, side by side, fists at each hip, palms up. That might bode well; it's a strong, solid stance but, some opine, a bit slow.

We'd see.

I assumed a jeet kune do on-guard position, a semicrouched stance with legs fore and aft, arms up near my chin, similar to a conventional boxing position. Milk Eye moved in, tried a front hand-snap punch at my face, which I checked with an outer forearm block. He hooked his left foot around mine and unbalanced me briefly, then connected a reverse punch to my chest, knocking me back a step, opening me up for a feint at my head. Caught off guard, I deflected the feint with my right arm, then blocked a straight left aimed at my eyes with the same arm, following up with a reverse of my own directed toward his anvil-like chin, which he speedily blocked, sending me off balance yet again, this time to the right, exposing my left side. He landed a hammer-hand to my ribs that vacuumed my lungs, then, my weight moving forward, followed with a roundhouse kick to the back of my head that slammed me to the ground.

I rolled out from under a stomping boot, regained my feet, and poked a finger jab at him, easily blocked but altering his momentum, enabling me to reset. As I did, like lightning he switched to a cat stance, unusual for a thickset man. *The Karate Kid*, I thought fleetingly, then chided myself for losing focus.

Losing focus with this guy could get my head handed to me.

I dodged and weaved, sidestepping, dipping, then a forward shuffle, retreat shuffle — doing my Bruce Lee impression. Negotiating a forward burst, I covered the eight feet separating me from my adversary in about three quarters of a second, sweeping upward with my lead hand for momentum and distraction, landing on my left foot, performing a side kick with the right, whacking him on his oyster-colored eye, snapping back his head. He retaliated with a flying side kick that missed, thankfully, then a flurry of punches, many of which connected, but none doing much damage until one slipped through my defences and split the skin along my cheekbone.

That pissed me off. I went low, reverse punch to the groin, pain bringing Milk Eye down low too. Springing up, I executed a spinning blade kick that put him in the dirt, shaking his heavy head to clear it.

Couldn't have that.

Front jump kick as the tough bastard started to climb back to his feet, catching him under the chin and snapping his head back with such force I thought for a moment it was all over. Not yet. Still on his knees, he took my next kick on crossed arms, protecting his face, then lumbered upright, blood streaming from his mouth as he spat something to the ground — a small section of tongue, bitten clean through. I danced some more, bobbing like a cork in stormy seas, sweat sluicing, dust in my nostrils. Darted in with a forward punch to his nose, back out, shuffling, weaving; in again, ridge hand to the side of the neck, taking a damaging left in return as he shuffled back out of reach. He still had some juice.

I reset and went back at him, side snap kick from a neutral position, connecting high over an ear. Did it again, then as he was toppling, a back kick this time, mulelike, looking past my shoulder to make sure of my target, *whap!*

And down he went, slow motion, like a short thick tree, full-length in the dirt, bloody, beaten, legs splayed.

There I stood, chest heaving, hurting in a

dozen places, staring at the man at my feet. "Hell . . . of a . . . fight," I said, ears ringing from blows to my head. "Just me 'n' you . . . when it came . . . down to it," I rasped.

"Don't think he can hear you."

There was Dave, holding Simmons upright by the loose skin at his jawline, below the ear.

I walked unsteadily over. "Where the hell" — gasp — "were you?"

"Inside making sure your clerk buddy didn't invite the police to our little party."

"He agree?" I wheezed.

"I brought him around to my way of thinking."

"How long before he'll wake?"

"Four, five minutes."

I looked at Feron. "Didn't soften me up much, did you?"

Simmons, still groggy, said nothing.

Dave nodded toward Milk Eye. "He did, a bit."

I glanced over at the Latino, prostrate in the bloody dirt and heat. "Did, didn't he?" I agreed, then walked over, picked up the unconscious man in a fireman's carry, and set him the shade.

Back in front of Feron Simmons, I said, "That one's too much hombre to leave lying on the sod. You're not. Where's Resovic?"

"Kiss my ass."

"Your pluck returneth. David?"

Dave flung Feron into the discarded shelving like a puppet, unzipped his jacket, withdrew the big .44 Magnum revolver. Feron's eyes grew large.

Snapping open the cylinder, Dave dumped the six cartridges into his palm, then into a jacket pocket. A little sleight of hand and one reappeared, the dummy.

The dummy on the ground didn't know it. "Hey," he said anxiously, as Dave inserted the cartridge into a chamber, spun the cylinder, closed it, cocked the hammer, and aimed the muzzle at the end of Feron's rather bulbous nose.

I squatted on my heels, head level with Mr. Simmons's, and reiterated, "Where's Resovic?"

"Fuck — "

Instantaneous *click!* of the falling hammer.

"Hey!" cried Feron, trying to jerk his head out of the way.

Dave popped open the cylinder, spun it again, slammed it shut. Pointed at our captive's runny nose.

"Quit it, man, I don't — " Feron began.

I grabbed his shirtfront, held him still, said through my teeth, threatening as all get out, "Where . . . is . . . Resovic?"

"I can't tell — "

Click!

He squirmed so fiercely I had to slip behind him and gain a choke hold.

Eyes big as hubcaps, he watched Dave snap open the six-gun, spin the cylinder once again, close it with a flip of his wrist, Hollywood style. Theatrical, but effective.

He pointed the muzzle, cavernous from my and Feron's point of view, and cocked it once again. The nose of the cartridge was not visible from where we sat. That meant it was either at the bottom of the cylinder, hidden by the frame . . .

. . . or directly under the hammer.

If I could see that, so could Feron.

Holding him tightly, but not so tightly as to stem the blood flow through his carotid artery, I said, "Where's Resovic?"

He looked once more into the muzzle of the gun, then gave such lucid directions Cullen could have followed them.

33

FERON SIMMONS and the parsnip were in the back seat of Dave's car, securely bound (duct tape) and gagged (more duct tape) and probably very thirsty, which couldn't be helped. While at the store, we'd called McElroy. He wasn't at his office; his car phone was out of range or unattended; his pager yielded no response.

Axel Mershon, however, had been standing by. A call to his cellular brought the squeal of his tires within minutes. He agreed to babysit my Hispanic buddies, lest they remember urgent business elsewhere. The three of us stood in the parking lot discussing options.

"If we call Fanner, he'll just arrest Resovic, let the criminal justice system deal with him," was Dave's view.

"He'd have no choice," I concurred.

"We sure as hell do," he said.

"You bet."

The Ax said, "You guys just go ahead. I'll sit on these wetbacks till you call or come back, don't care if it takes till Christmas."

So here we were — in a grove of trees about a half mile east of the farmhouse in which Feron claimed Resovic awaited our arrival — scrutinizing the place with binoculars. We'd brought along Simmons and his partner in case they had been disingenuous. Nearby, a crow

292

kept divebombing a rabbit carcass, plucking at its eye sockets, then alighting on a fence post to bemoan our presence. After a moment's raucous cawing, he'd repeat the procedure.

"As I see it," I thought out loud, "our primary problem is that you and I can't surround this place by ourselves, make sure no one slips the noose. If we go in and are spotted, there they went."

"Unless they're setting us up."

"True. This whole routine could be a trap. Or Resovic and Diaz might have a contingency plan in case those two bozos in the car botched their mission."

"Can you imagine a mission those two ol' boys *wouldn't* botch?"

I considered. "Good point. Why would Resovic send that pair to do anything more important than fetch grub?"

"At least they had competent backup. Those roughnecks would have trampled anybody else. Except me."

"And John Wayne."

"That goes without saying."

"You know," I went on, "my sparring partners just might have been the main event. Maybe Feron was there to finger me, so the Chicano Quintet could move in to extract Resovic's pound of flesh. Maybe things are getting too hot for him. Maybe the cops are closing in."

"And maybe his gun deal is coming up."

"Too many maybes."

"So," Dave said, "what's the plan, skipper?"

I sighed. "We still have to check the house."

"Then let's get to it," he said.

"Screw containment, maybe we should just take the car. If we go in by the driveway, we'll block egress in that direction, if anyone is there. I don't see an off-road vehicle, though there could be one in the barn. Can't see them trying to bulldoze that Nova through the kudzu."

"Egress?"

"Writer talk."

"Oh."

"Let's move."

From the trunk of my car, I removed my Benelli 12 gauge and a high-capacity 9 mm, which I shoved into my belt, right side, next to the hipbone. More secure there, in case I had to chase somebody, or dive behind a parapet. If I ended up using my guns, I'd probably also need McElroy's clout, or a very good lawyer.

Or both.

I circled around by the barn; Dave came in from the garage side. The house was one story, red brick at the front, vinyl siding on the other three sides. The roof had recently been reshingled; the driveway was littered with the resulting detritus. A doghouse rested in the shade of a maple tree. No dog, just a twenty-foot length of chain snaking out from one corner, choke collar attached.

Where was the dog?

I stepped into the barn. The smell of rotting flesh assaulted me, seeming to come from a large freezer. Walking over, I noticed its cord lying in the dirt, unplugged. No outlet to plug into. The stench was overpowering, but I opened the freezer's lid. And immediately wished I hadn't.

Two cadavers, both elderly, a man and a woman, each shot in the head. Holding my breath, I eased the lid back into place.

Pausing at the barn door before crossing to the north corner of the house, I saw Dave low-crawl out of a patch of weeds I wouldn't have thought could conceal a wharf rat. He disappeared around the south edge of the building as I made my run to the rear of the house.

With my back to the wall, I sidestepped along, peered in a window, sill at eye level. Kitchen. No one in sight. Stepped onto the back porch — screened, an ancient Maytag washer, no dryer, divan, straight-back chair, dust mop in the corner, cluster of pottery ready to be glazed, three empty cereal containers, litter box. Where was the cat?

I went in the back door as Dave came through the front, gun out.

Nothing.

No dog.

No cat.

No Resovic.

There was a telephone over by the TV on its own stand, the wire cut. Stink of ashtrays, beer, dirty dishes, toilet where men had urinated inaccurately and often.

Several magazines printed in Spanish were strewn on the coffee table, a pretty pastoral scene on the cover of one, low-country farm with a grape arbor.

Nothing else.

I went to call Axel.

Then Fanner.

Shit.

34

DAVE and I returned to Bobby Tew's Bait, Tackle, and Karate Shop to phone Fanner. We then stashed our weaponry in the trunk of Axel's Subaru and took charge of the tough guys, all of whom were in varying states of surliness and disrepair, and none of which made any difference to Dave or me, since they were securely duct-taped. Right before I placed the call to Fanner, I spoke intimately with my friend Milk Eye, whose name turned out to be Ralph Gonzales.

How come Resovic wasn't at home, waiting for us? I queried.

Probably because I wasn't supposed to be taken to the farm, but beaten to death right where I now squatted on my heels in the sun, Gonzales told me.

But Feron Simmons had indicated otherwise, I argued.

That ignorant gringo *pendejo* didn't know his anal orifice from an excavation. He was just there to finger me, him and his chowder-breathed crony, neither of whom could extort lunch money from a kindergartner, was the answer I got.

So Resovic was no longer at the old people's house when these five were dispatched to take care of me? I delved further.

El jefe had left yesterday with his bodyguard,

the formidable and vicious Hector Diaz, for parts unknown, I was informed.

And their pay for stomping a mudhole in me was to be secured how?

They'd been paid in advance, one thousand American, each. With that I got a look, and the comment, "For jew, eet should hab been twinny t'ousan'."

Did they do this kind of work often?

Yes, mostly going from place to place, keeping the migrants in line. Sometimes they accompanied illegals over the border, to stave off trouble.

Was he emotionally or philosophically attached to his comrades?

No. His group changed composition constantly. He didn't even know the names of two of them.

Why had he not entered the fight sooner, when his considerable skill might well have turned the tide against me?

He spat at my feet. I had insulted him. Obviously that wasn't his way of doing things.

I untaped him. He stood and looked at me, hard for him since his one good eye was puffy, nearly closed, leaving only a very narrow slit for vision. "I am bery good. Jew should not hab take me so easy."

"Easy? You nearly handed me my head on a plate."

He smiled, kind of; his lips weren't working properly. "Chure I did. I had four hombres to make jew ready, an' steel could not take jew."

"I lucked out. Look, you got five minutes

before the police arrive."

"And them?" He waved an arm at his compadres.

"They tried to kick my ass, for money. They can rot in jail, or be deported."

"I too tried to kick jour ass."

"To see if you could, not for money."

Again the sort-of smile, then, "*Vaya con Dios*," and he turned and walked into the woods.

★ ★ ★

Lieutenant John T. Fanner was not entirely happy with me. Not even moderately happy. He was in fact moderately miffed.

"After your little scuffle, who watched over these hooligans while you and Mr. Michaels checked out the house?"

"Several rolls of duct tape."

"And if they had broken loose and phoned to warn Resovic?"

"You ever try to get loose from duct tape? And the phone wire at the house was cut. Besides, one of the bad guys told me that Resovic had flown the coop. Dave and I went to verify it. He had."

"And what if you had been misinformed?"

"Then we'd have come right back here to call you."

"I am sure you would. And what if Resovic had set a trap for you? I am certain that you were not armed, therefore could not have shot your way clear."

"Of course we weren't. Didn't need to be. We

observed from a distance, using binoculars."

He glanced over at my prisoners. "Are you filing charges?"

"Absolutely."

"Right now, down at the station?"

"Sure."

"What about the clerk?"

"Accepting bribes from opposing factions?"

Fanner snorted, spun on his heels, and walked away, barking orders.

Soon we all went to the police annex.

*　*　*

It took hours and hours to handle the mound of paperwork at the police station-cum-annex. When Dave and I finished, I was worn out, had a black eye, the cut on my face was throbbing, and I was famished. So I went home to three peanut-butter-and-jelly sandwiches, a quart of two-percent, and a half-dozen Oreos.

I'm into exotic cuisine.

Then twenty minutes of news until I fell asleep on the couch, wondering what we were going to do next.

*　*　*

I didn't have to wonder long.

The phone woke me up. It was McElroy, excited. "We've got the bastard!" he exclaimed. "Or will have soon."

His exuberant mood was contagious. "So tell me."

"Not on the phone. You never know where a little bug may be lurking. Besides, I'm on a cellular. I'll meet you at the Bojangles on Battleground in fifteen minutes."

"Why not here at the house?"

"Walls have ears. This is hot stuff. Don't want to lead with our chins here."

"All right. I'll buy you a biscuit."

"We won't be staying, just leaving your car. We'll go elsewhere for breakfast, ensuring our tail is short."

"My treat, then."

"You're on," he agreed, and rang off.

★ ★ ★

We went to Shoney's for the breakfast bar after stashing my car at Bojangles. McElroy was so excited he could barely contain himself. After he'd filled me in, I was too. The gist of the conversation went like this:

The cash Resovic and crew had liberated from the bank was laundered drug money bound for a representative of a Bosnian Muslim faction who was to use the funds for a major arms purchase. The guns and ammunition were to be smuggled later into Bosnia-Herzegovina aboard a Red Cross shipment en route to the beleaguered and arms-embargoed Muslims in Sarajevo. Resovic had made the arrangements, agreeing to supply the arms and specifying the bank to which the money was to be wired for withdrawal by the Muslim delegate and his outriders, who would guard the considerable sum until the day of the gun buy. Instead, Resovic had intercepted the funds. Still intent on purchasing the guns — now with Muslim-supplied capital — and selling them to a different end user, bolstering his profits substantially, Resovic had enraged the double-crossed Muslims, adding to his reputation as a big-time wheeler-dealer to whom no hoodwink was too bold. It was a good plan. The Muslim contingent, unable to seek assistance from American authorities since the origin of their money was hazy, cast about in a frenzy, searching for Resovic, who meanwhile was busy trying to wreak retribution on one Tyler C. Vance for killing his brother and nearly foiling his dirty scheme.

Sources within the CIA and the BATF had narrowed down the prospective gun buy to three possible locations, only yesterday settling — through information extracted from a Serbian informant — on Florida's Dade County. The deal was to be consummated by exchange of cash and materiel on Friday next, or the guns would be sold to a backup purchaser already in line, dough in hand. Whatever else he was, Resovic wasn't a man to let a petty vendetta interfere with a multimillion-dollar deal. Thus, McElroy's sources reasoned, he had to show up in Miami personally, to oversee the orderly transfer of money for armament and the secure though illegal exportation of his illicit acquisition before returning his attention to making life hazardous for Mr. Vance.

"You mean to tell me he'll be in Miami this coming Friday?" I said, disbelieving.

"That's the word. And our source is very close to the horse's mouth. Guy like Resovic makes a lot of enemies."

"Do they know where the buy will take place, who's providing the items for sale?"

"BATF's working on it."

I thought about that, and other things. Voiced one niggling worry: "Something really puzzles me."

"And that is?"

"Why Resovic is so deeply involved himself, instead of having a faithful lieutenant perform his dirty work. We think we can place him in the bank at the time of the robbery. Now he's conducting an illegal arms transaction in person. Why does he expose himself needlessly?"

"Word is he does it for the thrill. We know he's got tons of bucks in several Swiss accounts, not to mention one or two offshore in this hemisphere. He should retire, right? Not Resovic. He's a hands-on kinda guy, loves to cheat and steal and swindle, see how far he can push the envelope against the law, other crooks, the world."

"So far he's been pretty successful," I said.

"Damn straight."

"Think I'll stick a rod in his spokes, see how hard a spill he can survive."

"Bingo."

"Can you get me in? And Dave?"

"I'm working on that."

"I have a contact in Miami, assistant district attorney. Will that help?"

"Can't hurt."

"I'll make a call."

"Do it. We don't have much time to get this show on the road."

We finished breakfast; Rufus returned me to my car; I went to make my call.

35

WE were at the Tarwheel Skateway just east of Asheville — actually in Swannanoa, Highway 70. Picturesque place. Cullen was on the hardwood floor with Stephen Sandford. Literally, the two of them entangled and laughing, buttocks or knees in contact with the unyielding surface. Dave and Web, obviously more experienced skaters, were circling at a good clip, Web with his arms out to the sides for balance, Dave just gliding along effortlessly, as he did so many things. Cullen helped the sergeant to his feet, or Sandford made it appear so, and they started off again, confident as two penguins in a logrolling contest.

Heather, carrying two Slushies, joined me at a booth — lime for me, goodness knows what for her. Red, whatever it was. She took a bite, made a yummy sound while watching our kids and their consorts.

"Cullen and the sergeant really hit it off," she said, her smile lighting up the room, for me anyway. "Look at them."

"I have been. The more attached they become, the safer I'll feel while I'm in Florida."

"Florida?" she said, eyes locking on mine. "What's happened?"

I filled her in. Afterward, she said, "You remember I said I wanted in?"

"Sure, but you can't go all the way to Miami."

304

"Why not?"

Well? Why not? I thought about it and couldn't come up with a plausible reason.

"We can get a motel room at a Holiday Inn or someplace similar. I'll run errands for you," she continued. "Look, this scumbag tried to have my son killed. I want to be near when you get your hands on him, hear the sordid and explicit details firsthand and fresh."

"Bloodthirsty wench."

Her face went hard. "It's my son we're talking about. And yours. You telling me you don't long to feel your hands at his throat?"

"More than anything I can think of."

"Well then. Besides, I can give you back rubs at night, keep you loose and stress-free."

"In a hot tub?"

She batted her lashes. "Wouldn't want to distract you from your work."

"It won't. Just keep me loose and stress-free."

She turned to watch the skating. We held hands, consumed our Slushies — my tongue growing cold and clunky in my mouth — and watched the boys at play. Michael Jackson's voice surrounded us: "Heal the World" at 110 decibels. Which was okay; I liked the song.

Colored lights, sounds of gaiety and rollers and the announcer over the public address system, advising us of an impending limbo contest.

How *low* can you *go?*

Resovic was about to find out.

Next day, an exchange of goodbyes at the Goodall farm, once again. Dad shook my hand, squeezed tight. "Come on back, you hear? I'm too old to take care of a little boy."

"No, you're not." I squeezed back. "But I'll be back, all right. You be looking for me."

"Every day."

Even Ethyl gave me a hug and a quick kiss, although most of her attention was devoted to Cullen.

To Lawrence Goodall, I said, "You don't know how much I appreciate — "

"Shush. None o' that," he interrupted. "Things'll be all right here, never you mind. Keep your thoughts where they need be, on that there Valentine feller. Grease his trolley and git on back. Your boy'll be waitin' right here. Safe and sound. I guarantee."

"Thanks, Lawrence. I mean it."

Cullen walked over. I knelt and hugged him hard. "How long will you be gone?" he asked in a small voice.

"Little less than a week, I hope."

"You've never been gone that long before."

"I know. And I wouldn't be now if I didn't have to."

"You're going after that bad man I heard you talk about, aren't you?"

"Yes, sweetheart. I am."

"You 'member you promised not to leave me, like Mommy did?"

"I remember."

"You always tol' me to keep my promises, right?"

"Right."

He leaned back and looked me in the eye. "So you keep yours." He hugged me again, tighter this time. Scared.

Me too. For him, not me. He'd have a long few days.

But at the end of that time, Resovic would be out of his life for good.

Or so went the plan.

★ ★ ★

Back in Greensboro, I called Fanner for an update. He had none.

We filled the Suburban with needful things, then climbed in — Dave, Heather, Rufus McElroy, and me. Jason took Nubbin to his place; I hoped his cat got along with dogs.

Then off for Miami, and points south.

36

WHEN Heather and I exited the River Parc Hotel, it was just before five in the afternoon. We walked toward Bijan's Fort Dallas Restaurant, where we were to meet my friend, the local assistant district attorney, a representative of the Bureau of Alcohol, Tobacco, and Firearms, and a suit from the Dade County Sheriff's Department. Dave stayed in the room, guarding our gear and gobbling shrimp à la room service. McElroy had gone ahead to the restaurant to make arrangements for our fete.

Heather held my hand as we strolled, pointing out a barge negotiating the nearby Miami River. It was filled with bicycles, to overflowing.

"Probably two tons of guns and ammo beneath those velocipedes," I said.

"What makes you think so?" asked Heather.

"Why not? Those boats are almost never checked by customs. Resovic could run a bargeful of A-bombs out to the ocean, let alone a few guns and grenades. Who's to care? They'd be on their way out, not in."

"In is tougher?" she queried.

"That's what I hear."

As we approached the restaurant, three well-groomed, professional-looking individuals stood waiting. I recognized the assistant DA immediately, despite the two decades since we'd last stood face-to-face. The years had been kind: no grey in the dark hair; relatively unlined face despite countless sun-drenched hours playing volleyball on a Miami beach; still trim, not going to seed, no telltale thickness in the middle. Dark suit, expensively tailored, two-piece, pinstripe.

The trademark lopsided grin was in place, and the square-shouldered go-to-hell body language. Mischievous glint in the eyes. I grinned back, offered my hand.

"Twenty years of nothing but letters and an occasional phone call and you stick your hand out at me?" came the response. Then, "C'mere," grabbing me roughly by the shoulders, pulling me in and kissing me hard on the mouth. After a moment, she leaned back, looked me over, asked, "How you been, stud?"

"Still got the tattoos?"

She laughed throatily, leaned forward, and whispered, "Both of them. Now shut up. Folks around here know not of such things."

The taller of her comrades, who looked like Paul LeMat doing James Dean, cleared his throat.

"In a minute, Braithwaite," said the assistant DA, turning to Heather. "You must be his sister, or possibly his accountant. You're too classy, attractive, and intelligent to be linked in any other way to this buffoon."

Heather displayed her perfect teeth and extended a hand. I said, "Heather Patterson, meet Lisa Craft Jamison. Lisa, Heather."

"I'm very pleased to meet you. What's this about tattoos?" said Heather.

Lisa shot me a look, answered, "Sorry. Privileged information," then turned to introduce her associates, Gerald Braithwaite of the BATF and Detective Jim Johnson of the sheriff's department. McElroy came over and herded us to a couple of wooden tables pulled together and surrounded by matching chairs. We sat, ordered our tipples from an engaging brunette in shorts and a Fort Dallas T-shirt, and scanned the menus. After settling on my order, I scanned our few fellow diners, all of us seated outdoors. I scrutinized the concrete floor.

"What are you looking for?" asked Lisa.

"Bugs. Especially those nasty fire ants I read about."

She chuckled. "They don't allow them in here."

"Never been to a picnic without a few ants to liven things up," I replied, then turned my attention to Debbie, our waitperson, who had returned with her order pad.

"Since the fodder is reasonably priced," I said, "I'll spring for these ladies and the guy with the buzz cut. These other two gents are on the government dole. They can pay for their own. By the way, can you take an out-of-state two-party check?"

"For amount of purchase only."

"Think my tab will run forty-five hundred bucks?"

"Only if you're a very generous tipper."

"Depends on the service. Now, what do you recommend?"

We decided on the conch fritters, Heather and I, followed by blackened redfish for me — slaw and fries — and mussels marinara for Heather. Bouillabaisse for Lisa. McElroy ordered Buckets O' Peel & Eat Shrimp (all in caps on the menu). We talked and ate and requested key lime pie for dessert.

"Debbie?" I said, as my portion was placed before me.

"Yes sir?"

"They forgot to put the green food coloring in my key lime pie."

"I'll speak to the pastry chef."

I poked at my plate with a fork, shaking my head. "I'm not sure I can eat pale yellow key lime pie."

Lisa made a grab for it. "I can." I speared her hand with my fork. She pulled back, rubbing it and saying, "You just assaulted a member of the bar. I'll have Jim here arrest you."

I leaned over, spoke into her ear. "He know about the tattoos?"

She whispered back, "Of course not. I'm respectable now."

I smiled at her, taking in her metal-rimmed glasses, the brushed-back hair, the sensible shoes. "You always were. Sometimes you just forgot to act like it."

I'd met then-Spec-4 Lisa Craft in the Korean DMZ, never mind how. She'd had a tough time after leaving the Army in 1976, but managed to return to college a year later. Married a used-car salesman in Chicago in '81. Moved to Florida to go to law school away from the cold and the wind and the snow, her salesman coming along. They were in love. Years of too much

311

studying, toeing the academic line, her husband, Larry, selling Volvos to yuppies and middle-class married-with-children, twelve hours a day, no time to start a family of their own. She was hired by a law firm that worked her to death, again leaving scant time for Larry.

In the mid-eighties, the tide turned a little. Both were making real money — Larry was now a sales manager — but long days still ruled. No kids, but talk of them anyway. Soon as they could find the time.

In 1986, while skiing with a Miccosukee client of Lisa's, Larry was hit by a powerboat piloted by a drug runner fleeing his third bust. Distraught, Lisa nonetheless had the presence of mind to have a urologist insert a needle into her comatose husband's vas deferens and remove a sample containing tens of millions of live sperm. The sperm were frozen in nitrogen and stored in plastic vials. Larry died two days later. By means of in vitro fertilization, Lisa bore two beautiful boys, one in 1987, the other in 1992. She was a devoted mother.

And there she sat, with her secret tattoos, brash manner, fine brain, and recently acquired authority. Two decades ago, she'd helped get me out of a fix. Now she was going to help with another one.

There is no substitute for friends.

* * *

After the victuals, a skull session.

Johnson briefed us. He had dun hair, took a

312

size 36 jacket and 44 slacks, wore Weejuns that had never seen polish, and had a complexion not unlike that of a link sausage. The air when he spoke smelled of oyster and vermouth.

"We have no idea where Resovic is," he said.

"Then we're in agreement. Neither do I."

"We've located the location of the gun buy, and expect to locate the guy in charge of the exchange, who is well known in this locale."

I did not make that sentence up, am quoting verbatim. I looked at Heather. Her mouth hung open. Repeticular shock, I suppose.

Unabashed, I forged on. "What will you do when you, um, locate this guy? Watch him, squeeze him, replace him with one of yours?"

"We plan to monitor the buy location and move in when the deal goes down," answered Johnson.

"Can you grab Resovic as soon as he shows up?"

McElroy said, "No warrant."

"Aren't the Fibbies looking for him? Bank robbery's federal, is it not?" I said.

"Not enough evidence to place him at the scene," offered the BATF man. "No one can positively identify him. We know he was there, just can't prove it. That's why the FBI isn't represented here this evening. They're leaving it to us Treasury types, and the locals." He cringed slightly upon uttering those final words, and seemed about to recant them.

Johnson again. "We've covered the airport, train depot, bus station, similar entry locations, but we've failed to locate Resovic as yet, and don't really expect to. We figure he'll come by car or truck. Tougher to locate him that way, so long as he avoids a traffic stop."

"What if he doesn't show at the gun buy?"

"He'll show," said Braithwaite. "He's too do-it-yourself-if-you-want-it-done-right not to. And he doesn't know we nabbed one of his lieutenants. Nobody does. We managed it on the QT, for once. He won't be warned. He'll show."

"Hope you're right."

"I am. You'll see. He'll show."

"Who gets him when he does?" I asked.

Lisa said, "We'll share, depending on how many rules he breaks when we move in to take him. If there's resistance, traffic violations in a getaway attempt, whatever, it will merely add to his account. The BATF will bring weapons charges, and the FBI may well decide to pursue the bank robbery aspect, depending on the information we acquire from whoever we net."

"Can I have five minutes alone with him?"

Lisa smiled, sharklike. "Not even five seconds, stud." She touched my arm. "I'm not privy to specifics about your military background, but I once saw you toss a big, tough Special Forces noncom around like he was a ten-pound sack of Martha White cornmeal. I heard stories, unpleasant ones, about you while I was in Korea. If we allowed you to get within arm's length of Resovic, you'd snuff him like a cheap cigar. McElroy filled me in on your recent escapades up in North Carolina, and I feel for you. Were I you, I'd want to make sure he didn't beat the system and walk, for my own peace of mind. If it were up to me, I might let you have his sorry carcass. It's what the bastard deserves. But it ain't up to me, so don't you try anything, at all, or your only son's daddy might wind up in a Dade County jail. Okay?"

"Can I at least watch the bust?"

I didn't like the way McElroy was looking at me.

She smiled. "Sure. From way back, and unarmed. Not even a slingshot."

Returning the smile, I said, "I wouldn't know how to use one."

"The hell you wouldn't."

She was right.

★ ★ ★

"You gave in too easy, old hoss," McElroy opined as we walked back to the hotel.

With her eyes, Heather agreed.

"At least I'll be on the scene. Who knows what could happen? He might make a run for it. I'll maybe have to make a citizen's arrest."

"Careful, or these South Florida cops are going to stick you in a cell," McElroy said.

And Resovic in the ground, I thought, but didn't say so.

37

"WAS the restaurant tony?" Dave asked upon our return.

"I suppose," I responded. "But I was disappointed. Didn't see Madonna."

"I did," Dave said. "On MTV."

"If I'd known you were going to watch MTV, I'd have made you go with us."

"Saw some Live, too. Thinking about doing that ponytail thing with my own hair."

"You'd resemble a pomegranate with a rope tied to it."

"How about dreads, like ol' Adam Duritz of Counting Crows."

"You'd have to take up the harmonica."

Heather looked back and forth, from one of us to the other. "What in the world are you two talking about?"

"You don't like alternative rock?"

"I can stand Weezer," she admitted, somewhat sheepishly, "if I have to." She retreated to the bathroom.

"'Happy Days!'" I said joyously.

"I loved the Fonz," she quipped, slamming the door.

Dave and I sat beside fresh coffee (Bed 'n' Breakfast), with me bringing him up to speed on the situation. "So what's our next move?" he asked.

"I'll try to get them to take me along on

316

a surveillance. Once I know the setup at the transaction site, I'll figure a way for one or both of us to get inside."

"Unseen by the police."

"Preferably."

"We likely to get in much trouble if we're caught?"

"Presumably."

"Get yelled at, threatened, tossed in jail?"

"Probably."

"I like it."

"Thought you would."

He hesitated. "We in agreement that Resovic doesn't walk away from this deal?"

"We are."

"No matter what?"

"No matter what."

"Any ideas as to how we might manage that without drawing attention to ourselves?"

"You bet."

"Don't keep me in suspense."

I didn't.

The more I explained, the more he grinned.

Directly, Heather rejoined us. Upon hearing my plan, she didn't grin. But her eyes grew large, and she licked her lips in carnivorous anticipation.

38

THE building was on the north side of Miami, squat and run-down and deserted. Huge. Only one other edifice stood within a quarter-mile, and that was another large abandoned warehouse. From the second storey of that adjacent building I now viewed through a pair of Pentax 8×50s the exterior of the warehouse in which Resovic was to exchange cash for weaponry on the morrow, if our information was correct. Rusted hinges, broken glass, rotting window casings, one curious crow pecking at something in the parking lot. No sign of human activity more recent than the first transatlantic flight. I panned the glasses away from the setting sun. A thin finger of trees extended from a densely wooded area to within fifty yards of the dilapidated peripheral fence, which was ten feet high and concertina-crowned.

"Can't see a lot from here." I addressed Detective Johnson.

"Don't need to. Only one way in, and one way out. For large vehicles anyway. You can't carry off a shitload of guns and explosives without large vehicles, now can you?"

"How about a big chopper?"

He obviously hadn't considered that. After a moment, he said, "They'd have to load it outside. Soon's we saw the copter, we'd move in. They'd never have the time."

"Any way to narrow the time frame tomorrow?"

"Friday's all we know. Don't worry. If they show, we'll nab the lot."

"You certain your source is reliable?"

"CIA says so."

"They have to squeeze the guy hard?"

"Way I hear it is money changed hands."

"One of his men sold Resovic out?"

Johnson nodded.

That wasn't what I'd been told, and I didn't like it much. Didn't feel right.

"How'd they find this guy?"

"I hear he just turned up, hand out. Claims Resovic did him dirty on a deal, something like that."

I grew even less happy, more apprehensive, as the afternoon dragged interminably.

* * *

Eight hours later, Dave and I negotiated the thin line of trees in the dark, dropped to our bellies, crawled to the fence. We were all-over black, from our clothes to the grease on our faces.

"You sure those gents don't have night scopes?" asked Dave as he cut the fence, *snip!*

"I didn't see any."

"Doesn't mean the night crew might not have brought some along."

"Quit griping and cut faster."

"Just keeping up my end of the conversation.

Wouldn't want you getting bored."

"Bored?" I said. "I'm so wired my navel's knotted."

He cut the last strand and pushed a section aside, allowing us to slither through. Inside the fence, we crawled the last fifty yards to one corner of the warehouse as fast as we could on knees and elbows. Once around back, we'd be on the dark side of the moon so far as observation from the adjacent building was concerned, although I had no way of knowing whether a cop or two might be stationed inside the woods to our left. If so, we'd likely be spotted entering the warehouse.

There was nothing for it but to go ahead. Using glass cutters, we removed a few panes of glass and presto! — we were inside looking out. I scanned the tree line, the roadway due south, the vacant parking lot.

Nothing. Even the crow was gone.

I went one way, Dave the other, searching the inside of the building, looking for a spot from which one or both of us could oversee the proceedings tomorrow. Dave had with him a newly purchased compound bow, a quiver of razor-tipped arrows, a blade that made Rambo's look like a paring knife. And his ever-present .40 Smith & Wesson.

I carried a silenced .22 semi-auto rifle, scoped, loaded with subsonic target-grade ammo. From fifty meters, I could put five bullets into a nickel, assuming I had a solid shooting position and a couple of seconds to aim. One in a man's ear or at the base of his skull was all it would take, while making little more noise than one of Dave's lethal arrows striking home. The plan was for us to nail our opponents without raising much of a ruckus, then slip away in the aftermath. It was the best I could come up with, given the situation.

In case things went awry, I carried my Browning 9 mm and four extra magazines.

My security blanket.

Linus, I'm not.

★ ★ ★

Dave had climbed up onto a catwalk twenty feet over my head for an elevated viewpoint when I spotted it in the middle of the floor.

An ancient Coca-Cola crate, upended.

Nothing else stood near the crate.

On top of the crate was a shapeless lump.

It was not there by happenstance.

Icy fingers played up and down my spine.

Over to the crate — knees so weak I could scarcely remain upright, the pit of my stomach a nauseous mass of seething, writhing worms — I walked.

Never, before or since, have I been so indescribably, uncontrollably stricken.

I scarcely breathed.

Could scarcely breathe.

Thirty feet from me.

Twenty.

Ten.

Oh God. Please.

I fumbled a small flashlight out of my pocket,

twisted its head, aimed the slender electric flame at the crate.

The object resting there was a yellow T-shirt.

Affixed to the shirt by a safety pin was a slip of paper with a phone number printed boldly in red. It also had a message . . .

. . . which I didn't need . . .

. . . because I knew the shirt . . .

. . . with the tag reading "Size — Boy's, Small" . . .

. . . the front saying: "YMCA Youth Baseball Program."

It belonged to Cullen.

The message said: "We have your son."

39

THE phone number was for an answering service in Fort Lauderdale. A pleasant senior citizen answered and read to me the following message:

The exact time of this call is now logged. You have precisely twelve hours to arrive alone at your home. Any deviation from these instructions, no matter how minor, will cause destruction of package we recently acquired.

★ ★ ★

My next call, from a pay phone near the interstate, was to McElroy's room at the hotel. He answered on the ninth ring. "I told you not to disturb me!"

I said, "It was a setup. They have Cullen."

He was silent for ten seconds. "How the hell . . . You positive?"

"No question."

Ten more seconds. "You calling from a pay phone?"

"First one we found. Northwest Hundred-and-seventh Street."

"How long until you get here?"

"Fifteen or twenty minutes. Traffic's light."

"Should I tell Heather?"

"No. I will."

"What you want me to do?"

"Get us to North Carolina as quickly as possible. I mean that literally."

I told him the situation.

"Son of a BITCH!" he said. "How? Tell me how!"

"It doesn't matter, isn't even important, not now at least. What is important is damage assessment and control. We need to be back up north ASAP."

"I'll arrange a jet out of Homestead immediately."

"For the four of us."

"If I have to route the request through the Pentagon."

"We're on our way." I rang off.

Dave drove because I couldn't. My hands were so shaky I'd barely been able to punch out the numbers on the phone. My breath came in short, ragged gasps.

Dave looked over at me, put a hand on my knee. "Hyperventilating won't help. You have to get a grip on yourself. I can appreciate that it's hard, but you've got to manage nonetheless. Dig deep, Cullen needs you.

"Think. Think hard, but only about solving the problem, not the problem itself. Don't dwell on what might be happening, only on what we can do to resolve the situation. If your dad's alive, and I suspect he is, he'll have found a way to protect Cullen."

Dave was doing all he could to reassure me, redirect me, accentuate the positive, keep me focused. My father might be dead. Resovic didn't need him to lure me in; he had Cullen for that.

What was my son doing right now? Was he hungry? Hurt? Scared? In despair? Worse?

I buried my face in my hands.

★ ★ ★

"Oh God!" shouted Heather. "OhGod! OhGod! OhGod!" She sank heavily to the bed, hand to her mouth. I sat beside her, held her to my chest, trying hard to keep us both from unraveling. Dave began packing for us. Deepening worry lines channeled tears down Heather's face.

I said, "Web should be okay. They've got no quarrel with you."

She looked up, said, "How can you deal with this? Look how calm you are!"

"Heather," Dave said, "he fell apart in the car on the way back. He's putting on an act. For you. Now I want you to put on an act for him. Because if we just fold up our tent, where does that leave the boys? They need us — *all* of us — functional. And functioning. Understand?"

She mopped up with a corner of the spread. "You're right. Absolutely right." She looked at me. "I'm sorry."

I gave her the best smile I could muster. Not much of one.

She stood. "I'll help you pack, Dave."

I didn't help them pack. I sat in a corner, facing the wall, plotting Resovic's downfall.

★ ★ ★

325

Lisa Craft Jamison stood in front of me on the tarmac, next to a C-141 Starlifter troop transport. She gripped my arms tight. "You get your son back, then kick that motherfucker's ass. Don't count on the cops with this. Do it yourself, the way Uncle Sam trained you. You don't and Resovic will pop up later, sure as hell."

"Yes, Ms. District Attorney."

"I mean it. I lost a husband, and nearly my mind. I couldn't take losing a child." She looked deep into my eyes. "Neither can you."

"I know."

"Wipe Resovic off the board, hear? You catch any repercussions, I'll use my pull, call in all my chits. If you get your tail in a legal crack, I'll come defend you, gratis." There was steel in her voice. "You hear me?"

I hugged her. "Seems like whenever I fall in a hole, you're there to pull me out."

"Go get him," she said, then turned and walked away.

At 0204 hours we lifted off from Homestead Air Force Base, climbing swiftly to thirty-five thousand feet. At 0436 our feet were on Tarheel soil.

My call to Fort Lauderdale would have been logged at 11:31 p.m., Eastern Daylight Time, by my watch.

I had just six hours and fifty-five minutes to find and rescue my family, and the most important part of Heather's.

I made the most of it.

40

WE'D set up our base of operations in the home of a cousin of my wife's, Willy Hawks, the only location I could think of that wasn't likely to be monitored by one of Resovic's thugs. It was just after six a.m. No one had slept.

The phone rang. Cousin Willy answered it. "Thank y'all for calling," he said, listening for a couple of seconds, then handing the phone to McElroy.

"Speak to me," McElroy barked; then he too mostly listened, interjecting an occasional short simple specific question. Holding the phone to his chest, he said to me, "There's been no outside activity, yet. My men have searched every wooded area within eyeshot of the place, including a knoll two miles away. Nothing. Each man has secured his particular area. No one can get in or out without being seen, and stopped or dropped if necessary."

"Okay. On to step two," I said.

He hung up to call Fanner, who at the moment was in a house just down the street from mine, surrounded by exotic surveillance equipment and a SWAT team. McElroy made a polite inquiry, got his answer, handed me the receiver.

"How's it look?" I asked Fanner.

"Quiet. Twice during the night we spotted a

pinpoint of light inside the house, probably a cigarette."

"Right. Step two is now in effect."

He hung up without saying goodbye.

An hour and four minutes later, one of McElroy's soldiers rang from up in the mountains. I took the phone from Cousin Willy. "Vance."

"Yes sir. There's movement outside the house. A short specimen, heavyset, wearing a shoulder holster with a big-bore auto, probably a SIG .45. No long gun in sight. These guys supposed to be any good?"

"Probably not your caliber, but let's not make the mistake of underestimating them. I doubt this is being run like a military operation. There may be a hired gun or two, but that type usually hits folks who are unsuspecting, and thus not likely to hit back. Which is fine by me. The lower the level of competence, the easier we can neutralize them, get to my son, my dad, the other hostages. Look out for the big Mexican and a lanky type with Elvis sideburns. The latter's the brains, the other's the heavy hitter, I'm told."

"Right, sir. I'll keep you — Wait! There's movement by the tractor shed . . . Yes . . . the sneaky shitkicker. Guy must've slept there all night and just woke up. Went outside to take a piss, then ducked right back in, out of sight. Sergeant Mueller may be able to get in close enough to acquire him. Gonna be tough, though. Problem is there's two small outbuildings which may block his view . . . " He was thinking aloud.

328

"There's an old twin-axle farm truck near the shed, and a blue van."

"If Mueller's good," I suggested, "bring him down the wooded west slope. That'll put him within thirty meters of the open back of the shed. Have him dig in like a tick and sit tight, but only if he's really good."

"He's very good, sir. He could crawl up that old boy's butt, given a little cover. I'll get back to you."

The hours dragged. Every now and then, the phone would ring, usually one of McElroy's men with an update. I called Fanner twice. Nothing new.

Ask anyone who's been in such a situation; waiting's the hard part.

Keeping my mind off what could be happening to my son was the even harder part.

41

IT was exactly 11:31 when I came up the walkway to my own front door.

I wore a lightweight nylon jacket with a 9 mm Browning P-35 under it, stuck in my waistband. A slender, sharp throwing knife rode in a scabbard at the nape of my neck. During training in Korea, I could draw and sink it point-first into an orange twenty feet away in less than a second, four out of five tries. Rusty now, I could still hit a cantaloupe, though it might take me a little longer. There was a chance the blade might go undetected in a hasty pat-down, so I'd brought it along.

After standing by the mailbox watching the house for a couple of minutes, I decided, what was the point? — I was going in regardless. Not sure what to expect, I rang the bell. No response. Tried the knob. Locked. I let myself in with the key.

Two steps into the room a voice stopped me. "Lose the gun."

"What gun?"

"If a gun doesn't hit the carpet in five seconds, I'm gonna splatter you all over the wall."

I counted to ten slowly, then stooped to lay down the Browning and straightened up. It's only in Hollywood that folks toss loaded guns around willy-nilly.

He stepped out of the hall, into the living

room with me, and pointed a long-barreled .44 Magnum revolver at my left nostril. "I told you to toss it, not put it down."

"You said five seconds, too. Have trouble counting in your head?"

"I'm going to enjoy popping your raggedy self."

"Only if someone holds me for you."

He took in a lungful of air, easing it out through his teeth. Good. It showed he possessed some degree of self-control, and had probably been told not to off me here. That meant I could prod him a little without his going over the edge and dropping the hammer on me.

Just as I began to ask, "What's the message?" the telephone rang. I nearly jumped out of my sneakers. He saw it and laughed. "Right spooky there, ain't you, boy?"

The phone again, *bbrrrring!*

"Better get that. It's for you," he said, still smiling, his crooked-toothed yellow grin dim in the weak sunlight filtering its way through the curtains. He was lean and serpentine, with a diamond-shaped birthmark distinguishing his acne-scarred face. He held the big Colt Anaconda negligently in his left hand, as if it spent a great deal of time there.

Bbrrrring!

He motioned with the Colt. "Answer it."

The nearest phone hung on the kitchen wall. *Bbrrrrin* — "Hello."

"Daddy?"

My heart sang. "Hey, babe."

"Can you come get me?" — in a small,

frightened voice. Trying to be brave.

"Very soon. Are you okay?"

"I'm scared. Strangers are staying here, and they hurt Paw-paw real bad . . . "

A new voice, adult, accented, spoke into my ear. "Come to farm. Leave now. Bring with you man who is there. Along dirt road leading to house someone will meet you, give instruction. My man there must be with you or your boy dies, everyone dies. If authorities come, everyone dies. If you try trick, everyone dies. You understand?"

"What did you do to my father?"

"YOU UNDERSTAND?"

With teeth set so tightly my jaws ached, I said, "I understand."

"Two hours." *Click.*

I hung up too.

Birthmark had moved up behind me. "We need to leave now to make it in two hours. I'll ride in the back, out of reach. Wouldn't want to tempt you."

I turned to face him. "Sure. Mind if I grab a quick Coke? I'm dry as a bone."

He stuck the muzzle of the big Colt right in front of my chin. "Fuck you, and fuck your Coke. If I already had my money, I'd — "

While his attention was on his machismo, I flicked up my right hand and grabbed his revolver, right where the cylinder sits in the frame. I held it tightly and hit him in the solar plexus with a short left that had all of my fear, strength, and frustration behind it. His breath left in a whoosh. Hurt but game, he yanked at

332

the trigger, the muzzle of the .44 still aimed at my face. But the trigger wouldn't budge; so firmly did I have the revolver secured in my grip that its cylinder couldn't rotate. As his knees gave way, I twisted the gun violently, jerking it free. He tried to resist, but my punch had removed his starch. Down he went and there he stayed, mouth opening and closing like a guppy lying beside a broken fishbowl.

I unloaded the Colt and put it in the refrigerator, the cartridges in my pocket. A quick frisk produced eight more rounds plus a wallet with a New Jersey license and fifty-three dollars, mostly in fives. The license claimed he was Leplin Carey.

After three or four wheezing minutes, he sat up and leaned against the fridge. His color was ashen.

"What's your name?" I asked conversationally.

"Eat shit."

I hit him on the bridge of his nose with the edge of my stiffened hand, crunching bone and showering us both with blood. Emitting sounds of outrage and pain, he reached for my neck, with both hands. I deflected the right and grabbed the left, turning it, separating his little finger from its neighbors then curling the digit inward so that its tip rested against his palm. I held it in that folded position with the thumb and forefinger of my right hand while he put his other hand to his nose, attempting to stanch the blood flow. Unsuccessfully.

"Listen to me," I said.

He still fretted with his nose. I applied

pressure to his finger, as if cracking a walnut. In spite of his battered nose, that got his attention.

"I'm going to ask you questions. You're going to answer them quickly and truthfully. If you don't, I will hurt you. The nose was for illustration."

His beady little eyes, dazed with pain, were on me.

"Now, what is your name?"

"Eat sh — " was all he managed, coherently anyway. His imperative expletive dissolved into a scream of pain as I broke his finger, ground the splintered bones under my thumb. The pain must have been excruciating.

I released his hand. As he clutched it to his chest, I grabbed his nose, slick with blood. He screamed again. Face-to-face, shouting to be heard, I said, "I'm not going to stop and no one is coming to help you!"

Letting go of his nose, I sat back on my heels to give it a few seconds to sink in. Then, "What is your name?"

"Leplin Carey."

"Have you been to the farm?"

He nodded.

"Is my father all right?"

He just sat there, bleeding. I jammed my right thumb into his open mouth, hooked it outward against his left cheek to keep from being bitten, and tried my damnedest to rip through. Heaving himself off the tiles, he clubbed at me with his right fist. I blocked that with an elbow, held him firmly in place by his cheek, then drove the heel of my hand into his ruined nose. His scream this time held not only pain but bowel-churning fear.

Good. Maybe I wouldn't have to hurt him any more.

I didn't. Over the next ten minutes, he told me everything he knew about the situation at the farm.

42

SEATED on my couch, Fanner said, "He gave you two hours to travel how far, one hundred miles?"

"Right."

He checked his watch: two minutes after noon. "Even with a Highway Patrol escort, it is very doubtful you could make that unless it is all interstate."

At that moment we heard the sound of a helicopter. A very powerful helicopter. "I'll make it."

McElroy left the room.

Fanner went on: "You want no assistance from any law enforcement agency whatever?"

"Correct."

"The Army has no jurisdiction in this."

"I'm sure a federal marshal or FBI agent will turn up."

"But only after the dust settles, I fear."

"It's not your neighborhood, Fanner. How many times did you tell me you couldn't help me when it *was* your neighborhood?"

He shrugged his heavy shoulders. "I cannot help it. I disapprove. I am a lawman, and I feel that apprehending criminals should be left to lawmen, not vigilantes, no matter how competent. If you get your hands on Resovic, he is a dead man. You should not be involved. You are insufficiently detached."

Dave said, following a sip of cocoa, "How detached would you be if it were a cop who was missing, or your own son? Would you veto your own involvement based on a lack of detachment?"

"We are not talking about me. I am an officer of the law."

"Oh, I see," I jumped in, "you can be 'insufficiently detached' and still shoot hell out of people just so long as you carry a badge."

"That is not what I mean."

"The hell it's not. That's *exactly* what you mean. It's the police mentality. Look at Waco and Ruby Ridge for examples. Cops think only they have the right to initiate shooting battles, no matter what the provocation.

"Well, you had it your way, Fanner. Now, God willing, I'm going to have it mine. Once, I did this for a living. The U.S. government signed my paychecks. It's like riding a bike. It'll come back to me."

Fanner just shook his head. "Of that I have no doubt. What if I retained you for questioning? That man we just arrested has a broken nose. You were the only one present when he received it."

"He broke into my house. Stuck a bazooka in my face."

"That is your story. I could quite reasonably hold you, if only as a material witness."

"Fanner," I said, "I really don't want to get crosswise with you on this, but you don't have enough men here to arrest me."

Dave said, "Or me."

Fanner looked at me very hard, growled, "Let me know how it pans out," then got up and stalked out, slamming my front door so hard the photo of my mother fell off its hook on the wall.

Five minutes later, I was flying again, this time in a very loud, fast helicopter.

★ ★ ★

"How many men?" — from McElroy, whom I could barely hear over the mechanical din.

"Carey said six, counting himself," I shouted. The vibration was making me queasy.

"Can we rely on that?"

"I impressed it upon him that if his information proved unreliable, he could expect a lengthy, private conference with me in his cell. While I was explaining that to him, I removed my throwing knife to pare my nails. I don't think he lied."

Dave yelled, "So, with one man spotted in the tractor shed, and the stumpy dude coming and going, that leaves Diaz and Resovic and whoever they plan to have meet you on the road."

"What worries me most," I admitted loudly, "is that the section of dirt road we're concerned with is one mile long, from blacktop to the farmhouse front yard, where it curves and climbs out of sight. The road is mostly bordered by woods, thankfully on one side only. If their guy is already in place, why hasn't one of McElroy's men spotted him?"

"That's been bothering me, too," agreed

338

Dave. "The most obvious stopping place is right after the final bend, about a quarter-mile from the house. You'll be out in plain sight. I'd've expected our soldier buddies to have that area thoroughly reconned by now, and have spotted the odd man out. But," he went on, "maybe he's staying inside the house until right before you're due to arrive. That would strengthen their defences should we toss a blitz at the farmhouse."

McElroy nodded, then yelled, "You could be right. Nonetheless, I'll get on the radio, put two or three guys to searching that stretch of dirt road. We need to find this jazbo. Can't have a loose cannon snafu the whole operation."

"Heather arrive yet?" I screamed at Dave.

"Yep. She called while you were, uh, interrogating the gofer. She's at the Mountaintop Restaurant with one of McElroy's men."

"How far's that from the farm?" shouted the colonel.

"Couple miles," Dave answered.

McElroy went up front to radio his squad leader, returning in three or four minutes. "We'll be there in less than half an hour," he said, glancing at his watch. "All we can do now is relax and enjoy the ride. We've hedged our bets as much as we can."

I sat back, but could neither relax nor enjoy the ride. I was too nauseous from worry and helicoptering. Something nagged, nibbling at the corners of my consciousness. All my life I'd had a sixth sense about looming catastrophe. It had saved my bacon more than once in Korea.

The night my wife died, I awoke sweaty and panicked from a sound sleep, heart racing, pulse pounding. It was a most unpleasant experience.

I wasn't sleeping now, but I felt sweaty and panicked. My heart was racing, pulse pounding.

Something was dreadfully wrong.

What had we overlooked?

43

WE landed on a closed-off section of the Blue Ridge Parkway five miles from our destination, out of hearing range of the farm. Eight minutes later, Dave, Heather, and I were finalizing plans in the little restaurant while McElroy made radio contact with his troops. Heather was saying, "I tanked up the Supra as soon as I arrived. I decided to carry the pistol here." She lifted the lower edge of her sweater, showing me the butt of the little 9 mm Smith & Wesson automatic. "I can get to it quickly without having to reach across my body."

I nodded my approval. "Remember, that's only for emergencies. You go right where I told you to, and stay there. You'll have a good view, at least of whatever happens out front. When it's over, one of us will come get you. Wait until we do, no matter what happens."

"I will. Promise."

McElroy joined us. "No luck finding the guy along the road."

"That means I'll have to drive on in, just like Resovic ordered. Oh well, have to play what's dealt. Your man getting dressed?"

"He's in the bathroom now. The shirt is still wet, but at least we got all the blood out of it. Why couldn't you have kneecapped the asshole? Not as messy."

"Must not have been thinking straight."

"Are the two of you referring to something unpleasant?" asked Heather.

"Very," I said, just as McElroy's man — a sergeant — walked in, dressed in the clothes I'd last seen on Carey himself. He was Leplin's size all right, but blond, freckle-faced.

He came over and held out a hand. "Good to meet you, Mr. Vance. Heard a lot about you. I'm York."

I looked at McElroy. "He kidding me?"

The colonel grinned. "Nope."

"Hallelujah," Dave said, climbing to his feet. "Sergeant York. Just who you need."

"I'll be on the left side of the road," he continued, "in the thick stuff uphill from the mailbox until I see how it's going. If you can't negotiate the hostages into the open, I'll crawl through the weeds to the north side of the house, wait to see how it breaks."

"I'll create as much of a diversion as I can, to give you time," I said. "Above all, don't let the shit hit the fan until we know where the hostages are."

"I'm gone," Dave said.

I got behind the wheel of my Supra. Heather climbed into the back seat to lie down. Sergeant York settled into the passenger seat, adjusted a baseball cap to hide as much of his face as possible, then lowered the sun visor, further obscuring his face from the front.

McElroy was behind me, at the helm of a battered Lincoln. We pulled off in tandem.

I'm coming to get you, son. Hold on.

342

44

MCELROY dropped back at the second curve, still out of sight of the farm but within less than a half-mile. He intended to slip up a steep hill and into the woods, then move as close as he could to the farmhouse while still observing the entrance road.

Just before the final curve, where the Supra would come into full view of the farmhouse a quarter-mile distant, a creek bed ran off to our left, perpendicular to the road. Its banks were about three feet high. I turned to Heather. "Remember to stay low. If you're spotted, that's the ball game."

She patted my head. "Fret not, dear heart. My son's in that house too. I will not, repeat, not, screw up. Worry about them, not me."

"Okay. Got your binoculars?"

She touched a lump under her sweater, beneath her breasts. "Right here, where they won't flop around or rattle against the rocks whilst I'm traveling on hands and knees."

"I don't anticipate your encountering the enemy. That decrepit feed shed offers very little cover and is far out of the way, a nonstrategic point. But you never know. Keep your eyes open. Except for the sergeant here, Dave, McElroy, and me, anyone on our side will be wearing camo fatigues. Bear that in mind — there's one guy unaccounted for. He could be anywhere."

"Bye," she said, patting my arm.

Sergeant York and I watched her safely on her way into the creek bed. "There goes a woman," he opined. "She's not scared a bit."

"Nope, but anyone who runs into her better be."

I shifted into first and we rounded the curve.

The farmhouse came into view . . .

. . . into bold relief, crystal clarity in the mountain air, sunlight streaming down from heaven onto the front yard.

In the yard stood a stately oak, its weathered branches extended beseechingly skyward.

The gnarled trunk of that ancient tree was twelve feet in circumference.

My son was tied to it.

45

FLOORING the accelerator, I fishtailed down the road, slewed into the graveled parking area of the yard, dust and rocks flying, and quit the car. York stayed put, not knowing exactly what to do. Cullen was sitting at the base of the tree, leaning back, legs crossed, head forward on his chest, the rope tied tightly around his middle. As I ran toward him, his head came up, tear-streaked and dirty.

"Daddy!" he yelled; then I was all over him and he over me, little arms around my neck, holding on for dear life. I felt for wounds, broken bones, examined every square inch in sight. He was okay physically. I reached around behind him, to where the rope was knotted.

"Don't even try to untie the rope," said a voice.

I glanced left, toward the southeast corner of the house, partially hidden by shrubs. Just inside an open bedroom window, a vague silhouette. On the windowsill something not so vague, the barrel of an M-1 Garand.

I said to Cullen, "Son, are you thirsty?"

The voice said, "He ain't been there thirty minutes. I give him a glass of tea 'fore I tied him up. He ain't hurt none, scared's all. He cried some, not a lot. Tough little guy, just didn't like being tied up. Kicked the fudge outen my knee, when I was just trying to make him more

345

comf'table. So I let him alone, come back in the house. Directly, the sun being so warm and all, he drifted off to sleep. Quit fussing over him. Boss man wants to see you, pronto. Go on in. I'll look out for the kid."

Cullen said, "Please don't leave me, Daddy. Please don't."

"Where's everyone else?" I asked him, low-voiced.

"Web and Grandma were in the den when they grabbed me and brought me out here. I fought 'em hard, Daddy. Hard as I could. That mean Payton slapped me in the face. That's why I cried, not because he tied me up. He's a liar. The big dark man is with Web and Grandma. I haven't seen Paw-paw since he hit him on his head real hard. He fell down and didn't move." He started crying softly. "Is Paw-paw dead?"

I pulled him to me. "I hope not. We'll have to see."

"I said pronto." The voice from the window again. "Is that Payton?" I asked Cullen.

"Sounds like him. Please don't leave me."

"I won't leave you, but I do have to go in the house and talk to the big dark man. Check on Web and Grandma. Look for Paw-paw. Then I'll come back for you."

"Promise?"

"Promise."

"You hard of hearing?" Payton yelled.

"I'm coming."

Rubbing Cullen's cheek with my left hand, I shifted my body a bit, moving between him

346

and the window. I dropped the throwing knife beside Cullen's left hip. He looked at it, then at me.

"Don't let him see you doing it, but cut the rope there," I whispered, pointing to the place he was to cut. "That knife is very sharp, so don't cut yourself. Do it as quickly as you can without letting Payton see. Then hold the rope in place with your left hand, so he'll think you're still tied up. Understand?"

He dipped his little chin.

"If you hear shooting, run to the milking barn, then out the back. Web's mother is in that run-down shed beside the creek. You know the one?"

"Yes."

"But stay here unless you hear shooting. If there's no shooting, I'll be back for you. And, son?"

"Yes?"

"If you have to run, run like the wind. Don't fall, don't look back. Just run."

"I will."

"I love you," I said, and left him, heading for the Supra.

"Where the hell you think you're going?" Payton yelled.

"To tell Carey to stay in the car. There's enough of you inside."

"Resovic said — "

"Screw Resovic."

Most of the car was obscured from the view of anyone in the house by the huge oak tree. I leaned on the windowsill, my head in the opening. "Can you see the window at the left front corner?"

"Only a piece of it," answered York.

"What are you carrying?"

"UZI with six mags, here in this bag at my feet. Standard-issue Beretta at the small of my back. Boot knife."

"Get out of the car, but keep the tree between you and the window, even if you have to climb out my side. Then just stand around. That's what Carey would probably do. Bring the UZI and the bag out with you. If you hear shooting, pepper that room. I won't start anything unless I'm sure no one is in there but bad guys. There's a Garand in sight. I don't know what else he has."

"That gives him only eight rounds to toss at me, then a slow reload. Piece of cake," York said cheerily.

"Love the confidence, but don't get cocky. Do him quick; you're pretty exposed here."

"You noticed that."

"Probably none of our people knows about him, at least his exact location. Hard to spot him in the shadows. He may well be their entire defense at this end of the house. They're spread pretty thin. So nail him."

"What do I do after?"

"Drop back to the milking barn, behind you. I'm sending Cullen through there and on to Heather. You're his rear guard."

"Nobody'll follow him."

I gave him a thumbs-up and headed into the house, noting that Cullen was already at work on the rope with one hand, thumping acorns with his other as a diversion.

Good boy.

I winked as I walked past him.

He winked back.

And kept on cutting.

46

THERE he sat, Valentin Resovic, like a monarch on his throne, in the same chair where Dave had worked on his miniatures, the harsh floor lamp above and slightly behind illuminating his heavy features. Across the room on the sofa, Ethyl sat holding Web in her lap, stroking his head. The boy's eyes appeared glazed.

Resovic said, "At last we are face to face."

"Yeah, well, yours isn't all that pleasant."

A fist the size of a mango came from somewhere and slammed into my head, knocking me over the coffee table. A glass of beer hit the floor. So did I.

I decided to lie there awhile, at least until the room stopped spinning, but such was not to be. The same huge hand picked me up like a bag of peanuts and slung me across the room into a wall. The movement must have cleared my head, because I saw before me quite clearly a monstrous face, large-pored mocha skin stretched tightly over heavy bone. A thin scar swept upward from one corner of the pear-shaped nose, disappearing into the scalp line.

A deep, grinding sound emanated from a mouth that seemed to have too many teeth, most of them pointed. The sound said, "Don' be disrespectfool."

I nodded in agreement.

"Jew hab keel hees brother."

"He tried to shoot — "

He slapped me very, very hard, then grabbed a handful of my hair. "Chut up. Talk when I say so."

I tried to nod, but with his meathook still entangled in my hair, it was difficult.

Resovic said, "Let him go, Hector. Watch woman and boy."

The menace moved away, but hovered so near I could smell his body odor.

Resovic said, "Sit down. We talk."

I sat in Lawrence Goodall's old rocker. My head hurt. My face burned. I had a cut on my lip. Aside from that, I was fine.

Resovic said, "You not only hard to kill, but hard to find. But my trick in Florida worked pretty good, huh? First you there, now you here. For my brother. You understand."

"Sure."

"You do not complain? It is not like American not to complain."

"I came here prepared to die, just as I presume you did."

The menace moved, feet heavy on the linoleum floor. I didn't need another rap on the head, and at this point I couldn't fight back, so I said, "Hey! All I'm saying is the truth."

Resovic raised a hand to stop Diaz. "You have brought authorities?"

"They're at both ends of the road."

Resovic slapped my face, hard. He said, "I told you no authorities. Now I kill all."

351

He slapped me again. My lip began to bleed in earnest. It was all I could do to stay in my chair, menace or no, but I managed.

"You kill us all and you'll die for sure. If all the hostages aren't out of here in five minutes, the Army will come in, for you. There's no media coverage, so they can do exactly what they want to."

"What if I keep only you?"

"That's the deal, you get me. They take the hostages and leave."

Resovic snorted. "They would not do as they say once hostages are safe."

"You'll have to trust me."

He slapped me again, rocking my head this time, opening another cut. I looked him in the eye. "You'll have to trust me on this too. If you hit me again, I'll kill you before your pet gorilla can make it across the room."

Resovic laughed. Diaz laughed as well. I didn't.

Resovic said, "Very good. I wonder how long you take such abuse. I am beginning to think you not much man. Now you show courage. Bravo!"

I said nothing, just bled some more.

Resovic said, "Here is how it will be. You will go out back and get van, bring it to front. We load hostages in van." He indicated Ethyl. "Then old woman drive away." He raised his hands, smiled. "No problem."

I wondered, belatedly, why they hadn't frisked me when I first came in. Neither of them appeared to be armed.

"Where are the other hostages?"

Resovic said, "In bedroom."

Ethyl shook her head almost imperceptibly.

"I want to see them," I said.

Resovic said, "When you come back."

"Now."

From somewhere within his clothing, Diaz produced a Walther automatic, *swish*, in about half a second. Fast, very fast. That was why they hadn't searched me; I hadn't worried them.

Diaz put the pistol to Ethyl's head and thumbed back the hammer for dramatic effect, unnecessary since the piece was double-action. Web watched. Ethyl showed no reaction.

Resovic said, "Get van now, or old woman die."

"Kill her," I said.

"What?"

"Kill her, then have him kill me. Then the authorities will come in and kill you and we'll all be dead. Look, you went to a lot of trouble to get me here, and I came in good faith. These old folks and kids are no threat to you, unless you fail to release them. You used them as the means to an end. It worked. I'm here, and I've arranged for you to walk away, assuming you can take me, which remains to be seen. Let's settle it, the two of us. Like men. Unless of course you plan to have your bean eater do it for you."

Resovic thought a moment, then nodded to Hector Diaz. The menace left the room. Soon he returned with my father, who was dressed only in his underwear, a filthy rag stuffed in his mouth, his bloody hands tied behind his back. I went over to him. He sagged against me, nearly falling, but Diaz held him up. I removed the rag from his mouth, raised his chin with my hand. The light was still there in his eyes. Hurt but defiant, my dad, and game.

"Why's he in such a state?" I asked Resovic.

"Like you, he has no respect. Hector had to teach him some."

I looked up at Diaz, taller than six and a half feet, roughly three hundred pounds of granite and gristle — despite his appetite for junk food — and said, "After I kill Resovic, it's me and you, *cholo*. If you have the *cojones*."

He grinned a mirthless grin. "Chure. Een a leetle wile. Jew and me, *amigo*."

I turned to Resovic. "Where are the others?"

"Others?"

"The old man, and the soldier."

He shrugged elaborately. "Casualties, my friend. You should be glad your tata is still alive."

I looked at Dad. He shook his head, eyes downcast.

"I want everyone on the front porch before I bring the van around. I'll cut my son loose myself."

Resovic said, "No problem."

"Come on, Ethyl," I said. She got up, carrying Web in her arms. Dad leaned into me, barely able to walk, and we hobbled out.

When all of us were on the porch, Resovic spoke to my back through the screen door. "Remember, we have guns on you, and not just those you know. There are others. You do not know where, so cannot defend."

"I'll do just as I said I would, as soon as I cut my boy free. Do you have a knife?"

The menace opened the screen door and tossed me a folding Buck, three-inch blade. I turned to Dad, whispered, "You as feeble as you let on?"

His eyes danced.

"Good. When it starts, go around the side of the house into the bushes. Dave's there somewhere."

"There's three besides those in the house," Dad told me. "Two outside, dunno where, plus the feller who went to fetch you."

"That one's in jail. The man over by my car is McElroy's. I'm going to cut Cullen loose, then go get the van."

Moving to the oak tree, I knelt beside Cullen, pretending to cut him free while I told him Paw-paw was okay. I took the throwing knife from him, slipped it into its sheath at the back of my neck.

Resovic spoke loudly from the front doorway. "Throw knife into grass where I can see, then leave boy there until you come back with van."

I considered. Would Cullen be safer where he was, covered after a fashion by Sergeant York's UZI, or around back with me? I had no gun, knew there was a gunny hiding in the tractor shed, and I'd no confirmation whether one of McElroy's men was in position to take him out. On the other hand, I wasn't completely

355

familiar with Sergeant York's skill level, and I was with mine.

I stood, tossed the knife well away from me, into the grass as instructed, and said, "Come on, son." He jumped as if he had a spring under him.

"I said leave boy!"

"We'll be back, Resovic. You think I'd leave my father?" I retorted, then turned, taking Cullen by the hand.

Walking around that building and out of their sight, with my only son exposed there beside me, was the longest walk I ever took.

47

"HOP in and climb over to the other side."

"What for? It's too hot to sit in there."

"We're going to drive around front to get Paw-paw and Grandma and Web. Go on, get in, quickly."

"It's broke," Cullen said.

"What's broken?"

"The van."

"No it isn't. Get in, get in!" I prodded him a little. "We don't have time for this!"

"Please don't yell at me," he said, clouding up as he climbed in.

"I'm sorry, but we have to go. Now, babe."

"This van won't go," he insisted.

"Son, we drove it to the store the day I left," I said irritably.

"I know. But after the strangers came, the big dark man spent a long time out here working on it. One day, the one who hit me wanted to take it and go for beer. The big mean one called him an idiot and said take the rental. What's a rental?"

I reached for the ignition key, ready to twist it. "A rented car. I'll bet this old heap starts right up."

"Then why wouldn't the big dark man . . . "

I didn't hear the rest. My mind was occupied.

357

Why would Diaz need to spend time working on a vehicle that ran perfectly? I took my hand off the key.

"Son?"

"Hmm?"

"Did you actually see the big mean man working on the truck?"

"Yes. Some."

"Could you see what he was doing?"

"Just working. Up there." He pointed toward the engine.

"Could you see what tools he used?"

"Nope. Sorry."

I thought some more, chewed my lip in concentration, but only for a millisecond, having found one of the splits Resovic had given me.

"I wondered," Cullen said, "what he was gonna do with the Play-Doh."

My heart skipped a beat. "Play-Doh?"

"Yeah. He had a big handful."

"What did he do with it?"

"Put it under there." He pointed toward the hood again.

My spine crawled.

At the open rear of the tractor shed, a man appeared, a pump shotgun held loosely in the crook of his arm. He looked at us questioningly.

Telling Cullen to get out of the van, I followed suit, stepping around front to open the hood. There it was, hidden low, nearly out of sight, wrapped around an unidentifiable engine component — unidentifiable by me anyway, since I'm no mechanic — a medium grey formless lump of plastic explosive. Maybe two pounds of the stuff.

Enough to clear your sinuses.

Level your block.

Protruding from it was a small cylindrical object with two wires running from the exposed end back to the explosive. A remote-controlled detonator. There were no other wires in sight. I could start the van, then drive it off a cliff and the bomb wouldn't explode. But Resovic could flip a switch on a sending device and reduce the truck and its occupants to a fine red mist from five miles away.

The guy with the shotgun said, "What's your problem?"

"Engine won't turn over. I'm checking the battery terminals."

"Hurry the fuck up."

Where was Mueller! He had a clear shot — why didn't he take it? Maybe he'd been told not to unless all hell broke loose.

Well then. I was on my own.

I needed a gun. A shotgun would be fine. Like the one that doofus over there was cradling so negligently.

"Can you jump in and give it a try?" I asked him.

"Try it your fucking self."

"Why are you being such an asshole? Resovic wants this truck around front. I can't help it if it won't crank."

"Who you calling an asshole? Come over here!"

Bingo.

I put my hands up, near my ears, and walked over, looking contrite. I hoped. At eight paces, he said, "Close enough."

I glanced toward the house. We couldn't be seen unless someone came outside.

"Now, who were you calling an asshole?" he was saying.

I turned to face him. "You, you nose-sucking gob of spit."

"Suck this . . . " he said, taking a step forward, raising the shotgun to chest level, one hand at the pistol grip, the other on the fore-end, intent obvious: the good old horizontal butt stroke, taught to basic trainees everywhere. Effective if you didn't telegraph it and you were very quick.

He did and he wasn't.

I concentrated on his left eye, focused, tunneled my vision as I drew the knife and flung it from me with all the force in my body. It missed his eye, got the cheekbone instead, perfectly point-on, driving through bone, slicing deep into his skull, piercing the brain.

He fell as if poleaxed.

Grabbing his belt, I dragged him into a corner of the shed and relieved him of his handgun, a monstrous Desert Eagle .41 Magnum autoloader, of all things; if I stuck that one in my belt, my pants might fall down. On a stool nearby were an extra loaded pistol magazine and a box of number one buckshot. I took those, too. I might have to fight this war by myself.

Running back to the van, I whispered loudly,

if that isn't a contradiction, "Mueller! Where the hell are you?"

Some bushes moved and a soldier appeared, camouflaged from head to foot, even camo makeup on his face. Leaves and twigs poked out from under his campaign hat, were sewn all over his fatigues. Toting his M-16 at port arms, he hustled over.

"You sleeping? Why didn't you grease that guy as soon as he stepped out?"

"Nobody told me to do that."

"Don't you have a radio?"

"Battery's dead."

"Come here, son," I said. Cullen popped up from behind a bush, taking in the soldier.

"Wow! G.I. Joe. He on our side?"

"You bet. I want you to go with him, into those woods. He'll take care of you while I finish this thing."

"I wanna go with you." Clouds again, lower lip you could dive off of. I knelt on one knee. "Listen, sweetheart. I have to go get the others. It shouldn't take long. Then I'll come right back for you."

He looked at the soldier. "He won't take me away from here, will he?"

I turned to Mueller. "Take him just far enough up the hill to keep him safe."

"Will do."

"Okay, honey?"

"I guess so." Still not entirely happy, he gave me a kiss, then followed Mueller into the woods and out of sight, safe at last.

48

WHEN I rounded the corner from the side of the house to the front, I stopped the van between the house and my Supra, blocking York from their view. I said, "I'm driving right through the front door. Soon as I hit the porch, Payton's yours, so keep him occupied. I neutralized the one out back. Mueller's got Cullen. Watch your ass," and floored it.

The back end of the van came around, dirt spraying out from under the rear tires as I spun the steering wheel counterclockwise, jumped the grassy verge, and gunned the engine, aiming for Lawrence Goodall's old house. At the right side of the porch, Ethyl had Web in her arms, Dad at her elbow. Diaz and Resovic were just inside the screen door — silhouetted by light coming from the rear of the house — as I roared across the yard, straddling the walkway. Dad grabbed Ethyl and jumped off their end of the porch. As they went, Diaz kicked open the screen door and aimed his Walther at them. They were still within his line of sight — and the porch still ten yards from my front bumper — when I poked the Desert Eagle out the window and cut loose, sending splinters flying from the door and its frame, blowing holes in the outside wall near Diaz's head. He ducked instinctively, getting off two shots toward Dad's little group, then bringing the gun to bear on me. Resovic opened up with a pistol of his own, starring my windshield. Too late. I rammed into — then onto — the porch, crushing it, then crashed through the doorframe, causing the roof to sag and scrape the top of the van as it lurched into the living room. Grabbing the shotgun off the floor, I hit my seat belt release, dove behind the passenger seat and out through the open cargo door. Diaz jumped toward the parlor after unloading his Walther into the van. Resovic had dived to the floor to avoid being run over, was just rising as I exited. He swung his depleted handgun, whacking me hard on the temple. I took the hit while moving, mercifully lessening its effect, but still tumbled head over heels to land flat on my back with my feet jammed against the piano.

As I lay there slightly stunned, still gripping the shotgun across my chest, the staccato sounds of big-bore rifle fire rattled down the hallway from the southeast corner of the house, undoubtedly Payton blasting at York. Resovic came across the room toward where I lay on my back — head aching from the bang he'd given me — poking a fresh magazine into his handgun, kicking a table out of his way. I shoved the muzzle of the shotgun at him and pulled the trigger, its roar deafening, recoil digging my fist into my stomach, the load of buckshot pellets barely beginning to spread as they struck his knee and smashed the patella, blood and bone speckling the floor. He dropped his gun, fell screaming and writhing. I rolled over to get up, just as

Diaz stuck his head around the front of the van and shot at me, his bullet impacting the linoleum near my shoulder, kicking up a divot as I planted my right elbow solidly and pumped six shells at him as fast as I could jack the slide back and forth, the thundering cacophony in this confined space momentarily reducing my hearing to nil.

With my hearing gone and my head throbbing and fuzzy, I looked frantically for Diaz. On my right, Resovic was still twisting like a beheaded reptile, holding his knee, moaning. I grabbed his pistol and went after Diaz. Just as I cleared the front of the ruined van, I spotted movement down the hall to my left, someone going into the bathroom. In hot pursuit, so did I, finding a short, squatly fellow trying to squeeze through the bathroom window. I grabbed a handful of his shirttail and hauled him backward, continuing the move with all my body weight behind it, slinging him into the bathtub. There he lit with a thud and a curse. "Payton?" I yelled and he yelled "What!" identifying him as the man who'd slapped my five-year-old son, then tied him to a tree.

I jerked him upright and slapped him, backhand with my left, his head snapping sideways from the blow, then forehand, like smacking a tennis ball, *whap!* — his head now jerking the other way, him hollering "Quit!" and raising his hands to ward off more blows, me having none of that, a rage rising in me, dropping the handgun in the corner, slugging him right, left, right, going to his midsection when he lifted his hands — the breath leaving his body in a rush — to his face when he dropped them, with him trying to slide down into the tub to escape the punishment, me grabbing his shirt with my left hand, shoving him against the wall, punching his face again and again with my right fist — DID . . . punch . . . YOU . . . punch . . . LIKE . . . punch . . . HITTING . . . punch . . . MY . . . punch . . . SON? — popping him hard, but not enough to induce unconsciousness — until his face was a pulpy mask bereft of sensation or awareness and my frenzy had abated.

I let him crumple soddenly to the porcelain at his feet; then as I turned away, reaching down for the pistol, the menace was there, slamming me hard with a right, following with a left to my ribs that snatched my breath, then an overhand right with nearly three hundred pounds behind it that sent me reeling through the doorway into the hall — not much maneuvering space there, so I scrambled crablike down the hall and into the living room, where Resovic had moved over against the piano — leaving a bloody smear — to sit unmoving, holding the ruined leg, his sweat-bathed face a mask of pain.

And then Diaz was on top of me, fist in my hair, twisting my head backward as if to break my neck, rancid breath hot on my face as I stabbed upward, felt his eyeball squish as my thumb found the socket, hearing as if from a distance his grunt of pain and anger. I brought my hands up to knock loose his hold on my hair — to no avail — so I spun catlike to face the floor, encircled his thick legs with both my arms and drove upward, tackling him high, near his hips, trying to overbalance him, doing it, feeling him spill over my back like an overbalanced sack of fertilizer, and continue on, still pulling my hair, taking me with him, nearly snapping my neck, his groin near my face when we landed, locked together, my scalp feeling as if it was being ripped loose, and there was his groin, inches away, vulnerable, so I pounded him there, once, twice, three times, like an adder striking, my fingers rigidly extended, his response being to cross his legs and twist my neck again, as if trying to wrench free my skull, but I went with it, crawling up his body, going for his huge neck, throat, locking my hands onto it, thumbs digging into the Adam's apple, his heavy-metal groan harsh in my ringing ears, his right fist hitting me on the side of the head, over and over, ineffectual because of our closeness.

Abruptly, he let go of my hair and flung me from him, ten feet through the air, into the parlor, me crashing into the television, knocking it over, Resovic shouting demonically KILL HIM!KILL HIM!KILL HIM! in the background, then Diaz was coming again, arms reaching to gather me up, and I scissored my legs to snag an ankle the size of a ball bat, jerking, then sprang to my feet when he dodged, ridge hand to the bridge of his nose with everything I had — no effect — then a spinning blade kick to the jaw that rattled the giant but didn't stop him, prompting me to cast frantically for a weapon, any weapon, but he was too fast, crowding in, towering, delivering a left that put me down again as if I'd never been up, then moving in for the kill until a voice said, "Remember me?"

My dad's voice.

From the kitchen.

He must have come in through the breezeway beside the old springhouse. He just stood there, bloodied and bruised and glorious and holding my Benelli 12 gauge.

"*Tu madre es puta!*" Diaz roared, lunging toward the living room.

He didn't make it.

The first load of shot took him in the left shoulder, spinning him away from the hit, exposing his frontal parts, which bore the brunt of the next two blasts, one to the upper right chest, the next spraying fecal matter all over the wall. He hit the floor in a sitting position, so hard he bounced; sat there frantically attempting to hold together the gaping hole in his abdomen from which spilled bloody loops of intestine. The look on his face was more of bewilderment than pain, as if he couldn't understand what was happening.

From across the room, Dad looked at Diaz dispassionately, then said, "*Adiós hombre malo*," as the big man slumped to one side. Then he walked calmly into the living room and surveyed Resovic. Over his shoulder, Dad said to me, "You okay, son?"

I walked over and stood beside him. "Never better."

"This fellow here planned to kill us all."

"Yes," I agreed.

Through his pain, Resovic managed to grin defiantly. "Someday soon. I will not stay in jail forever."

"You're right," my daddy said, and blew the grin off his face.

★ ★ ★

Three minutes later, in walked Dave, gun in hand. Dad and I were on the sofa bleeding together. Dave surveyed the carnage. "You two don't fool around. Is this everybody?"

"The child beater's in the bathtub, resting but still alive," I said.

"Want him to stay that way?" Dave asked.

"Reckon so. He's a minor player, I think. Besides, he may have a change of heart."

Dave went to check on Payton. In a moment he was back. "Nothing six months of plastic surgery won't fix." He examined my face. "Looks like you got some wear and tear too. Diaz?"

I nodded.

"Would you have taken him?"

"Who knows? Dad butted in right when I was beginning to get my rhythm."

"Fathers never just step aside to let you handle things on your own, do they?"

Dad smiled. "I would have, but I owed the big 'un for a bruise or two myself. No need him" — he indicated me — "havin' all the fun."

Dave looked at the messy hulk in the corner. "Looks like Diaz didn't have much."

"Had his fun earlier, beatin' on me. Knocked

368

out one of my few good permanent teeth, the son of a bitch." Dad touched his jaw tenderly. "Think I'll go over and shoot him again."

"Don't," Dave said. "It'll make my ears ring."

McElroy came in, gun in hand. Looked around. "Hope you nailed that bastard in the back corner. He shot York up pretty bad."

"Sorry to hear it," I said.

"That damned .30-06 full-jacket stuff went through your car's sheet metal like a needle through steamed okra. York took one in the lung, another in the thigh. Medic's working on him now. I saw Ethyl and the other little boy outside. Where's Cullen?"

"With Sergeant Mueller up the west slope. Your men all accounted for?" I said.

"Except Mueller. He hasn't checked in."

"His radio's battery is dead."

"How you figure that?" asked McElroy.

"He told me. After I put a knife in that jerk out at the shed, I called into the bushes for Mueller to come out. He did and I sent Cullen with him, up the slope in back of the house."

McElroy looked puzzled. "Mueller told you his radio battery was dead?"

I suddenly had a horrible sensation.

"Did you ever find the fifth man?" I asked.

McElroy shook his head. "Neither hide nor hair. We figured he saw where things were heading and took off."

I jumped to my feet, said, "Describe Mueller."

Dave said, "Oh, shit!"

McElroy said, "He's about six one, medium

369

build, blond hair like most Krauts . . . "

I didn't hear the rest. Dave and I were running out the door.

49

WHILE McElroy fanned out his troops, Dave and I began our search, beginning where I'd seen the bogus Mueller enter the thicket. Any trail would be tough to find in the thick woods behind the house, so heavy was the carpet of fallen leaves and debris, but here and there an occasional foot had slipped, leaving a telltale smear on the forest floor. After traversing perhaps a hundred yards, we topped out on a little promontory which offered a pretty good view through the trees to the house below. There we discovered a freshly dug circular depression in the rich dirt, about six feet in diameter by three feet deep. It was partially hidden by branches into which leaves and smaller twigs had been interwoven, making a rudimentary but effective sliding cover.

"Obviously this guy's an outdoorsman. He dug himself a hidey-hole, even made a lid for it. He could lay in it, covered up to his nose, and watch the house all day. So long as he didn't smoke or scratch his ass, he'd be tough as hell to spot," Dave said.

"Let's look for the real Mueller," I said, and we began a semicircular swing. Within two minutes, I found the body, stripped to his shorts, shoved underneath a blowdown beside a mountain laurel. There was a tiny hole behind his left ear, most likely a bullet's entrance, though it could have been made by a long pointed instrument such as an ice pick. I pointed to it when Dave came over.

"If that's a bullet hole, then this guy probably used a silenced piece," Dave opined.

"Um-hmm. Likely a .22 from the looks of the wound. Whatever it was, it had to be subsonic to silence effectively."

"What was he carrying when you saw him?"

"M-16. And a sidearm, but I didn't examine it closely. My mind was on other things."

"Well, maybe it isn't a bullet hole."

"Or maybe he left his quiet gun in the woods when he came out to meet me. What puzzles me is why he didn't just drop me right there, or pretend not to hear me when I called out."

"Resovic probably had him out here to cover the back door, with instructions not to shoot unless the shooting started. Maybe when you called out to him, he figured you knew Mueller was supposed to be nearby, and that you'd be suspicious if someone didn't show his face. Taking a chance that you didn't know Mueller on sight, out he trots. He likely didn't know exactly what was going on at the moment. After seeing you take his buddy out easy as pie, maybe he was hoping you'd give him a clue as to how things stood."

"I gave him more than that. I handed him my son for a hostage. His ticket out."

"Don't start beating yourself up over that. There was no way you could have known."

"Regardless, my stupidity took Cullen out of the pan and tossed him right into the fire."

"Right. It would have been *much* better for you to take Cullen with you in a vehicle that was filled with high explosives and that you intended to drive into a building, during which activity you were certain to be shot at by as many as three people, one of whom you knew to be armed with a battle rifle. Sure. That makes sense."

"I could have dropped him off with Sergeant York."

"Oh, York, yeah. Excuse me, but is that the same Sergeant York the medic is working on right now? The one shot to dollrags by a guy with an M-1 Garand, while he was crouched behind a fucking car?"

"Can we go find Cullen now?" I said, capitulating.

"Sure. Just lay off yourself."

We found one small track in a bald spot at the edge of the promontory. It led into deeper cover. We plunged on.

For twenty minutes we searched, often on hands and knees. And found nothing. Not a clue. Not a trace of anyone's passage. We returned to the last certain spoor — the footprint in the dirt — and began again, moving northwesterly in ever widening arcs.

Another half hour crawled by.

Nothing.

A few more steps, eyes to the ground . . .

. . . and there it was.

Bright red, glistening in the sunlight.

There, on top of a rock.

Easy to see.

It nearly stopped my heart.

I ran over to it, touched it with a finger.

A Gummy Bear.

Dave ran over. "What is it?"

I held out my hand, the red Gummy Bear in my palm.

"That boy never stops thinking, does he?" Dave said, shaking his head in awe.

I couldn't speak for the lump of hope in my throat.

"The Gummy Bear was lying on its back," I managed to say.

"So?"

"Its head pointed that way," I answered, extending a finger.

Dave was incredulous. "Ty, that's probably a coincidence."

I shook my head.

Within thirty yards, a broken twig, just at Cullen's height, something he could have done easily without drawing attention.

Two dozen paces farther, another Gummy Bear, lying on its back, ears pointing forward. A short while later, a wet swatch of leaves dug up by a child's toe. Then a tiny yellow rubber ankylosaurus, maybe an inch and a half long.

And so on.

Until we entered a big cluster of rocks edging a pine thicket. There the trail ran out.

Completely.

Maybe he ran out of Gummy Bears, I thought.

Maybe his pockets are empty, I thought.

Maybe his captor caught him in the act, I feared.

And broke out into a cold sweat.

50

CULLEN told me later:
He was scared some of the time   not all   the sholjure grabbed his wrist right after they heard a big crash down at the house   made him run as hard as he could up this steep hill   he fell twice but the sholjure jerked him up and made him run some more   he hurt his knee falling once   it bled but he didn't cry   not any   if he hadn't of had on shorts his knee prob'ly wouldn't have been skint at all   the sholjure kept stopping and looking back and all around   then they would run some more and stop again   he said why are you taking me away   you told my daddy you would stay down there   the sholjure said to shut up or I'll pop you one   he tried to think of a way to leave a messhage where his daddy could find it but he had nothing to write with   so he thought how his daddy had taught him about following a trail   what to look for   he figured he could leave a trail for his daddy to look for so   he did whenever the sholjure wasn't looking   then they came to a wire fence   the sholjure said to crawl under and not touch it or it might electricate him   so he crawled under very carefully   as the sholjure was crawling under the wire he jumped down this steep hillside and fell and rolled like a log just like at granma's house till he was dirty and

dizzy down at the bottom   the sholjure was
coming after him but he fell too   he heard
him say a bad word   and so he ran into the
woods and hid   he watched the sholjure when
he got to the bottom of the hill   the sholjure
didn't know where he had gone   but he was
afraid he had left tracks so he snuck deeper
into the trees and ran some more   after a
while he stopped to rest   he took his shorts
and shirt off and dressed up a little bush
to look just like a boy   that ought to trick
him if he sees it   he took off again and
soon at the edge of the woods there was a
green field   across the field there was a line
of trees   he didn't know where to go once
he reached those trees   then he remembered
the creek   it was beyond the trees down in a
kind of ditch   he could get down in the creek
and wade toward the house   the sholjure might
not see him way down in the ditch   so he ran
across the field and under a bob wire fence and
into the woods and down into the ditch   the
water was very cold and up to his tummy and
made his cut hurt   the rocks were slippery and
hard to walk on   he fell a lot of times   once
onto his hurt knee   he did cry just a little that
time 'cause it hurt so bad   no one saw him
though   after a while he climbed out of the
creek to see farther   there was the sholjure
pretty far away but coming after him   he
looked if daddy was at the house but couldn't
see much through the trees   he started to run
to the house then but was afraid the sholjure
would see him   he went back into the water

and kept going wondering what he would do if
the sholjure caught him   he had the little Swiss
Army knife his momma had given him when he
turned four   it was in his hand   closed of
course like she taught him   he didn't know
how to fight with a knife and the man was
too big   he just kept moving through the cold
mountain water toward his daddy . . .

51

WHEN I find the little turd, he thought, *I'm gon' break his neck. He went through there,* spotting some long-stemmed grasses that had been disrupted, trod upon, bent to one side. There were marks of slippage in the wet black mud leading to the water's edge.

Damn, it's hot, slapping at a horsefly, one of plenty. Not to mention fresh cow patties near about the size of sofa cushions. He jerked off the fatigue top — stupid-looking thing with leaves and twigs and shit, itchy as hell — and tossed it among the cattails. His orange T-shirt, pale from washings, was emblazoned with the creed:

I Don't Date Girls
Who Use
4-Letter Words
DON'T
QUIT!
STOP!

He eased into the water — which rose high and cold enough to send his balls right up into his belly, seeking warmth — and stepped away from the bank, rocks large and small underfoot causing him to teeter precariously, lurch to starboard as he headed into the current.

Kid couldn't a gone far. He's bound to be

tired. Prob'ly hiding in some bushes along the bank. I don't find him and Resovic'll hang my handsome young ass out to dry. A sudden flurry of brown caught his eye. He swiveled fast, at the hips, reaching for the rifle slung over his shoulder.

Fucking groundhog. The animal ran twenty yards and zipped into its hole. He let the rifle flop back into place.

"I find that kid, I'm gon' rip his arm off," he said aloud, squinting into the blazing sun, crow's feet and perspiration on his brow.

He didn't know how close he was.

Didn't know that fifteen feet away five-year-old Cullen Vance cowered in the shadowy weeds at creek's edge, hunkered down and shivering from fright and frigidity and fatigue, praying over and over, *Please, Jesus, don't let him find me. Please, Jesus . . .*

The man in the orange shirt and camouflaged face drew abreast, moved on past, eyes swiveling from bank to bank, searching, seeking . . . him.

And then the man was gone, round a bend, no further sound to mark his movement.

I need to wait, need to wait, need to wait . . . Cullen thought, but he couldn't any longer, his youthful patience stretched past endurance as he waded across, splashed up onto the bank, muted footfalls stirring the grass as his stout little legs churned, mud flying from his heels, heart pounding, his refuge in sight, the farmhouse, not so far . . .

. . . when a hand shot out and struck him from behind, spinning him around and down and

380

onto the ground — falling hard, lungs emptying from the force, terror naked in his eyes.

The soldier towered over him triumphantly, his leaf shirt gone, as Cullen tried to suck air into deprived lungs. "Try to get up and I'll hit you again, boy."

"Then again, maybe not," the woman behind him said. He turned to face her standing there, wet up to her crotch like he was, holding a small autopistol in one hand.

Look at that. The bitch is too dumb to hold the thing in both hands. Don't she ever watch TV? he thought.

What he said was, "You'll never hit me from there."

The woman took five long-legged strides as he unslung his rifle and brought it around, fumbling for the safety.

"How about from here?" she said, and shot him in the chest.

Twice.

Aftermath

WEB examined and sedated, Dad patched up, Sergeant York evacked to a West Jefferson hospital, Mueller's body recovered. A medic gave me Tylenol XIII or something, to sooth the headache Resovic had initiated with his pistol and Diaz exacerbated with his fists.

Cullen was warm, fed, asleep. The only mark on his body aside from a skinned knee was a half-moon cut from landing on a rock when the Mueller imposter knocked him flat. Heather had carried him all the way to the farmhouse. Dave and I, having heard the shots, met them there.

"Daddy! Heather saved me!" Cullen yelled joyously when he saw me, running into my arms. Once more he was hugged and kissed and carefully scrutinized by his father, and held tightly, so tightly he objected, "I can't breathe!" I put him down, whereupon Dad snatched him up and repeated the foregoing, Ethyl standing there tapping her foot, waiting her turn. Directly: dry clothes, hot food, bed.

McElroy made a few calls. The FBI showed up, stoically examined the blanket-covered bodies, migrated to the living room to posture and ask questions, receive curt, noncommittal answers, finally settling at the kitchen table with an iced-tea pitcher and a mess of fried apple pies, an indication that they were almost human.

I phoned Fanner and gave him enough details so he'd know the situation had been defused.

"Did you kill Resovic?" he asked.

"Not exactly."

"Diaz?"

"No."

"You did not shoot anyone?"

"Resovic, but just in the knee."

"Your shooting abilities are on the wane?"

"I was in a hurry. Another guy's a little abraded and contused."

"Your handiwork?"

"What can I say?"

"Good to see you were not totally idle during what must have been one damnable fray."

"Not totally, no. I took a short drive in a booby-trapped van, went hiking up the mountain . . ."

"Hiking?"

"Tracking, actually."

"Someone attempting to leave the scene?"

"Yeah. With Cullen."

"I suppose you dissuaded him."

"Heather did."

"Fine lady."

"For a fact."

"Both boys are well, then, and your father?"

"We're not certain how much trauma Web suffered. He's out of touch right now."

"Oh. A pity."

"Yes."

"Do not forget our other matter, when you get back."

"I won't. How is my pal Leplin?"

"He has been singing, despite your having deviated his septum. Two arrests have been made already, based on information he provided."

"Give him my best."

"Of course. He will be delighted to hear from you." He cut the connection.

★ ★ ★

I was sitting in Lawrence Goodall's old rocker, missing him, lamenting bringing terminal trouble into his life. Ethyl walked in from the kitchen and handed me a cup of coffee. I nodded my thanks. She stood there a moment, looking at the rocker, and me in it.

"He was a gentleman, God bless him," she said. "And he thought the world of you. Don't be too hard on yourself. Cullen was your primary concern, and this was the safest place you knew."

I intertwined two of her fingers in mine. "I know. But that doesn't help Lawrence."

"Diaz shot him, you know. Walked right in the front door there and shot a hole in him. For no reason. He fell over against the couch, put his hand on my knee and tried to rise, me trying to help him . . . " She had to pause. "Then Resovic shot him and down he went again. I got down on the floor to hold his head up. Odie ran down the hall from Cullen's room and Diaz knocked him out, just like that.

"Lawrence saw it, tried to get up to help. He simply couldn't. He pulled me close and said, 'Tell Tyler not to blame hisself, it's not his doin'.' Then he died. Right there." She pointed at the floor, crying openly now. "In my arms."

She looked at me. I squeezed her fingers. "He was right. It isn't your fault," she said.

"He's dead all the same."

"But you didn't kill him, and you'll do poorly by his memory if you shoulder the blame."

"I know."

"Grieve awhile, then get on with life," she said, her voice stronger. "For Lawrence."

I whispered, "Thanks, Ethyl," then sat for a long time, rocking.

* * *

Much later, Heather came in. We sat on the couch, arm in arm. She offered me some Coke. I declined.

"Web asleep?" I asked.

"Finally."

"What'd the doctor say?"

"It's too early to tell. Web was unresponsive to anyone until he saw me. Even then, he was withdrawn. Thank God he's not comatose like that little boy in *The Client*."

I nodded. Fishing for words of comfort to offer, I was too emotionally drained to find any.

I did say, "Thanks for Cullen."

"My pleasure," she responded, leaning against me. "I'm just glad that I saw him run across the lower pasture and into the woods. It was pure luck — I was headed for the road. Then I saw the soldier come running after him and thought, *What the hell is going on here?* So I went to see, wading in the creek at one point because I didn't know what to expect. I thought I might do well to arrive unannounced. When I saw the creep hit Cullen, and heard him threaten him, I decided the man was not with Social Services."

"How right you were."

"I expected killing him would bother me."

"It hasn't?"

She shook her head. "He was involved in kidnapping my son, murdering two men, and I saw him slug a five-year-old child. He obviously intended to shoot me with his rifle. No. It hasn't bothered me a bit."

We were silent a spell, enjoying proximity, the diminution of stress. Then she said, "I called my mom. Told her things were fine, we'd be home soon." She shook her head. "But things aren't fine. Web is . . . " She didn't continue.

"Don't despair. All of us will do everything we can to help him get through this."

"You want irony? He called my mom at three in the morning the day after we left. Told her he was fine and would be seeing her soon. And now . . . "

I hesitated a second, then asked, "He called your mother in the wee hours of the morning?"

"He told her he was having trouble sleeping, and that I had gone off for a little while. He said he missed his family."

"He knows how to call long-distance?"

"He carries a little wallet. Their phone number is in it, and mine, in case he gets lost in the mall or something. He likes to make phone calls, do the dialing himself. Show me how grown-up he is."

That explained a lot. I'd been puzzling over how Resovic could possibly have found us. So far, I'd drawn a blank. Now I knew. He'd bugged phone lines, including Heather's parents. Once a call came in, it could be traced — with the right device and connections — to its origin. Never, as long as I lived, would I tell Heather.

★ ★ ★

I was back in the rocker after everyone else had gone to bed, when Dave joined me, iced-tea glasses in hand. He gave me one. If everyone kept plying me with caffeinated beverages, my bladder would defect.

"Well," said Dave, "things didn't turn out too badly, all things considered. What puzzles me is how Resovic found this place."

I told him of my deduction.

"After all that careful planning . . . " He shook his head sadly. "Who'd have thought a little boy would get up in the middle of the night to call his grandma, and set off a chain of events that led to seven deaths? Maybe eight."

"York?"

He nodded. "McElroy just told me he isn't doing so well. But it's too soon to know."

"It'll be a long night for those men," I said.

"How're you feeling?"

"Delighted that Cullen and my dad are safe and well. Ethyl too."

"Your head hurt? Old Diaz gave better than he got."

"For a while."

"Until your dad took a hand."

I smiled. "Never mess with a man's son. Especially when the man has a shotgun."

He grinned back. "And is standing nearby." He reached over and patted my shoulder. "I'm after a nap. Come read me a bedtime story?"

I aimed a kick at him. Missed.

An hour later I lay down beside Cullen. He was sleeping peacefully, snoring a bit, his beautiful little face placid. No bad dreams, not now at least.

I hoped never.

I had enough for both of us.

And then, for the first time in weeks, I slept without a gun at arm's length.